She tried to move away, but he stopped her with two hands. There was heat in his voice. "What are you asking me for, sweetheart?"

Trembling started at his touch, and it spread through Gem, caused a shaky hollow in her belly. She couldn't meet his eyes. "Nothing," she said. "I don't want anything from you." She *couldn't* want anything. Not what he was offering.

A large, calloused hand slid into her hair, cupped the back of her skull. Blue's thumb rubbed gently behind her ear, making her weak, and he stared into her eyes. He seemed to come to a decision and said, "Well…I want something from you. I've wanted it for a long time."

His kiss was seductive, possessive. It was a flame that threatened to burn out of control.

Other *Love Spell* books by Autumn Dawn:

NO WORDS ALONE

When Sparks Fly

Autumn Dawn

LOVE SPELL NEW YORK CITY

To the One who made me a dreamer,
The teachers who taught me to read
and the librarians who keep the treasuries
of books. Thank you.

LOVE SPELL®

June 2009

Published by

Dorchester Publishing Co., Inc.
200 Madison Avenue
New York, NY 10016

ISBN 10: 0-505-52802-9
ISBN 13: 978-0-505-52802-5
E-ISBN: 978-1-4285-0689-3

The name "Love Spell" and its logo are trademarks of Dorchester Publishing Co., Inc.

Printed in the United States of America.

10 9 8 7 6 5 4 3 2 1

Visit us on the web at www.dorchesterpub.com.

ACKNOWLEDGMENTS

I want to thank my editor, for his determination to keep the cell phones and the speed dial in our century where they belong. Also my agent, for the guidance.

And thank you, John, for letting me keep the van warm in the garage, even though you're the one who has to drive to work at -50 below. It's so much easier to type when my fingers aren't frozen.

When
Sparks
Fly

Chapter One

A Zzel dragon looked in her window. Gem Harris-daughter screamed as the huge reptilian eye blinked and focused on her with malevolent intent, knowing she was going to die. Then she heard a snort. The huge native reptile was laughing. At her.

With a growl of ire, she stalked to the kitchen door, ripped it open and walked outside. "All right, who wants to die?"

The neighbor's punk son Bijo and his green-haired Kiuyian buddy pelted out of the scrub-covered side lot, laughing like miners on a drunken spree. Dressed in shabby jackets and with their hair razored like wannabe rock stars, the pair had been bugging her with pranks since she'd told their fathers she'd seen them ditching class. It wouldn't have been her concern, but they'd been doing it on her property and had nearly gotten into a brawl with some customers.

The Kiuyian boy tripped over his big feet and crashed into a thorny bush. He yelped and jumped out.

Gem smirked. Served him right for pulling his shape-changing pranks on her. He'd be picking thorns out of his hide for the next half hour. Maybe she ought to plant a few carnivorous bushes out there while she was at it—or just leave whatever grew naturally. Saints knew they weeded enough dangerous indigenous species out of the struggling garden to form an entire hedge.

She watched the kid dust himself off. Gem didn't mind Kiuyians in general, but they could get up to serious trouble with their shape-changing abilities. The talent had helped them survive on their hostile home world until they'd learned enough to colonize other planets. Luckily there were few Kiuyians who could change into fully humanoid shapes other than their natural form, or she'd have a bar full of underage drinkers. Mostly they stuck with animal forms or humanoid/animal crosses.

There'd been an influx of Kiuyians to Polaris in the last seven years. Most of them were dirt poor, brought in as cheap labor to work the mines. Gem still hadn't made up her mind about the aliens as a group. Sometimes they came in as customers, and those who spent money behaved . . . for the most part. There had once been a drunk who changed into a three-headed serpent and puked all over the floor. She'd had the sot working odd jobs ever since, to help pay off the damages.

She reached for the thick wooden door, letting herself back into the spacious kitchens of The Spark.

Like the Kiuyians, Gem's family had come to Polaris for the mines. Unlike the Kiuyians, Gem's father had decided that building a business to cater to the miners was more profitable than grubbing around with the ore. Her father, Airk Harris, had homesteaded their land and built this inn on it. Until his death last year, he'd called the inn a work in progress, and it showed. The fortresslike building was still mostly un-painted. Both interior and exterior walls were striped with multihued layers resembling sandstone, a result of the pouring process of construction. It was a mark of the inn's cheap, if sturdy, materials; more expensive buildings on Polaris were one color, often glossy, even jewel-hued.

For herself, Gem liked the stripes. The look was earthy and unpretentious, much like her family.

The tables were inexpensive antigravity tiles that doubled as screens. The menu and drink list appeared in several languages on the surfaces, allowing guests to touch-select their orders. These orders were beamed directly to the bar and kitchen, streamlining service. Or it usually streamlined service, assuming the servers weren't flirting with the customers. Gem had a terrible time keeping the girls who worked for her from turning the place into a brothel. There had been one incident last year . . .

Well, it was hard to find good help. Polaris was a very reserved community, and it was vital that the family maintained its reputation, both business and personal, if they wanted to succeed. Those who didn't toe the line here were ostracized. A business run by three sisters could easily be ruined.

The antigravity tiles could be used as lighting, lined up to form banquet tables or stacked against the wall if she wanted to turn the bar and dining area into a dance hall. The inn had a private room that doubled as a family dining room and parlor, but most of the time Gem and her sisters just ate in the kitchen. They charged extra for guests who wanted the private room.

The floor was actual sandstone, polished to a high

sheen. A couple of robotic floor-cleaners the size of dinner plates zipped around like miniature flying saucers, sucking up dirt and vaporizing sticky spills. Occasionally they'd zoom over to the incinerator hidden behind the bar and eject a stream of waste before going back for more.

The inn had one type of all-occasion, oversize mug used for its soups, drinks and desserts, and one size of plate; all were formed of self-cleaning glasstic. If a food type needed a knife, it wasn't served, which was okay, as most guests were happy using spoons or their hands.

Gem's father had had big dreams. He'd once considered naming the inn after himself, but since he had no sons and his unmarried daughters were properly addressed as Harrisdaughter, he'd settled on *The Spark*. He'd promised his still young family that it would be the starting point for any and all business on the newly colonized planet of Polaris. Now that he'd died, it belonged to his daughters.

As she surveyed the room, Gem took in a table that was a little too raucous and grimaced. A woman was holding court with a table full of miners. Too much longer and there'd be trouble. Gem shuddered, knowing she'd have to deal with the situation before it got out of hand.

They were in an odd position for three single women. They'd inherited the inn, of course, and their father had been well-liked, but if they weren't careful how they conducted themselves, respectable customers would shun them, Then they'd be forced to accept seedier clientele if they wanted to survive. She didn't want to see her father's memory dishonored that way. Although he'd come from a planet with more relaxed

standards, Airk had chosen to settle here. It was a
good place to raise a family, what with its high ethi-
cal standards, and he'd taught his daughters to respect the culture.

Gem didn't really mind, anyway. She didn't want
the uncertainty of a casual relationship. When she
finally did find a man, she planned to keep him. That
way, she'd only have to train a husband once. She didn't
have time to fritter away on emotional upheaval and
broken hearts. She'd seen enough of her customers
drowning their sorrows in liquor to give her a distaste
for the dramas of the lovelorn.

Before Gem could intercept the hooker and send
her packing, her sister Brandy came up from the cel-
lar toting a small keg. She glanced at Gem with her
mismatched blue and brown eyes as she walked toward the bar. "We've got rodents in the tubers again.
I set traps. Rissa's in the taproom, and those miners
are at it early today."

Gem grimaced, already heading for the L-shaped
hall that separated the rooms. "I see her. Why didn't
you deal with it? You can knock heads just as easily.
You have the red hair."

"It's nearly brown." This was Brandy's standard response to the old argument. "You have a better touch
than me. Quit whining."

It was midmorning, but the taproom was already
half full, thanks to the new trainum mine that had
been found. The blue ore was a crucial ingredient
in the starship fuel used by the Galactic Explorers,
the corporation famous for exploring—and some said
exploiting—most of the newly discovered planets in
the last thirty years. Of course, most of the ships in
the Interplanetary Council's jurisdiction relied on

the energy-rich mineral as well. Any new discoveries were a boon to the local economy, and the recent claim was causing a huge influx of visitors, the side effects of which were not all pleasant. A case in point was this brazen chit perched on a miner's lap.

Gem pointed to the hooker, Rissa. She jerked her thumb over her shoulder. "You, get out. We're not running a brothel."

Rissa pouted her full green lips and leaned over to whisper in the miner's ear. Her wildly curling green hair slipped forward over her chest, doing a better job of covering her than her low-cut dress. She knew better than to cross Gem, though. She didn't linger.

As the hooker slunk off, the miner set up a protest. "Hey! We were just having a little fun. Lighten up, cutie." His skin was tinged blue with dust from the ore he worked, and he and his two buddies exuded an unwholesome aura.

Before the man's mind could travel farther down a road she didn't like, Gem warned him, "I'm the owner of this inn, and I have the best drinks in town. If you ever want another drop of alcohol here, mind your manners and don't hassle me or my help. I won't hesitate to have you blacklisted." She paused a moment to let her threat sink in, then walked off.

She hated dealing with riffraff, but that was part of being the owner of this place, and her father had made certain she knew how to do all aspects of the job. It had gotten harder lately. The lunar mines had turned Polaris into a boomtown, and the influx of transients was mostly male. Women like Rissa were in demand, and growing bolder about plying their trade. Once a place got a rep for tolerating hookers, it was hard to clean up. The Spark didn't need that kind of attention. If Gem and her sisters wanted to remain respectable businesswomen, they had to stay vigilant.

Polaris was a gas planet. "Planet" was a bit of a misnomer, actually, when considering the areas where people lived. All the inhabitable land masses were made up of huge orbiting chunks of rock, floating islands formed from asteroids that had been pulled into orbit around the planet's core. The atmosphere here was breathable, a belt of air somehow comfortable for most life-forms. While there was no sea, colonists had mined ice from the moons and formed lakes in available craters. They'd filled those lakes with fish and sea life. Water was valued and carefully recycled; hauling in more from the moons to form new reservoirs cost money.

Colonist farmers had used that original shipment of ice to turn the barren surface of their asteroids into islands of lush growth, gradually adding small livestock as grasses took root and flourished. Each asteroid had an electric biodome over it to keep the precious water vapor inside. Individual climates ranged from hot and humid to warm and arid, depending on the crop grown. Land that was not farmed was either residential, commercial or used for mining trainum, platinum or gold. People like Gem and her sisters were getting rich from the influx of new business, but increasing lawlessness meant they also paid for it. Polaris was an exciting, if dangerous, place to be.

Gem was joint owner of The Spark with her two sisters, but as the eldest, she was in charge. She had the temperament to deal with trouble, manage the kitchens, the taproom and their accounts—and it was a good thing, too, because in addition to the inn, they had two rental cabins and the huge garden to oversee. Polaris had only been settled for forty years and its farming industry occasionally struggled. Anyone who wanted variety and independence grew their own produce and spices. Only the very wealthy purchased off-world food, because shipping prices were insane.

Gem and her family worked hard and their business thrived, catering to whoever arrived at the nearby spaceport and appreciated good food and excellent brews, whether they were locals or passing through. The brewmaster The Spark used was so good that Gem had recently made arrangements to export some of his goods—for a share of the profit, of course. She was always keeping an eye on the family business.

"Gem!" Her sister Xera stomped down the stairs, a fistful of wadded linens in her hands, her short black waves of hair bouncing around her face. "That stupid Guok you rented to last night threw up in the bedding! I told you he was drunk." Xera had a temper to match her Amazonian build. She probably would have chewed out the hapless alien if he hadn't already skedaddled.

Gem leaned back as she got a whiff of the offending sheets. Guoks were flabby white bipeds that looked like walking sacks of jelly. Gem knew little of the aliens, though she'd heard they were usually harmless. Now she knew they had vomit to rival sewer sludge. Lesson learned.

Eyes watering, she waved her sister off. "So, go toss them in the wash. What do you want me to do, hunt him down and shoot him?" The Spark had forty rooms, and Xera and her maids were in charge of cleaning them. The trouble was, Xera wanted out of the job.

"The puke ate through the sheets. We'll be lucky to salvage the mattress." Xera handed the sheets to a passing maid and followed Gem's retreat into the kitchens. The cooks were busy preparing the noon meal. Hungry, Gem helped herself to some seafood salad and tried to avoid her sister by heading for the office.

"Don't think you're going to dodge me," Xera called out, following her inside and shutting the door. "I'm twenty years old, Gem, old enough to know I don't want to be head housekeeper anymore."

Gem sat behind her battered desk and crossed her feet on top of it. She was twenty-five, herself, and still had no idea what she'd rather be doing. Why should Xera want to change all of a sudden? All she'd done for the past two months was whine. "You know we need you," Gem tried to explain.

"I want to be a pilot for the Galactic Explorers," Xera replied.

"No, you don't."

"Gem!"

Gem groaned. They had a rule about disparaging each other's dreams. "Okay, I'm sorry. Go on." She waved weakly, disgruntled by the idea of replacing her sister, concerned that Xera was going away where she couldn't have tabs kept on her. Since their father died, keeping tabs had been Gem's job, but her sisters were growing up.

"I already have my private pilot license. I've been shuttling between the islands every chance I get. I'm ready for deep space now. I talked to the recruiter . . . He can get me off-world next week."

Gem's face darkened. She didn't like to be reminded of how often Xera fled their asteroid island to go exploring. It was dangerous. There were too many claim wars to go rambling around alone. And now she was planning to go even farther away?

Xera forged ahead. "I've trained Rosa. She's capable and very eager to get the raise."

Gem looked around at the walls, which were painted a restful white-sage, and sighed. The office doubled as a sitting room, with a few well-worn and overstuffed chairs and a long, leather-covered bench that provided space to crash if anyone needed a place to sleep. The bow window behind them looked out over the garden. It was open at the moment, and wisps of flower-scented air stirred the linen curtains. How many times had she stared into the fireplace, watched the flames burn as she dreamed of the future? She and her sisters had spent many evenings here, talking, fighting, laughing. They were her family, but now everything was changing.

She focused on her sister's face. "Are you sure, Xera? You'll end up a long way from home for a long time to come."

Xera snorted. "I've only talked about it since I was sixteen. The flying lessons, the weapons training . . . You knew where all that was leading!"

"I'd hoped you'd change your mind," Gem admitted.

"I haven't."

Gem blew out a breath of air. "Okay. Let's look at what you need to do to get your affairs in order. You said a week?"

Xera looked surprised, then grinned.

So Gem helped the first of her sisters prepare to leave home, spending the next hour with Xera, going over her plans and finding no flaws. It was hardly surprising, she realized; of her two sisters, Xera was the more levelheaded.

It was late that day when Gem finally wandered down to the taproom. There were a few regulars, but the place had quieted. Her bartender was there, polishing glasses, so she wandered over and took a stool. "Hey, Jaq. Where're our guests?"

The elderly man raised bushy white eyebrows. "Races today. Forget?" In his late sixties, Jaq had a head that was bald as an egg, yet he still managed to grow an impressive handlebar mustache.

The races. Of course. The Simian-Goat Runs were held once a week. Lemur monkeys were trained to ride goats. Clinging to miniature saddles, the monkeys would burst out of starting gates, whipping their goats to high speeds with riding crops. It was funnier than a squirrel drinking whiskey, and drew huge crowds. Bigger crowds than simple alcohol, at least.

Gem pinched the bridge of her nose and shook her head, leaning her elbow on the chrome antigravity slab that served as the bar. "Long day."

"It's not noon yet."

"It ought to be." In no mood to do her usual work, she looked around and spotted one of The Spark's regulars. In the corner beyond the fire, he leaned back in his chair and watched her with eyes that were probably already bloodshot, given the way he usually looked.

She turned to Jaq. "How many's he had today?"

The bartender glanced at the corner, then filled

two mugs with hot mulled Poizi berry juice. "One. I told you he's not a drunk."

Gem raised a sardonic eyebrow and collected the mugs. "Weaves when he walks, eyes always blood-shot . . . He might only order one or two in here, but he's drinking more elsewhere."

"If you're so sure he's a drunk, why serve him?" Jaq asked. He gave her a knowing look.

"Shut up," she replied good-naturedly, then took over the drinks.

Hyna Blue gave her a crooked smile as she approached, squinting up at her through his wild black hair. "Hello, Blue-eyes. Come to save me today?"

She ignored his flirting and put the mugs on the table. "Have something that won't bite you back, Hyna."

"I told you to call me Blue. I've never gone by my first name." He smiled crookedly. "Makes me think you're talking to my uncle." He considered her through indigo eyes as dark as hers were light. "You know, we'd make beautiful babies together. Just think—they'd all have blue eyes and your good looks."

"Sober up and ask me again," she said, ignoring what his words did to her pulse. She was average-looking, with dark hair and a medium build. In spite of his habitual slouch, she'd seen him stand straight a time or two, and he was a big man. Maybe he did hard labor somewhere, because anyone who sat around like he did should have had a paunch. Hyna didn't.

There was something alluring about his ruined beauty, though the drunken stagger tended to tarnish the shine. He'd been coming into The Spark every day for two months now, ordering one drink and nursing it for hours. Nobody knew where he lived, or even if he had a home.

He smirked. "Would you say yes?" he asked.

"No."

"Then there's no point in putting myself through the torture, is there?" He glanced at the glass of juice she offered and shook his head. "Why do you always bring this hot? It's just not normal." As he looked at the liquid, his eyes turned winter-gray. One touch, and the drink frosted over.

"I just like to watch you cool it off," she said, watching his cybernetic implants work. It was kind of sad; they gave him super strength and control over temperatures, but it meant he'd lost his arm somewhere. His eyes, too. She wondered if they'd been blue before the surgery. Using his cooling ability was a lot like waving a wooden leg around, advertising his disability. Maybe that was why she had a soft spot for him.

He took a swallow from his original glass and savored it. "You do serve the best liquor in town. And the beer you guys brew . . . You sure you're not bootlegging it?"

She sighed. He always asked her that. "We distill it right here, and yes, we pay our taxes. Why, do you want a tour of our distillery?" She grimaced at her tone. Intolerance and snark were no way to reach a lost soul.

"Sure," he said with relaxed interest. "I always wanted to be a brewmaster. Missed my calling."

She regarded him skeptically. If he'd wanted to be a brewmaster, he'd have asked to see the brewery, not the distillery. A master distiller produced liquor. If he'd wanted to be one, he should have at least known the proper term. Of course, both facilities were housed in the same room here, and their brew-master was also a certified master distiller; but Blue might not realize that. "What do you do now, other than haunt my place?"

He wagged a finger. "You're trying to distract me. You don't want to give me the tour."

She didn't. Talking to him in the bar was one thing; inviting him physically into any part of her life was another. And yet she found herself saying, "You don't have a job, do you? Do you want one?"

Those dark eyes actually looked surprised. "You want to hire me?"

Disinterest seemed the best way to achieve her goal. "You smell. If you're going to work for me, you need to shower, shave more than once a week and show up in clean clothes."

"Ouch! So much for the angel-of-mercy disguise. What if I don't have another pair of clothes?"

"Don't you?" she asked without blinking. She'd suspected something of the sort.

He took a meditative drink. "I suppose I could steal some."

"Do, and you'll not step foot on my property again."

He looked down, not quite hiding a grin. "Now that's serious."

She blew out a breath. "I could advance you a set of clothes against your first week's pay. We need an extra hand to see to some chores that slip through the cracks. There's gardening, some handiwork, help around the kitchens . . . whatever's needed."

He blinked at her. "Are you going to buy me underwear, too? I need them extra roomy in front, you know."

A blush caught her by surprise. Embarrassed that he'd thrown her good intentions in her face, she stood.

He stopped her with a light touch to the hand. Surprised, she looked at him. "I'll take the job," he said. There might even have been an apology in his eyes.

Mollified, she nodded. "Tomorrow. Show up sober or the deal's off."

She'd only taken two steps before trouble came her way in the guise of a redheaded storm. Brandy planted herself in front of Gem and growled, "What's this I hear about you letting Xera run off to join the Galactic Explorers?"

The coals of a headache had been lurking in Gem's head all day; they now flared to crackling life. "She's of age, and she's worked toward it for years."

Her sister's eyes flashed. "I don't care if she's a hundred! You know what the death rate is among their crews. Two ships disappeared this year alone, and nobody knows what happened to them. That's not including attacks by pirates, mechanical failures, bloody alien plagues . . . You're mad to let her go!"

Gem bent her head and massaged the back of her neck, letting her short, straight hair cover part of her face. Why did Brandy always have to rake her over the coals at the times she was feeling most worried? "You have some way to stop her?"

Her sister started tidying a table, working off her anxiety. "She won't listen to me. She said you helped her with the paperwork! You've always overindulged her."

"That's not fair," Gem said quietly. Brandy could be nasty when nervous, but she usually had a sense of justice. Already Gem could see her start to feel remorse.

Conscious of the interested ears at her back, Gem took the opportunity to formally introduce Blue to her sister as newly hired help. Brandy stared at him, then looked at Gem as if she'd lost her mind. She threw her towel down on the table and walked off with a muttered, "She's lost it. Lost it!"

"She likes me," Blue said, and polished off his drink.

Gem's day did not get better. The inn filled back up in the afternoon with loud guests celebrating or bemoaning their wins and losses at the Simian Runs. Jaq and his girls were on alert, ready to deal with anyone who got out of hand.

Anyone who had too much to drink was cut off. This had started as Gem's father's policy and remained hers. To prevent drunken protests, the policy was posted at each table along with the drink list, and carved in a sign above the bar. In spite of this, there were still a few belligerent drunks who thought they could intimidate an old man into giving them more. It was times like that when Jaq's military training saved the day. He might be of advanced years, but he was deadly. The inn wouldn't be what it was if not for him.

Gem had retreated to her office and was trying to focus on accounts when the fire alarm went off. Her pen left a streak on her document as she jumped up. She ripped open the door and watched the guests race by, babbling as they went. She waited for an opening then dashed up the stairs, pushing past people who tried to knock her down in their haste to escape.

As she gained the second floor she found the smell of smoke everywhere, but she couldn't tell where it was coming from. Using a master key, she started opening closed doors, going room by room to make sure each of the guests had evacuated. Brandy was at the other end of the hallway, doing the same.

"Empty!" Gem called as they met in the middle. "All empty. The ventilation system must be spreading the smell around. Let's check upstairs."

The smoke became visible as they raced up to the third floor, making them cough. Jaq was already there, kicking in doors. Gem winced, but they didn't have time to be careful. The fire extinguishing system should have turned on by now. It hadn't, and that worried her.

"Down here!" Jaq called. Smoke billowed out of a door he'd just splintered. Using the fire extinguisher he'd grabbed off the wall, he sprayed all around as he walked in, likely unable to see.

"Jaq, no! The floor!" Xera rushed in from nowhere, armed with her own extinguisher. "You don't know what it's going to do."

Gem shivered at the thought of Jaq crashing through a burning floor, then ran into a different room and grabbed a towel, soaking it in the bathtub. Brandy had found an extinguisher herself and was using it, but the actual blaze wasn't what Gem was considering. She was worried about the people putting out the fire. If their clothes or hair caught, they could be seriously injured.

Sirens sounded, announcing the volunteer fire

department's appearance—too late, as it turned out. The fire was almost dead by the time the men rushed up the stairs, ready to save the day. Coughing, Gem, her family and Jaq let the new arrivals take over, grateful to retreat downstairs and find cleaner air. Outside, the paramedics checked them over, treating their minor burns while a crowd of neighbors and guests looked on.

Gem sat on the grass and rested her elbows on her knees as she watched the circus unfold around her. It was going to be a late night getting everyone resettled, and they'd all sleep with the scent of smoke in their noses. Why hadn't the fire extinguishing system gone off? That room should have been coated with foam before the blaze even got started.

The fire chief had the answer. "It was turned off."

"Excuse me?" Gem said, unable to believe her ears.

Chief Puyta looked grim. "Someone spread oil on the rug and set it on fire. You're lucky they didn't use something faster burning or the damage would be a lot worse. Have you checked your till to make certain nothing is missing?"

Jaq had locked the till in the bar and it was untouched. Gem's office had been the target. Her petty cash box was missing, and a pile of dog poop sat squarely on her desk. A fork was stuck in it. The message was pretty clear.

The chief's almond eyes narrowed. His green hair was graying, but he was still plenty sharp. Tall and usually quiet, the Kiuyian had been a friend of Gem's father until Gem's father had passed away.

"Someone has a sick sense of humor," he said.

Gem's stomach churned, but she tried to lighten

the moment. "Yeah. You know how long it took me to balance that ledger?"

"It's on the computer," Brandy snapped, coming forward with a plastic bag. When she was angry, she cleaned.

"Leave it a bit," the chief ordered. "Let the crime scene techs do their thing. Maybe we can catch the guy who did this."

Xera cracked her knuckles, her face dark.

Knowing they needed to work off some steam, Gem started giving orders before her family dispersed. "All right, let's start settling guests. I'm going to talk to the police and find out which rooms they need to look at. Xera, you're in charge of damage control. Anything that can be done to mollify guests, do it. There's going to be smoke smell all over the rooms, so if you can find any fresh linens, please replace what you can. Get the rest in the wash and have the maids start scrubbing.

"Brandy, find Jaq and tell him to close the bar for the night. Tell the kitchens they're on light duty and have them air the place on that end."

Her sisters bolted off to do as they were told. Gem sat at the bar and watched the organized chaos unfold around her, stuck where she was answering questions for the police. No, she had no known enemies, no obvious suspects—though if she were going to put her money on pranksters, she'd consider the neighbor kid, Bijo. She could see him and his buddy pulling a stunt like this. Still, he was a kid and she didn't like mentioning him to the cops. It was a necessary evil, though. Someone could have been hurt. If it was Bijo, he needed a wake-up call.

Mentioning his name didn't stop the flow of questions, though. They kept coming, adding stress to an already tense situation.

Brandy brought a pot of herbal tea, earning herself a grateful smile. Gem's sister had managed to wash her face, which only reminded Gem of the soot coating her own. The moment she could slip away, she washed up, watching the grime twirl down the drain, just like her evening.

Ah, well. No doubt tomorrow would be better.

Chapter Two

"Stinks like smoke in here."

Gem looked up from her consultation with her head chef, Jamir, and blinked. Blue had showered. He'd shaved. He was standing there in her kitchens, dwarfing her and the tiny Latq at her side.

"How tall are you?" she asked before she thought. She might come up to his collarbone. The Latq was barely four feet high and fine-boned, making Blue seem even bigger.

He grinned. "Impressed?" He'd pulled his black hair off his face and bound it with a piece of twine, and while his clothes were the same, they smelled a lot better.

"I am. You're walking straight and everything."

He smirked. "So, you got something for me? I know you can't wait to get me out of these clothes." His voice was lazy, suggestive.

She sighed. "I've had a busy day and haven't gotten to it. We had a fire here last night."

"I heard. You still owe me clothes," he replied.

She stared at him. "I've yet to see you do any work."

"Baby, I can work you right into the ground," he

replied, looking smug. "Get me some clothes. I wouldn't mind some breakfast, either." He eyed the lizard egg quiche Jamir had just taken out of the oven. "That'll do." And before they could say a word, he'd grabbed some potholders and snatched the whole pan.

"Hey!" Jamir yelped, then started cursing in his language. He waved a wooden spoon threateningly, his milky-hued face turning pink, but he didn't dare strike Blue, who sat at the table, arms protectively circling the pie dish as he wolfed down the food. The quiche was steaming hot, and Blue gulped air into his open mouth to cool it before swallowing.

Gem grimaced and murmured an apology to Jamir. "We'll teach him manners."

"I heard that!"

Jamir bared his sharp teeth and started banging pots around.

Casting an irate glance at Blue, Gem picked up her communicator and keyed in the code to a clothing store. She talked to the clerk for a few moments, describing what she needed, then pressed the comm to her shoulder and told Blue, "They need to know what sizes you wear."

He shrugged. "Tall."

She rolled her eyes. "Just send me several sets for tall men, in different sizes. I'll send back what I don't need. Yes, thanks. I'll expect you."

Blue looked up with interest, having wolfed down the entire quiche. "Must be nice to have someone do your shopping for you. That a regular thing?" He grabbed an unguarded drink on the table and gulped it down.

Gem frowned. "Not really. I'd take care of it in

person, but I don't have time today and I don't trust you."

"You think I'd walk off with your money?"

"Would *you* trust you?"

His smile was answer enough.

"Fine. If you're finished eating, let's go to the gardens and I'll give you your first task."

"After you," he said. He grabbed a fried dumpling on the way out.

Birdsong and the heavy smell of barbed melon flowers greeted them as they stepped through the rusted garden gate. Herbs and buju berry arbors lined the dirt path to the vegetable patches, providing shade for less heat-tolerant plants. Past them, just before the main garden, were piles of jumbled stone that served as the egg-lizard huts. Several reptiles were out seeking bugs or sunning themselves on the rocks, while a few brooding females flicked forked tongues, staring out of darkened nooks. A few hissed irritably as Hyna and Gem walked by.

The Spark employed two full-time gardeners during the height of the season, a father and his son, but the son had hurt his back two days ago and hadn't been in to work. Blue would come in very useful, provided he put forth decent effort.

Gem led him to a cart and handed him a shovel. Thanks to kitchen scraps and specially designed toilets, they had an abundant supply of aged compost. "Here you go. All the raised beds in this back section need a side dressing of compost, about three to four inches deep. When you've used up this cart, pull it back to that pile there and get some more." She pointed. "When you're done with that, you can use the weed burner to torch these thorn starts and carnivorous weeds between the rows." She kicked at a clump in illustration.

Hyna looked around the large garden. "This is a two-day job."

She shrugged. "Job security. You could leave."

He stared at her for a moment as if tempted, then stuck his shovel into the pile. "When's lunch?"

She laughed. "Noon, if you can find room after that quiche. There's a hose at the head of the path if you get thirsty—you saw it on the way in. Have fun."

Brandy met her at the gate with a sour expression. "He actually showed up?"

"Shaved and bathed, too," Gem said cheerfully, plucking a flower on her way out.

"I heard he ate a whole pie."

"He'll work it off."

"You don't know that. You might go out to check on him and find him leaning on his shovel."

"Might. We'll see. Meanwhile, I have some insurance forms to fill out and I have to call the carpenters back. Did you finish tallying what needed to be replaced?"

The day flew by as usual, and it was hours past noon when she had a moment to check on her new worker. When she asked Jamir if Blue had been inside to eat, the cook shook his head in annoyance.

"He ate an entire roast fowl, a tart, a huge plate of fruit salad *and* half a loaf of bread. The man is a pit. A pit!"

Well, she hadn't really been worried that he would skip out on lunch, she realized as she entered the garden. She wondered what he was used to eating. He wasn't skinny, but wherever he'd been getting his food, it probably wasn't anything like Jamir's dishes.

She came to the garden and stopped in her tracks. Blue had taken off his shirt and was on his way to a wicked sunburn; though deeply tanned, his bare skin was no match for Polaris's fierce afternoon sun. "Hey! You're turning red, you know."

He twisted and leaned on his shovel. "Didn't feel it."

She averted her eyes from his bare chest. "You'll feel it tonight. Better put on your shirt before it gets worse. I've got some salve that will take the burn away, and tomorrow I'll give you some blocker."

"Good idea. I'll cut these pants into shorts and work like that."

She glanced at his ripped jeans and imagined him running around in cutoffs and nothing else. Not a good idea. "Why don't we see if your new clothes are here? Let's hope they'll have the right size. I'll order you some shorts as a bonus."

Hyna grinned and stuck his shovel in the ground. "You must like me."

"You appear to be worth the cost," she allowed, looking at the amount of work he'd gotten done. "Nice job."

He just shrugged and followed her up to the inn, shirt slung over his shoulder.

The newly purchased clothes had indeed been dropped off, but Gem held them out of reach as he grabbed for them. "Whoa! Shower first or I'll have to pay for the whole lot." She couldn't imagine the clothing store would accept ill-fitting returns that smelled like compost.

At first Blue looked mad, but then his expression became calculating. "Your place or mine?"

Gem shook her head and showed him to the employees' bathroom. "Soap and towels are inside.

Clean up, find the clothes that fit and I'll take care of the rest. Dinner should be ready soon."

Her words apparently spurred him. He was out of the bathroom in five minutes, dripping water and dressed in black pants that fit a little too well. The short-sleeved indigo shirt, meant to look plain and utilitarian, looked nothing of the kind as it hung open down the front. He was buttoning his pants as he came out.

Gem twitched uncomfortably. She'd had warning, but she hadn't been braced for how well he would clean up. Giving herself a mental slap, she said neutrally, "Better, but we'll have to add shoes to the list. Yours are shot. Hungry?" She led the way to the kitchen table without waiting for an answer, then left him to Jamir's tender mercies. She had to get away.

Brandy walked in as Gem walked out, saw her expression and glanced into the kitchen. She paused, annoyed. Her eyes were mocking as she stared at Gem. "What did you say you hired him for?" she asked.

Gem flushed. "You know why I *didn't* hire him. Stop your teasing."

Brandy's face grew serious. "I wasn't teasing, Gem. Be careful. He's not lover material."

The room got hotter. Without a word, Gem hurried to her office, shut herself inside and stared at the wall. She *hadn't* hired Hyna Blue for his looks.

A nagging started in her brain, a warning that circled like a pack of taunting children. She hadn't had a boyfriend in a long time. Blue looked a little too good. He was her employee. Making him anything more would never be right.

She needed a husband. Blue was the leaving kind. Maybe she'd better put Xera in charge of him.

"Not in this millennium," Xera said firmly. "He looks like an ex-con to me."

They were standing at the bar, and Jaq just laughed when Gem looked at him in mute appeal. "He's your project."

"Fire him," Brandy suggested brusquely.

"I'm not going to fire him. He did good work today," Gem said firmly, hating that she was digging her hole of responsibility deeper. "I do have a lot of things to do, though, and he was hired to help pick up the slack that gets missed. If you guys have any extra chores for him, speak up."

Xera snorted. "You want to turn him into a maid? He'll quit. I know the type."

"He could help carry in the new mattresses we ordered, haul in the firebricks for the guestroom hearths, that sort of thing," Gem suggested. "You don't have to arm him with a duster and apron."

Xera smiled but looked thoughtful.

"Brandy, you could introduce him to the brewmaster. He showed an interest. I'm sure he'd be of use cleaning vats and pipes."

Brandy propped her hip on a table and took a sip of her drink. "You do it."

Stymied, Gem sighed and gave up. There was no other option. She'd hired him; it was either fire him or put him to good use. She'd do the latter.

It was easy enough to keep him in the garden over the following few days. That way she saw him only a couple of times, when she checked on his work. It was always perfect, which was a surprise, given her early impression of him. His manners did not improve, though.

He winked at her when she showed up in the garden that day. Dressed only in a pair of cut-off shorts, and barefoot besides, he wasn't shy about showing off his flexed muscles. "You come out here just to see this, don't you, Blue-eyes?"

"I come out here because no one else wants to deal with you," she retorted. Looking at the work he'd done, she added, "Looks like you'll be finished with the garden today. Tomorrow I'll introduce you to our brewmaster. Brandy is his apprentice. When he retires, the distillery will be hers."

Hyna's eyes gleamed.

"I hope you like scrubbing floors," Gem growled. "Jean Luc will have a mop in your hands for weeks before he lets you do anything else."

Blue shrugged. "I did worse in prison."

"Prison?" Gem echoed.

"Theft." He met her gaze defiantly. "My father kicked me out at fifteen. It was either steal or let strangers bugger me for a twenty. Which would you rather?"

She looked down.

"Don't worry, they knocked the thieving out of me in prison. I volunteered to join the Space Corps then, and aliens kicked my ass for a couple of years. Ended up becoming a POW for six months on Platoos." He was silent a moment.

Gem felt sick. Platoos had been the site of one of the ugliest battles in the galaxy. The Galactic Explorers had tried to lay claim to a planet that was already spoken for by a particularly vengeful race. The Intergalactic Council, a group of representatives from different planets formed to promote peace, had finally gotten involved and forced the GE to sign a treaty. The surviving POWs had been released, most given immediate medical discharges.

She took a deep breath. "You look pretty good for having spent six months in a prison camp."

He smiled without humor. "I was seventy pounds underweight when they released me. These eyes aren't mine. They'd plucked mine out and chopped off my ears. My lips were sewn shut just two days before I was released."

A wave of faintness washed over her. She sat on the empty compost cart. "Your arm?"

He waved a hand—not the cybernetic one. "I lost it in battle before all that. Crushed under a track truck. There was nothing left to salvage." His expression was dark with memory. "The government was kind enough to replace my eyes with cybernetic implants. I can see colors, but my depth perception will never be what it was."

He didn't have to explain his lack of scars—she understood about skin regeneration. "You weave when you walk," she said softly, finally understanding. "But you haven't been weaving lately."

He grimaced. "I finally checked into the clinic the other day. They activated my compensation chip. I haven't wanted it installed—there were bugs in the early versions and some of the vets went insane. I was finally . . ." He shrugged. "I had it installed."

She digested that. "I'm sorry I thought you were a drunk."

He smiled crookedly. "So, I'm not. Does that mean you'll go to bed with me?"

"No!" she gasped.

"So much for the aid and comfort due a suffering vet."

Her eyes narrowed, for she was suddenly suspicious. "Did you make all that up?"

He opened his eyes innocently. "Did I?"

Growling, she turned and headed for the house. He was a liar! Or was he? Maybe it was time she called in a favor.

"Have you got everything?"

Xera looked at Brandy and half smiled. "You asked me that three times already."

"Well, it's a little far to come back for something you forgot," Brandy snapped. "You'd better send us mail every chance you get, and don't leave anything out."

"Would I do that?" Xera smiled, in a good mood now that her day to leave had finally arrived. "Are you sure you don't want to come to the spaceport to see me off?"

"Why? I'd only get to see you for an hour more, at best. Besides, somebody has to look after this place." Brandy gave her a hug and managed a strained smile. "Be good."

"I will. I'll make you proud," Xera promised, misty-eyed.

"You already have," Brandy replied, her own eyes shimmering. "Go on with you. You'll miss your flight."

Gem picked up one of Xera's bags and grunted. She dropped it back on the ground with a thud. "What did you pack in here, bricks?"

Xera smirked and hefted the bag onto her shoulder. "You can get the carry-on, shorty."

"Watch it, squirt. I can still take you," Gem warned, though she doubted she could. Her sister was six feet tall and built like a tank. She'd also been in martial arts training for years.

The smaller bags were heavy, but Gem made sure she didn't look like she was straining. It wouldn't do to let the young ones think they had anything on her.

Hyna Blue met them in the front drive, next to the waiting transport. "I need a few hours off," he said. "I have some things to do."

Gem was distracted, so she demanded out of habit, "What?"

"Things," he replied.

"Like what?"

"Stuff at the clinic," Blue said. He sounded irritable. "I have an appointment."

"Oh. Sure," Gem decided. "I guess Brandy can introduce you to Jean Luc later. We've got to go before Xera's late."

She wondered why Blue hadn't mentioned his appointment yesterday but promptly put it out of her mind. She had more important things to consider than what her gardener did with his time. She'd put in a call yesterday to an old school-friend at the cop shop, as the locals referred to their police station. The friend had looked up Blue's record and confirmed he'd served time in prison with a military transfer, where he'd fought in the Interplanetary Council's peacekeeping forces. As for the rest, the friend couldn't say.

"Will you stop thinking about him?" Xera made a face as the transport moved away from The Spark. "At this rate I'll come back and you'll be engaged. Gem Harrisdaughter Blue. What a stupid name."

"You make it sound like I'm in love. I'm not," Gem retorted. "There's a mystery about him, is all."

"A fatal fascination," Xera agreed dryly. "Forget it. I'm sure I'll have my share of bad love stories, too. We can laugh about them when I get back." She grinned. "I can't believe I'm actually going! Sometimes I thought this day would never get here."

"We'll see if you're still excited when you're running around at five AM, dressed in that truly ugly uniform." Gem smiled, knowing her sister better than she implied. Xera would mind neither the schedule nor the clothing.

"I'm not the one who has problems with mornings, remember? I just hope the guy who set the fire gets caught. At least you still have Brandy and Jaq to help you . . ."

"Don't worry about it," Gem said. "The police think it was a one-shot deal. We can hope they'll know more soon. At any rate, you need to focus on your studies. If you want to learn to pilot a starship, you'd better pay attention. Daydreaming about home might send you crashing into an asteroid or something."

The transport pulled up at the field. There was a dizzying amount of traffic taking off and landing, both airships that hopped between Polaris's island asteroids and craft designed for deeper space. Off to the side Gem and Xera could see the construction of a coming spaceport expansion.

They paid the transport driver and entered the far terminal. A stream of passengers lined up for Xera's off-world flight. A voice came over a loudspeaker, announcing that the ship was boarding.

Gem's sister took a deep breath. "This is it. Thanks

for everything, sis. I love you." She gave Gem a crushing hug.

Gem sighed and willed her tears not to fall. "I hope the GE appreciates what they're getting. I'm sending them half my family. I love you. Be strong."

Her sister gave her another hug and got in line. Gem watched until Xera boarded the big blue ship, then turned away. Xera couldn't see her now, anyway, so there was no point in waiting.

She could hardly focus as she shuffled out to hail a transport home. Her sadness was overwhelming; it would be at least a year before she saw her sister again, maybe longer. There was no point in hurrying back to mope around the inn. Maybe she should take the day off and just shop or something. Distracted as she was, the first stinging blow to her head was a surprise and she lurched sideways. It felt like she'd been grazed with a small rock. She reached for the bruise—and got tackled by a gorilla.

Gem grunted in pain as the sidewalk caught her hip, but the grassy strip beside the pavement absorbed the worst of the fall. Whoever had grabbed her now rolled and dragged her up behind him, ran them back toward the terminal. He ducked them behind a concrete pillar and pressed her between his body and the stone.

She caught a glimpse of his face. "Blue! What are you—?"

A chip exploded off the stone right by their faces. Hyna Blue moved them to the other side. "Be still! Don't you know we're being shot at?"

Shot at? Gem froze, then gingerly reached up to feel her head. A smear of blood came away on her finger. Water replaced her knees.

"Not now," Blue hissed, holding her upright. "You can wet yourself later."

That roused her. "I'm not going to—!"

"Wait." He looked around the pillar. Whatever he saw made him ease out from behind it. "It's clear. Looks like my buddy Zsak winged him."

Confused, Gem let Blue drag her out from behind their concrete shield. A big blond guy in an old transport waved at them. "He shot the guy?"

"Just a graze, but we don't want him coming back for a second try at you. Your attacker shot at you from a transport on the street. As soon as Zsak fired on him, he raced off."

"Did you see? What are you doing here, anyway?"

Blue towed her toward it, using his body to block hers. "Let's get out of here before the cops swarm the place. I don't want to stand around answering stupid questions."

She didn't see why not, but he hustled her into the backseat of the roofless transport and slammed the door.

"Hi," the blond guy said. He had a handlebar mustache and goatee, but his hair was close-cropped.

"Who are you?" Gem demanded, trying to get her bearings. She touched her wounded head again.

"Get down!" Blue hissed, and shoved her down on the floorboards between his legs. He leaned over where she crouched, covering her. "You don't need to make it easy for them."

"Zsak. Nice to meet you," the blond guy said casually, driving like a maniac. They narrowly missed hitting a big fuel transport.

"Here, let me see that." Blue shifted so he could

inspect her head. He whistled. "You're lucky the guy wasn't a better shot."

"Who would want to shoot me?" Gem asked, bewildered.

He shrugged. "Maybe the guy who tried to burn down your inn?"

"The police thought that was random."

He looked at the blood on his hand. "This doesn't look random to me."

Faintness caught her again.

"Wow, I didn't know a woman could turn that white." Blue pulled her against his leg, steadying her. "Relax. If Zsak doesn't get us killed, we'll make it to the inn and get you patched up. It's just a scratch, anyway."

A fuzzy whiteness was swallowing all her good sense, but one thing nagged at her. "Why were *you* there?"

His words came from a long way off. "I finished up at the clinic and caught a ride with Zsak. He wanted to check if his bags had arrived yet. They sent them to the wrong planet, you know? Hundreds of years of spaceflight and the idiots still can't get the luggage on the right ship."

"I think she passed out." Hyna Blue tapped Gem's cheek, but she didn't move.

"Rough day for a little lady," Zsak said knowingly. "Probably hasn't had so much excitement in years."

"Either that or your ugly face did her in," Blue agreed. "She's lucky we showed up when we did."

"Yeah, lucky." Zsak laughed.

"Watch it," Blue warned.

They pulled up the circular drive in front of The Spark with a squeal of brakes. Blue glared at Zsak for the rough stop, then eased out of the vehicle, careful not to bang Gem's head. She roused as he moved, and looked around fuzzily, but he didn't dare set her on her feet. By the sickly look of her skin, she was just shy of another fainting spell.

Funny, he hadn't thought that anyone as feisty as Gem would give in to a little bullet scratch. Must be more fragile than she looked.

Nobody could say that about her sister. Many heads swung around as the trio entered the bar and dining room, and a buzz started up as people speculated on what was going on, but nobody offered useful help until Brandy ran up.

"What did you do to her?" the redhead demanded. She reached for Gem as if she could take her out of Blue's arms.

He looked at her doubtfully. "She was hurt. Unless you've got more muscle than it looks like, sweetcakes, you'd better let me carry her to the office."

She shot him a look of pure venom but led the way, unlocking the door for him. The family had been more careful about security since the fire, a move he approved of.

He looked around as he set Gem down. It was the first time he'd been in here. The lace and floral tapestry chairs made it seem more like a girlie living room than an office, and it gave a man shivers to think about trying to relax here.

"Gem, are you all right? Do you need a doctor?" Brandy was asking.

Gem blinked and reached for her head. "No. I think."

Brandy batted her hand out of the way. "Let me look." She looked around and spied Zsak. "*You*. Tell them to bring the first-aid kit out of the kitchen."

"Yes, Your Highness," Zsak muttered, heading for the door.

Blue crossed his arms and watched Brandy work, fighting annoyance. It wasn't as if her sister were dying.

"What happened?" Brandy demanded.

"She was shot," Blue said.

She ignored him like she would the devil's kin. "Gem?"

"I was shot," her sister repeated.

"What do you know?" Blue drawled.

"Shut up!" Brandy glared at him and then looked at Gem. "Why?"

"I don't know. I dropped Xera off and walked out to get a ride home. I thought someone threw a rock at my head; then Blue tackled me." She frowned. "I think he saved me." She glanced at him as if searching for confirmation.

He looked lazily at her. "Was that a thank-you?"

She frowned. "Thank you."

Zsak came in with the emergency kit, a bottle of booze and two glasses. He tossed the kit to Brandy, who caught it awkwardly. He filled two glasses with generous helpings of liquor and handed one to Gem. "You look like you need this." He took a healthy swallow of the other and sighed happily. "Good stuff."

"You could have brought me a glass," Blue grouched.

"Get your own. Clearly the little woman needed it more."

"How chivalrous of you," Brandy said between gritted teeth. No doubt the reference to *the little woman* was too much for her.

She started cleaning Gem's head. "Why would anyone shoot you? What are we going to tell the police?"

"Why bother with them? They haven't been any help so far," Blue noted. "Assuming this is connected to the fire."

"They've probably seen the spaceport surveillance cameras and are on their way. For myself, I'm glad. Unlike you, we don't have anything to hide."

Zsak belched. "I love good *brandy*. Goes down like honey." He leered playfully at Gem's sister.

"Give me that!" Brandy snapped. "You're wasting it. Do you have any idea how much a bottle of that stuff costs?" She snatched the container and put it out of his reach behind the couch.

"What do you mean? Don't you distill that stuff right here?" Blue asked, surprised.

"We don't make that kind. It's imported. Certain guests are willing to pay a fortune for a glass and so . . ."

"That good, eh?" Blue took the barely touched glass that had been poured for Gem and tossed the contents back like water. "Nice," he admitted.

Brandy looked at both men and bared her teeth in a fierce smile. "If you two are done celebrating your male splendor, kindly get out. We don't need you underfoot."

"'Male splendor.' I like that," Zsak mused. "Okay, Toots. I'll see you around."

Blue followed his friend, then hesitated. He glanced back at Gem. "Seriously, girls, I wouldn't stand around in front of your windows if I were you. And if you make enough to hire a good bodyguard, do it."

Brandy looked sharply at Gem as Hyna Blue walked out.

"Wait and see what the police have to say," Gem said slowly. "Maybe they will have caught the man who did this."

But they hadn't, as she and her sister would soon learn. The police came and left, imparting very little of use regarding the shooting except the advice to "take care." They'd made headway in the arson case, however. It turned out that the neighbor kids who'd been harassing Gem were to blame. The boys had agreed to community service to avoid going to trial and were supposed to pay back the money from the cash box. If they didn't, they'd serve time in jail.

But the cops had no leads on the shooting. The surveillance tapes Brandy had mentioned were a dead end. They showed a transport that turned out to be stolen. It had been discovered in a warehouse parking lot, still smoldering. There were no witnesses. They promised to let Gem know if they came up with any suspects. Other than Blue and Zsak, of course. It was clear by the way the detective looked when Gem said they'd rescued her that he considered the two men to be prime suspects. He also offered to patrol Gem's neighborhood more often.

Which was peachy, except that in the meantime she was still in danger.

"Maybe we *should* consider a bodyguard for you," Brandy said slowly. It was dark and they were again sitting in the office, blinds drawn, self-conscious of the windows at their back.

Gem considered morbidly that snipers had devices that could see through walls. They certainly had bullets that could punch through them. "Why just me?" she muttered. "Why do you assume you're not targeted, too? Maybe we should hire a whole platoon to guard us. I can see them now, filling the inn, making all our guests feel right at home."

"You're not funny," Brandy said broodingly. The fact that she didn't argue further said a lot.

Gem lifted her shoulders. "I will be as careful as I can be, but I can't live in fear. I have a life to live, an inn to run. People depend on me. The best I can do is be careful and pray."

"Pray," Brandy repeated, poker-faced. She'd had an ongoing argument with God since their father had died. "Pray for what?"

Gem heard her sister's disdain, but she never argued theology. Brandy was free to think what she would. The three sisters all had the same knowledge, but the difference was how they thought and felt. Their father had been old. He'd been ready. Even Xera had taken it fairly well. The only one not ready for his death had been Brandy; she'd loved him too deeply.

Gem shrugged and took a sip of calming libation. "Since you're been nagging me for years, let's kill two birds with one stone. Let's pray he sends a man to take care of me. How's that for a leap of faith?"

Brandy snorted and muttered something into her tea.

Unperturbed, Gem leaned back and closed her eyes. "Stranger things have happened."

Chapter Three

"I'll be your bodyguard, but I don't come cheap."

Gem looked up from her list, her mind blanked by surprise. They were hosting a wake in the bar that night and she wanted to make certain everything was ready. "Excuse me?"

Blue stood in front of her with an expression she'd never seen on him. He was stern and businesslike. "You heard me."

She shook her head. "I don't need a bodyguard. I know that yesterday was scary, but it was probably some random thing. There's no reason for someone to be stalking me. Besides, the police are looking into the case. Give them some credit."

"You were shot at last night. Did the police save you?"

"No, but . . ." She couldn't think of a good response to his implication.

"That guy was serious about killing you. It was a freak of luck that you got away. If we hadn't been there, you'd be dead. If he comes back, you don't have a chance."

She'd been bent over her desk but his words made

her straighten and face the thought she'd been avoiding all night. "You're saying that someone hates me enough to hire someone to kill me. Why? And the police didn't say anything about that." She knew she was grasping at straws.

"The police here are used to dealing with misdemeanors and small crimes. Whatever you're involved in is bigger than transport violations."

She fought back annoyance. "I'm not 'involved' in anything!"

He waved that away. "Whatever. He was bold enough to come after you in broad daylight, so I doubt this was his first kill. If I'm right, he has some experience at evading cops. He's not likely to be caught. Not by the cops around here, at any rate." He met Gem's gaze straight on. "I can keep you safe."

"Can you?" Angry and unsettled, she stared back in challenge. "Why should I trust you, anyway? What do I know about you other than that you were in the military? Ah, yes—that you're a convict. That's likely to inspire confidence." She cringed a bit at her tone. She was starting to sound like Brandy. Apparently she had reserves of anger and spite she didn't know about.

Blue's smile was slow and sure. "I was special ops."

"An ex-thief was given that sort of expensive training?"

"I was bright and willing to take risks."

She looked hard at him. "You can prove that? Until five minutes ago, you were a drifter I took pity on."

"Until five minutes ago, that's all you needed me to be."

He had the best poker face she'd ever seen: she

couldn't read a thing in it except determination. "Why are you doing this?"

"I like money," he said. "You have it."

Well, Gem decided, Blue was being honest about that, at least. "How much of my money are you wanting?"

He named a figure.

Her eyes bugged out, and she sat on the corner of her desk. People just didn't walk up and ask for that kind of cash. Not from her, at any rate.

A humorless laugh escaped her. "Get out of my office."

"You know where to find me." He turned and walked out.

Gem shook her head in disbelief. She'd never heard such arrogance! The man was a fool. The number he'd named might not beggar her and her family, but it would come close. She had plans for that money, plans to improve The Spark and secure their future. She wasn't about to hand it over to some virtual stranger just because a drunken miner had taken a potshot at her.

No, she decided, she was on her own.

She worked a bit longer before going to look for food. In the kitchen, she was surprised to be openly glared at by the head chef. For a moment she wondered if the fruit in her hand had been destined for a cook pot, and she asked, "What?"

"Your man has eaten the cheese tarts for the wake! All of them! I want his *head*." Jamir slammed his cleaver down, burying it in his chopping block.

Gem glanced at the empty serving tray and frowned. If Blue didn't stop his raiding, he really was going to get a cleaver in the back. "I'll speak to him," she promised. She ignored the reference to Blue being "her man." Jamir had called him that for some time, but he only meant her "hired man." Since nobody else gave Blue orders, she supposed it was a logical conclusion.

Ignoring the grumbling behind her, she entered the garden and searched for Blue. Past the garden was the shed, and she could see a man with a bare chest out there, working. As she got closer she could see he was hitting a punching bag that had been strung from a stout post and beam. It hadn't been there the last time she'd walked out that way.

He ignored her as she approached, sweat making his body gleam. While she was no judge of martial arts, she was glad she wasn't the bag. It didn't take an expert to realize one blow from him could kill.

Which made her consider the cops' suspicions. But if Blue had been behind the shooting at the spaceport, why not just kill her outright? Had he been staging it to get money later through an offer of protection? Could that shooting have been an elaborate hoax?

Gem touched the side of her head and shivered. It was doubtful. That bullet had come too close to be a ruse. Another inch or two and it would have been buried in her brain. It would have been easier to shoot at her feet or something if the intent had been to frighten. And, badly as she wanted to believe that the incident was random, she couldn't. Somebody wanted her dead.

She sat on a bench and watched Blue work out, unwillingly mesmerized. He was a beautiful man. When she saw him like this, the urge to touch him was stronger than she liked to admit. Instinct made her want to lean on him, made her want to let him hold her. Maybe he really could make it better.

Yeah, right.

Blinking at where her mind was going, she changed the track of her thoughts. "You have to stop raiding Jamir's special trays. One of these days he's going to fricassee *you.*"

Blue snorted. "He can try."

"You like to annoy him," Gem pointed out.

"He's a righteous little prig."

"I'm asking," she clarified.

That made him turn. "What's my incentive?"

"I won't have to fire you."

Blue grinned. "I'm not on your payroll anymore."

"What?"

Hyna Blue slowly shook his head. "I've given up being your errand boy. That's not what you need from me."

She let that dangerous comment simmer, then said slowly, "This is an inn, not a flophouse for ex-cons. I won't have a loose cannon on my property. You can't stay here unless you're working or being served, Blue."

"Then it's time to get serving." He moved toward her, his eyes full of hot intent.

Gem stood up in a hurry, ready to ward him off, but he only reached for the towel beside her. She noticed it was one of her good towels, and he was using it as a sweat sop. Her blood burned with both adrenaline and anger. At least now she had a good reason to tremble. "You're going to ruin that! We'll never get the smell out."

He smiled, his eyes glowing as he stared at her. "Do you really care?"

She gritted her teeth, hating his arrogance. "I care. I care that you're mocking me. And if you won't work, you can't stay."

"I plan to work—hard," he corrected, a gleam of humor entering his gaze.

"Not the way I want you to," she ground out. "I'm not paying you to be my bodyguard."

"You'll realize I'm worth it," he promised, and took a swallow of water from a bottle near his feet. "Your security system is archaic. With all these miners running amok, I'm surprised you haven't been robbed blind already. The way you take risks, you'd think your address was Pleasantville, Nirvana. I've got a list of surveillance equipment that needs to be set up to make you current. If you can open your wallet wide enough to buy it, I'll save you the installation fee and set everything up myself. I know just the place to pick it all up. I figure I'll go this afternoon . . ."

Bright fury rose in Gem, making her fingers shake. He was assuming power that wasn't his, taking liberties he wasn't due. Since her father had died, she'd answered to only one authority—her own. She'd compromise with her sisters, because this was a family establishment, but the final say was hers. Now, here Blue was, offering advice, making criticisms, trying to take over and pushing too hard.

As she opened her mouth, he placed a finger over it. "Before you say something nasty, consider. I'm trying to help you. Who else is doing that?"

She jerked away. "You're an ass!"

"I *saved* you." That serious look was back.

Gem calmed a degree. "I don't want your help."

"You have someone else lined up?" he asked. "Show him to me and I'll back off."

Scary, how that reasonable response shook her. "You know I don't."

Blue remained calm. "Then let me show you what I can do. You have nothing to lose but your life."

"Fine." She was caving and couldn't stop it. "Fine, but you're not installing anything in the guest rooms or bathrooms. No surveillance equipment anywhere like that. Not in my room, either!"

He smirked. "Something interesting going on in there?"

"No!" Color stained her cheeks. "You're just not going to invade our privacy."

Blue rested his weight on one leg. "I don't need to. The cameras are for the grounds and the public areas. I don't need to see you strutting around naked. I have a good imagination." His smile was sly.

Gem's eyes narrowed. "That's the only place you'll ever see me like that."

His light touch on her arm stopped her as she turned to go. "I'll come to you with the list later. Then I'll head to the store."

"Fine." She forced herself to walk away. She stumbled on a rock, cursed, and kept going.

Forget the sniper. Blue is the dangerous one.

Chapter Four

The wake started at six that evening. While Gem's presence wasn't required, she liked to look in and make sure things were progressing smoothly. The band—a bunch of moonlighting miners—had already arrived and arranged themselves. She could hear them warming up, and they weren't half bad. Maybe she'd talk to them about doing some work for her. She could envision a small corner stage in the bar. If they brought in enough business, she might even be able to expand the taproom. Maybe they could even try having an open mike some evenings, host a dance . . .

Her head full of ideas, she showered quickly and threw on some clean pants and a slinky, sparkly shirt. A touch of makeup and a sparkly clip later and she was done. She hadn't known the dead miner, but this wasn't the first wake they'd hosted at The Spark. Mine accidents were common enough, and the inn made a good place for both celebrating and mourning. They were hosting enough events recently that she was thinking of adding a complete banquet room. Maybe she'd see about getting some estimates in the morning.

Brandy had taken the night off, rightly assuming the staff could handle things. She'd been spending more time tinkering in the distillery lately, trying new recipes for sodas and ales. At least that's what Gem hoped she was doing. For all she knew, Brandy was carrying on an affair with the brewmaster.

Gem frowned and decided to take a walk through the distillery later. A girl ought to know what was going on in her inn.

Her family's private apartments were on the south side of the inn, above the office. Each sister had her own bedroom, and they shared the sitting room. Their father's room remained vacant. They dusted it from time to time, but that was it. Gem supposed whichever of them married first would take it over.

It suddenly occurred to her that Xera might not come back. It was very possible that she would find a man in the GE and settle down somewhere else, maybe even off-planet. Her sister Brandy showed no signs of doing so, but what if she left also? Gem would be stuck alone in the old family suite, no husband in sight. What a depressing thought!

Shaking it off, she left her room and headed for the private stairs that let out by her office. Opening the door at the bottom, she froze. She'd locked her office door but now it stood open. Someone was inside.

She glanced over at the kitchen, which was full of people coming and going. That, to her mind, narrowed the suspects. A peek around the corner confirmed her suspicions: Blue.

He glanced her way as she pushed the door wide, then continued fishing things out of his box and laying them on her desk. Packing material was scattered around like confetti, along with bits of electronic equipment. Zsak was there, too, and he was preparing to drill a hole in her wall.

"Hold it!" Gem thundered. "What do you think you're doing?"

Zsak was standing on a ladder with his power tool, poised to do untold damage. He lowered the drill at her bellow. "Wow! You look tasty," he said with appreciation. She ignored him.

Blue leaned his hip against her desk and crossed his arms. "Setting up your security system. I assumed you'd want it centralized in your office. We need a place to monitor everything."

"I don't think so! You're not turning my office into some kind of . . . of . . ." The idea of Blue and his overgrown buddy constantly underfoot was unacceptable. "Find someplace else."

"Okaaay. Which one of the guest rooms do you want me to use?"

She glowered at him. "None of them. They're all let out."

"You have forty rooms here!"

"And they're all in use," she repeated. In fact, she was making plans to build a new inn on the other side of the property. They certainly had the demand. "We're at full capacity. Go use the potting shed or something," she grumbled.

"Unacceptable."

She huffed. "Look, if I'd realized your little project was going to cause so many problems—"

"We're not doing this slipshod, girlie," he said sternly. "We need a room to work in, something with access limited to a very few people. What else do you have?"

"The only other spot is our private suite, and I'm not interested in you tromping in and out of that at all hours."

"You'd rather be shot?" he asked politely. "You did approve this list and spend a bundle on this stuff, and we've already installed the cameras and sensors. We can't return them."

Sometimes she hated him. This whole thing was being blown far out of proportion, considering there hadn't been any new attempts today . . . But he was right: She'd paid for the stuff and wasn't one to waste assets. "Fine. You can use my father's room. But I want to know exactly what you're going to do before you do it. Everything."

"Well, first Zsak is going to run to the bathroom. Then we'll do a perimeter check—"

"To the room," she said crossly, knowing he was deliberately misunderstanding. "I have to check on things in the banquet hall, but then I'll be up to supervise. Don't make any holes in the wall until I arrive."

"Yes, ma'am." Zsak saluted her with the drill.

She muttered something nasty under her breath and headed for the door, then turned suddenly. "And don't ever pick my lock again!"

"I'd like to pick her lock," Zsak said mildly after Gem left. "She has no appreciation for what a deal she's getting. You work too cheap, you know."

Blue snorted. "She won't find out from you."

"What you mean is, she won't believe a word I say, considering I'm a friend to your own charming self."

Blue threw monitors back in their box. "I *am* charming."

"Not around her. It would smooth our way if you could be a little slicker. I've seen you do it."

"I don't want to do it. Not with her."

"Now that's a lie if I ever heard one." Zsak laughed as he folded his ladder. "Try again."

Blue sent his friend a dark glance, then continued packing. "We're going to leave here when this assignment is over. She's the type who would want me to stay. You know how the women are on this planet. They have strict moral codes. And me? I'm a professional."

"Never stopped you before. Remember that little Ispian princess? You said she was worth the official reprimand."

"This is different."

"Ah."

"Bite me," Blue said. "Grab that ladder and let's go."

Chapter Five

Gem assumed a pleasant expression as she entered the bar. She'd been looking forward to a little socialization until Blue had thrown her into a foul mood. It'd take effort, but maybe she could salvage the evening. The place was starting to fill up, and there were a couple of good-looking men present. Mourners milled around the buffet tables or socialized in clusters. She wouldn't stay late, of course; miners' wakes could get wild as the night rolled on. Jaq and the servers would handle anyone who got too crazy.

They'd turned on the bar's sparkly lights for the occasion, making the ceiling look like a shifting nebula of stars with pink and blue swirls. They'd just installed the lights, and Gem was proud of them, like she was proud of the new kiwi arbor near the inn's entrance. She and Brandy had strung some sparkly lights out there, too. The look was simple and not sophisticated, but it was beautiful. She had dreams of someday transforming The Spark into something special and artistic, something more than just a watering hole and flophouse for migrant miners.

"Gem. How lovely to see you this evening."

Gem stiffened at the familiar voice. There was no reason for *him* to be here; she would have been content never to hear that deep, cultured voice ever again. Memories of what might have been made her fight for a neutral expression.

"Cirrus," she said, and slowly turned. "I didn't know you were a friend of the deceased."

He smiled affectionately, lingeringly. "I came to see you. You look lovely this evening."

She suddenly felt like crying. At one time she'd had hopes this man would marry her. They'd spent a great deal of time together. Anyone might have thought he was courting her. Unfortunately, she must not have been an attractive enough proposition, because suddenly he'd become distant, gently discouraging. It hadn't taken much to make her back off. She wasn't the sort to pursue an uninterested man.

Drawing in a deep, discreet breath, she smiled politely. "How's your business?"

He lifted his shoulders in a shrug. "We import, we export. Today it is Aliskan sea worm caviar that is hot. We've had an influx of Calisti immigrants. They have a soft spot for such delicacies."

"Well, best of luck with that." Having exhausted her stash of polite business conversation, she gave a polite nod and prepared to make a dignified exit.

"I am having a small party at my house this Friday," Cirrus said slowly, making a polite little bow. "I would be honored if you would join us."

She allowed herself to frown. "I doubt that would be wise. Sadly, I must decline." He always brought out formality in her, as if she had to live up to his standard of polished speech. Sure, she was educated, but she didn't usually speak so stiffly. She wasn't sure she even liked it.

He stared at her from beneath lowered lashes. "I was the one who was unwise, my dear. I have under-estimated many things. However, I will not press you at this time. Have a good evening."

As if she could, now.

Keeping her expression neutral, Gem made her rounds, giving her regrets, and then returned to the family apartments. She didn't hear any yelling as she entered, so Brandy must not have come back. Just as well. She didn't want her sister asking questions.

The suite's kitchen and living room were grouped together in an open design. Their father had favored simple yet comfortable furniture, so the room was chock full of overstuffed, dark leather chairs. The upholstery was fraying, but Gem hadn't gotten around to replacing it yet. Such furniture cost money that could be better used elsewhere. Nonetheless, Gem suddenly wanted to toss it all and start over.

Voices came from her father's room, and she made herself walk over to see what was going on. Not that she cared so much what they were doing at that moment, but she knew she would later.

Blue took one look at her face and stiffened. "Did someone shoot at you again?"

She looked away. "No. It was nothing."

"Something happened."

Knowing he would press, she nonetheless insisted, "It was nothing." Then she admitted, "An old suitor was at the wake. Just . . . memories."

Blue's gaze narrowed. "That rich importer guy?"

Gem stared at him. "How did you know?"

Blue shrugged. "Heard about him when I was still

hanging out in the bar. A couple of guys were discussing your . . . assets. One miner thought a man
could take it easy if he married you. His buddy piped
up and said you were practically engaged to a rich
importer already. 'Nother guy said, Nah, he'd broke
with you, that he wanted a girl with more money."

Brutal but accurate, Gem guessed. She looked
away, her eyes stinging. She canted her head in farewell and headed for her room before any tears fell.

She should have locked her door. She was just drawing breath for a really big sob when it opened. Blue
poked his head in and saw her sitting on her bed.

He winced. "My big mouth. Look, he's scum and
you shouldn't be crying over him. What you need is a
stiff drink and a good boxing match."

She choked, and swiped quickly at the tears that
hadn't quit falling. "I don't box." She laughed.

He snorted. "To watch, then. Or . . . I could teach you
some dirty fighting, if it would make you feel better."

A picture of them wrestling on the floor came to
her mind, which made her shake her head. No, that
wouldn't be good. Not now.

Blue muttered something, moved close and knelt
at her feet, pulled off her shoe.

Startled, she jerked back, but he had a firm grip.
"What are you doing?"

"Sacrificing myself," he muttered. "It's better than
spending the evening cursing my flapping gums. You
ought not take seriously everything that comes out of
them."

"How—? *Ohhhhh.*" She didn't want to relax, but he
had gentle hands, and that was a tender spot he was
massaging.

"See how your foot is all curled up? Nervous habit

with your toes, I'd bet. You need to quit that. One of these days your foot will cramp in your shoe and stay that way." For him, he was using a solicitous tone.

"I don't . . . need you to do this," she whispered. Her throat was too tight to say anything else.

His fingers gently worked each toe; then he moved up to her ankles. He took his time, and his motions made her relax against her will. Slowly, he brought her foot to his mouth and kissed it.

"What are you doing?" she gasped. .

His hands moved up her calf and worked the muscles there. Sure and strong, they soothed away the tension—and made her shudder.

"Stop!"

He did, but he also went to work on the other foot, easing it a couple of inches away from the first and continuing to knead.

Gem fought the muddled morass of her feelings. More than just her foot hurt, and here Blue was, invading her space, a perfect scapegoat for her wounded heart. "What is it you want, Blue? My inn? Think you can make a fortune through me?"

He kissed her foot, moved up to her ankle and then her calf. His eyes lifted, meeting hers. Their blue color was smokier than normal. "It's not money I want," he said.

A sob caught in her throat. Warring feelings buzzed through her blood, made her dizzy. "You want to bed me? Is that it? The way you always talk to me—"

His admission slid through her like hot steel. "Bed you, kiss you . . . lick my way up one leg and down the other . . . with a lengthy pause in between." He widened her thighs an inch by moving her foot, and stared between them.

She gasped. "I'm n-not . . . I . . ." She couldn't make her brain work. Instead, she pushed at him, but she had no strength. She was shocked. That was what it was.

"One kiss," he said darkly, and then crawled atop her, dragging her up the bed. He settled himself between her thighs, making her gulp. Her lungs were working so hard, and it felt like she was trying to drag wet, heavy air into them. She'd never felt the weight of a man before, never known what it would do to her body.

"Hyna!" she gasped.

"Blue," he growled against her mouth. "Just Blue."

They heard a door slam, then Brandy's voice rising in anger. Blue had left Gem's bedroom door open, but it was Zsak her sister was yelling at . . . for now.

Blue cursed. Vividly and thoroughly. For a moment he refused to move, maybe couldn't. Then he rolled off Gem, getting to his feet with another oath. Disoriented, Gem sat up, staring at the door with confusion.

Brandy appeared. Her angry expression grew suspicious. "What's going on in here?"

Gem struggled to look normal, though it was difficult to focus. "Nothing! He didn't even kiss me." She made it to her knees and glanced at Blue. He rolled his eyes and looked away.

Brandy shot Blue a look of disgust. "You were seducing her, weren't you? I knew it! Wrecking my father's room, worming your way in here . . . you just want to get into her bed, don't you?"

He folded his arms and stared at her.

"Have you no shame? You're diseased, aren't you? You'll bring disease to my sister—and babies! You'll get her with child and leave. How dare you? Don't you have any . . . ?" Brandy ranted on and on. She just wouldn't shut up.

Blue glanced at Gem's belly, then her face. He looked away. A tiny smile began to play at the corners of his mouth. Soon he was fighting an actual grin.

"What are you smiling at?" Brandy screamed. She looked ready to hyperventilate.

Zsak walked up behind her, listening. He gave her a wide-eyed look and drew her forcibly from the room. "I think they need to talk," he told Gem's sister. "And you need to breathe."

"He . . . he . . ." Brandy wheezed.

"We'll leave the door open. Come here. I'll find you a bag." He took her across the room and made her lie down on the couch, coached her to slow down and breathe.

Blue looked at Gem. She was sitting on the bed, still dazed. "Well, that was a near thing. Guess it was a good thing your sister was here to save you from my big bad self."

She blew out a breath and looked away.

"I'd better get back to work," he said. With one last scorching look, he shook his head as if with deep regret. He sauntered to the door, hesitated in the doorway. There he turned, scanned her again . . . and winked.

She drew a deep, shuddering breath. Eyes closed, she spared a moment to wish Brandy had taken longer to get home. That he'd closed the door. That . . . something. Well, maybe a closed door would have been bad. He wasn't "the one," but at least a kiss would have ended the tension between them. Of course, giving an inch to a man like Blue would be like tossing him the whole mile. A fool's bet—that's what he was.

In the sitting room, Brandy hadn't calmed down. She'd reached full steam and was now beginning to boil over. Taking pity on Zsak, who was murmuring rather helplessly, Gem slid off the bed and went to calm her sister before she sprang a leak.

Brandy had at least started breathing normally, if not talking coherently, but at the sight of Gem she started to hyperventilate again. Seeing that reinforcements had arrived, Zsak fled.

"Touchy chick," he muttered as he entered the command center that he and Blue were setting up in the girls' father's bedroom. The two men exchanged a look and a silent laugh. Blue got back to work.

"Was she worth it?" Zsak asked. His tone was casual.

"Never found out," Blue replied. He paused, screwdriver in hand, and stared at the wall, unseeing.

"There'll be a next time," Zsak assured him. "Hand me that clutch of wires, would you? No, the yellow ones."

"How could you? We hardly know him!"

Gem considered which subject to tackle first. "All our rooms are rented. I already agreed to pay for the equipment and it won't do any good sitting around."

"But Daddy's room?"

"He's not using it, sis, and I think Dad would approve. He'd be pretty upset if I were shot."

Brandy nodded, allowing for that. "But you still don't know anything about these guys." She lowered her voice. "What if they're behind it all?"

Gem considered for a moment. "Well, I can't say I didn't wonder that myself. The detectives didn't like either of them being around yesterday. Still, when I checked with my friend about Blue, he really didn't have much to tell me other than things Blue admitted himself. I suppose I could make a call about Zsak, though if there'd been anything in his history to report, the police probably would have given it up."

"It's not just me who's worried," Brandy pointed out.

"No. You're being reasonable and looking out for me. Look, Blue was in the IC's peacekeeping forces, and Zsak was, too, from what he says. So, here's what we'll do. I'll make a call to the on-base IC military police and explain what—"

"No calls," Brandy cut in. "We'll go in person first thing tomorrow. Both of us. I'm sure between the two of us we can find a cop who's interested in our case."

"Either that or look extremely silly," Gem muttered.

Now that she had a plan of action, Brandy seemed to be feeling much better. She sat up and said, "I don't care if we look dumb. I'd rather be seen as a flake than be killed by a psycho."

Gem raised her eyebrows, letting the moment pass. She wasn't going to go into any other issue right now.

Her sister stood up, steadying herself on the back of the couch. "Gem?" she said. "No more kissing."

Gem raised her brows again and looked away. She wasn't going to say anything. She had a feeling she shouldn't be making any such promises.

Chapter Six

Kissing seemed to be the last thing on Blue's mind the next day. He met Gem and her sister on the front drive as they prepared to enter a rented transport. Gem took a moment to regret not owning her own vehicle—they were imported and hideously expensive—so she could have raced out of her garage before he saw them. Then again, owning a car might not have given them enough time. The new surveillance system was working.

Blue opened his mouth.

"Don't start," Brandy butted in. "We have some private business to see to, and we don't need you."

His eyes glittered, but his tone was mild. "You willing to bet your life on it?"

"Today? Yeah, I am." Brandy gestured to the holstered guns she and Gem wore. "We're armed and alert. We'll be fine for one short trip."

Blue slanted a look of contempt at their weapons. "Those won't stop a *real* assassin. You agreeing to this, Gem?"

She sighed. "We can't take you with us. Not this time. I'm sorry."

He glanced to the side. "Take Jaq, then." He looked

back at Gem, his eyes hard. "He's an old man, but he's still good in a fight."

"You getting in, ladies?" their driver called out.

"Just a sec," Gem replied. Brandy climbed into the vehicle.

For a moment, Gem looked at Blue. She pondered the dangers she'd already been subjected to, and what might yet lurk in her future. After only a second she said, "Go get him."

Blue ran inside the inn and came out with Jaq in under a minute. Whatever he'd said to the old man must have been persuasive, because Jaq looked obstinate. The old man took one look at Gem's gun and held out his hand. "Give me that before you hurt yourself, and get in. I don't have all day."

Gem did as he asked, slid into the transport and watched as Jaq buckled her holster around his slim hips. By the time she glanced out the window, the transport had already pulled away from the curb. Disquiet settled in the pit of her stomach.

"What did Blue say to you, Jaq?" she asked.

The old man looked at her sideways. "He said, 'That damn fool woman is leaving with her brainless sister and thinks she's protected.' I put Helda in charge and came out to babysit." A small smile played at his mouth.

Brandy snorted in disgust and looked out the opposite window.

Gem closed her eyes and smiled. Helda was a formidable woman—skinny, silent and fierce, the old blonde could terrorize the meanest drunk with a look, just by opening her eyes wide. But that wasn't why she was smiling.

"Do you like him, Jaq?"

The old man glanced at her sidelong. "He's all right."

It was high praise, coming from Jaq. Gem looked out the window and tried to think reasonable thoughts.

The town whizzed by, sleek glass-and-steel blocks capped by some domes and spires. Here and there an old stone-fronted building elbowed aside more modern structures, testament to some rebellious architect. Gem loved the chaos, the mix of styles of Polaris; it fit the residents. Human and alien, all lived together in harmony most of the time.

There were a lot of people out and about, many of them stained blue by mine dust. Some walked, some rode motor boards or electronic bikes, and there seemed to be more of them every day. Polaris was changing. It wasn't much like when she'd grown up.

She shook her head, dislodging the disquiet growing there. It was only the recent troubles that had gotten to her. She loved this place, never wanted to leave. It would take more than an assassin out for her blood to drive her off. She planned to hide herself in The Spark and let it protect her. She'd never need anything else.

It was a fifteen-minute drive to the military base that was their destination. Gem was belatedly glad they'd brought Jaq: he made the check-in easy by flashing his military ID. They were waved inside.

Jaq raised a brow as they stopped at the cop shop. "You checking up on Blue?"

Gem met his eyes. "Wouldn't you?"

The old man shrugged and got out. Wondering at his unconcern, Gem paid the driver and followed.

Like most such places, the military police station

was strictly utilitarian and unfriendly. The austere atmosphere of the base combined with the air of authority intimidated her, but Gem concealed that fact as she walked up to the receptionist and introduced herself. "I need to see someone in charge," she added.

"Concerning?" The woman looked at Gem expectantly. Her short brown hair was held up with a number of clips and matched the brown spots on her camouflage uniform.

"Concerning an ongoing investigation about someone who's shooting at me, and about a veteran I have working for my family."

The woman hesitated, her finger hovering over a buzzer. She got up instead. "One moment. I'll see if the chief is in."

They watched her knock on the chief's door and then disappear inside. In a moment she popped back out and motioned for them to enter.

The chief of military police was middle-aged, lean and very reserved. His face hinted at American Indian heritage, as if he'd flown straight from one of Old Earth's reservations. Strands of silver streaked his black hair. As he stood to greet them, Gem saw he was of average height, but he reeked of authority and command.

"Hello. My name's Chief Blackwing," he said.

"No joke?" Brandy muttered under her breath.

Gem discreetly pinched her. She smiled and extended her hand. Security Chief Blackwing took it carefully and shook, his grip hinting at controlled strength. He performed the same act with Brandy, and nodded to Jaq. "Mr. Cole. I remember you from The Spark. You serve good beer."

Jaq nodded. "Chief."

The security chief moved back behind his desk. "What can I do for you?"

Brandy glanced at her, so Gem explained what had been happening and why they'd come.

Chief Blackwing looked at her, his brown eyes steady. "I see. What is it exactly you fear? You think this Blue is the one shooting at you?"

"He might be," Brandy said stubbornly. "But it's more than that. Somehow he convinced my sister to let him be her bodyguard. For all we know, he doesn't have a clue what he's doing."

The chief digested that, his eyes going to the door. "And where is he today? Did you bring him with you?"

"We made him stay home. How were we supposed to check his story if he was with us?" Brandy explained.

The chief cleared his throat. "I see. Well, I'm afraid I can't release his records to you without good cause, ma'am. *Very* good cause. The military respects the privacy laws, as I'm sure you can appreciate."

Gem considered that. She hadn't really thought they'd make any progress this way.

Brandy gave the chief a hard smile. "Have you seen his records, sir? If you can't give us anything specific, maybe you can venture an opinion as to whether our lives are in danger by having him on our property. How would you like it if your wife or daughter were in this situation?"

His smile cooled a degree. "I'm not married, ma'am. However . . ." He looked at his computer screen and typed in a few commands. Whatever he was looking at took a couple of minutes to scan, but his grim expression gave nothing away.

He looked at Brandy again before he addressed Gem. "I feel confident in his ability to set up and maintain a surveillance system, and to form a protective perimeter around your property. He has no history of crimes against women."

"What about dishonorable conduct? Is he a violent man?" Brandy demanded.

A faint smile turned up the corner of Blackwing's mouth. "All military operatives are violent men. It's in the job description, ma'am."

"You know what I mean," Brandy replied. But her voice held a false sweetness that signaled she was losing patience.

Blackwing clicked a button on his keyboard and laced his hands over his stomach. "If it would ease your mind, ma'am, I can make an informal visit to The Spark this evening. You can introduce me to Blue and I'll let you know what I think."

Brandy looked to the side and blew out a slow breath.

Gem looked at her sister and tried not to smile. She was sure the chief had been as helpful as the constraints of his office would allow, so she stood up and gave him a polite smile. "That won't be necessary, but thank you for your time."

He came around his desk, walked her the two steps to his door and opened it. Then he said, "I don't mind coming tonight. I never need an excuse to stop in for a good beer."

The front door to the military police outpost had barely shut behind them before Brandy growled, "Well, that was useless."

Gem laughed.

"What?" her sister snapped.

"Sometimes you remind me so much of Xera," Gem said teasingly. She elbowed Brandy. "He was cute, though, wasn't he?"

"He's too old for you," Brandy said.

"I meant for you. And old? Looked to me like he was still in pretty good shape. Besides, he put up with your mouth without losing his temper. Maybe that's just the kind of guy you need."

Jaq guffawed. Their transport was pulling back up, and he moved to open the door.

"I'm trying to protect you and no one is taking me seriously," Brandy complained as she slid in.

"I'm here, aren't I?" Jaq responded, closing the door. He gave her a dark look. "Blue tried to be here, too, but you wouldn't have him."

"I don't trust him," she muttered.

Jaq looked at Gem. "He's gone out of his way to help, even though you refuse to pay him."

Her eyes widened on learning that the old man was privy to so much information. She flushed. "I was being bulldozed, Jaq! I barely know him, and he asked for a fortune. What was I supposed to do? For that matter, *he* told *me* he was no longer on my payroll."

"Man's got to eat," Jaq said, settling back in his seat.

"He eats," Brandy remarked. "Jamir is about to quit over how much he eats. Apparently he's also got a free room now, too—conveniently near Gem's." She gave Gem a black glare.

Fed up, Gem glared back. She was tired of her sister's recent attitude. "What are you so afraid of? That I might get a man while you keep chasing them off? Get a life, girl! I'm not Dad, and I don't plan to drop dead on you. Even if I were Dad, you can't protect me all the time."

Brandy crossed her arms and looked out the window.

Gem grimaced, regretting her harsh words. She needed Brandy to back off—she couldn't deal with the hysterics right now—but she didn't want to hurt her sister. She searched for a peace offering. "Look, we can give him one of the guest rooms to use as soon as someone clears out. That will get him out of our suite."

"You won't get him out," Brandy predicted grimly. "You weren't going to let him be your bodyguard, either. You've got putty for a spine where he's concerned."

"I don't!"

"Yeah? I've seen the way you look at him. All he has to do is smile and you blush like a teenager. You *want* him near you."

A betraying heat crawled up Gem's neck. "That's not true."

But was it?

Determined to prove Brandy wrong, Gem planned to confront Blue as soon as they got back. They sprinted into The Spark, coached by Jaq, who swore they ran like a couple of girls. Disgusted, he turned them over to a tense Blue and resumed control of his bar.

"Congratulations," Blue said coolly, his expression as hard as quartz. "You're alive."

Brandy glowered at him and took off, likely headed for the bowels of the inn, to bang around something fragile.

"That girl needs to get laid," Zsak said, passing by. He was wearing a tool belt and a perturbed expression.

"Excuse me?" Gem demanded.

Zsak held up his hands and kept going, though he spun and walked backward, dodging tables. "Hey, not by me. I'm not suffering from cold sheets." He turned around and strode off. Gem barely caught his muttered, "Besides, she'd freeze it off."

Gem opened her mouth, but Zsak was already gone. Frustrated, she turned her attention to Blue. "We need to talk," she said.

She walked toward her office, but halted when she realized he wasn't keeping pace. A glance showed he was following, walking with the same control he seemed to be exerting over his expression.

Straightening her spine, Gem entered her office and motioned for him to close the door. She glanced at the log of visitors. "We've got a guest moving out this afternoon. You can move your equipment to that room."

"Why?" he asked. His stern face and bright eyes were making her nervous.

"We need our privacy. Besides, Brandy and I have reputations to maintain. We don't bring men to our rooms, and they don't stay overnight. You can't be seen coming and going from our suite at all hours. As a former employee—or current one, whatever—it would look doubly bad."

"So you'd rather look good than live?"

Gem took a deep breath to lock down her temper. "We need another solution rather than having you camped outside our door."

He smiled without humor. "As I recall, we tried to

install the equipment in here. Close, but not under-foot. Discreet."

A slow burn of chagrin started in her gut and spread to Gem's head. He *had* tried, and she'd screwed it up. She'd forced him into working in her family suite.

She fiddled with her wristwatch, giving herself a moment to find her voice. "I apologize. I don't do well when things are sprung on me. I'm a planner; spur of the moment things confuse me. In the fu-ture, if you have something you want to do like this, please warn me. *Is* there anything you need to do?"

He shook his head, a glitter in his eye. "You don't want to go offering me carte blanche like that."

She rolled her eyes for show and slipped behind her desk, needing its bulk between her and Blue. Needing a chair to rest her weak knees. She was three seconds from sinking to the ground before him and begging him to finish that aborted kiss. It was appall-ing, but she couldn't seem to wipe the fog from her mind.

"Probably not," she finally said. Her faintly shaky voice made her frown. Clearing her throat, she added more sternly, "About your pay—"

"I told you, I'm not on your payroll."

"And then you asked for a huge amount of money," she pointed out. There, that was better. Business was clearing her head.

"That was before," he remarked.

"Before what?" She shook her head. "As Jaq pointed out, you are actually doing the job. Of course, how does he know anything? He's a great listener, but I hadn't pictured you spilling everything to the first available ear."

Blue canted his head. "Jaq's no ordinary ear, and I asked him to be our backup. He's the closest thing you have to muscle around here, and he already knew what was happening. He's smart and capable. I trust him."

"Lucky thing for you that I do, too," she said with a hint of amusement. Then, realizing that there was no easy answer and she didn't feel like dealing with the situation, she added, "Well, I'm sure you have things to do." Pulling some paperwork in front of her, she glanced down at it.

"One last thing," he said. He placed both hands on her desk and leaned close. "That was the last time you leave this place without me." His eyes offered no compromise.

"Blue . . ."

"I'm discreet," he said. "If you have someone to meet at night, or you need to be alone and—"

"Blue!" she choked out, realizing what he was implying. "I don't go out at night and I don't 'meet anyone alone,' okay? Back off! I'll take you with us next time. Now, go . . . do something." She waved him away before she died of embarrassment. She didn't know how he'd been raised, but her family had been much more traditional and very strict. Not to mention that she'd be ruined personally and professionally if she did the things he suggested.

"Fine." He straightened.

She waited until the door clicked closed behind him, then put her head in her arms. She had to do something about this. He was turning her into something she was not—a spineless shadow of herself. She didn't know how to deal with desire this strong, but giving in wasn't an option. What was the solution?

For the first time, Gem started to realize what drove Brandy. Her sister had always been a passionate person. Maybe she really was frustrated, as Zsak had implied; maybe they both were. They were both getting older. Perhaps it was time Gem admitted certain needs to herself and got serious about a search for a husband.

Unfortunately, the only true candidate had broken her heart. But while she wasn't stupid enough to go back to him, maybe investigating the reasons behind Cirrus's new interest would give her a new direction.

God help her, she needed something.

Chapter Seven

"What are you doing?" Blue asked.

Gem looked up in annoyance. Brandy was right about one thing: Blue hadn't surrendered his real estate in her office. In fact, he'd taken it over as he originally planned, ignoring her protests and the offered guest room. And every time she brought up this fact, he changed the subject.

He was nosy and inconsiderate, too. He had a nasty habit of walking into her office unannounced. She was going to have to move her desk just to get some privacy. Where, though?

Irritated at the thought of giving up her sunny office, she frowned at him as she put away her communicator. "Taking care of personal business."

"You were talking to Cirrus." Not exactly accusing, his blue stare still made her uncomfortable. Blue was carrying a box of equipment, which he set down on the now-cluttered couch.

"When are you going to shift your stuff out of here and into the guest room? It's distracting, sharing my business space with your surveillance equipment." She didn't want to talk about her personal life.

He was undistracted. "Later. We were talking about Cirrus."

Gem shifted in her chair and looked for some paperwork to do. Rats, she'd cleared her desk not ten minutes ago, finished for the day. "And?"

"You were planning to go to his party tomorrow."

"With a guest," she said pleasantly. "We'll have to buy you something suitable for the occasion."

He gave her a forbidding stare. "I'm going as your bodyguard. I won't pose as your lover just to get your old boyfriend riled."

She blinked at him innocently, enjoying his jealousy. "Okay."

He drew a breath and looked aside, muttering something too soft for her to hear.

Gem grinned and got up from her desk, feeling better after putting him in a foul mood. "I'm going to get some fresh air."

"Wait a minute," he ordered. He slung a gun holster around his hips.

It was the first time he'd been openly armed in front of her, and she frowned in question.

He gave her a mild look. "It's time I stopped playing the waiting game and threw out a card. By now, the assassin has been watching. If he doesn't know who I am yet, he will."

She raised an eyebrow. "And who exactly are you?"

He didn't warn her; he just took her in his arms and kissed her for about five seconds. It was enough: whatever she'd been thinking went right out the window.

Disconcertingly, the kiss didn't seem to affect Blue at all. "Ready?" he asked. Taking her hand, he towed her to the door, opened it and let her go first.

It was a wonder she could walk. She'd felt just the barest hint of tongue in that kiss, and it wasn't cold and slimy like she'd been telling herself it would be. Nor was it merely pleasant. Warm, male, *heady*, the kiss had taken her softly like a butterscotch shot, sliding deliciously down her body and causing a shiver.

She still wasn't breathing right when they stepped out into the garden. Blue had been moving her along with a hand at her elbow, but he stopped when they were out of sight of the kitchens. Figuring the air was fresh enough where they were, Gem found a bench under an arbor and sat. She was facing a small clutch of flowers, but didn't really see them.

Slowly, the sound of wind in the leaves cleared her head. She looked up.

"Don't look at me like that," Blue said grimly. His eyes scanned the area, restless, his hands loose and ready. Very un-loverlike.

She looked back at the flowers. "Don't kiss me."

"I only kissed you once," he said.

"You know what I mean," she snapped. "You know what you're doing. Stop it. If you want to protect me, start with protecting me from yourself."

Silence greeted her words. "What is it exactly you want?"

Gem thought about it. Finally she said, "Stop flirting with me. Stop saying the things you say, doing the things you do . . . Keep your hands to yourself."

"You don't want much," he said with a hint of sarcasm. "If I'm to help protect you—"

She stood up and interrupted him. "You've got your freedom, Blue. There are lots of women in the world. Find one that would suit you better. I'm under a lot of stress right now, and I'm going to make a bad decision if you keep this up. I'm not strong enough." The honest words tasted bitter, and she turned back toward the inn.

His touch on her shoulder stopped her. "What do you mean, you're not strong enough? What else is going on besides that person trying to kill you?"

Gem blinked in surprise, and fought annoyance that he was playing coy. "*You're* going on. Brandy's going on. Xera and Cirrus and . . . and a thousand other people. Life goes on, Blue. I'm a part of all that, and I can't afford the energy I've been burning on you. Do your job protecting me if that's what you've decided to do, but let's leave it at that."

This time she made it all the way back to the inn without being stopped.

Sometimes Blue hated himself.

He cleaned his gun, ignoring Zsak, who'd come into Gem's quiet office. Blue had been crashing on this couch at night, despite the fact that he'd been offered a guest suite, so he supposed it doubled as his bedroom. They might be flowered, as he had once bemoaned, but there was nothing wrong with the couch's cushions. Unfortunately, he was too keyed up at the moment to appreciate their comfort.

Zsak slanted a look at him and threw himself into a chair. "Rough day?"

Blue grunted.

His partner sighed. "If it helps, I don't think she's guilty. We've been all over this place, through all her files, and found nothing. The drugs might be connected to The Spark, but *she's* not involved."

"They've been going out on the same shipments as

the beer she exports. The inn has become extremely profitable lately. We can't prove the how or the who yet, but it's close to her."

" 'Close' is not necessarily on target. They work hard around here, and business in general is good. It's not surprising things are looking up."

"With something this explosive, it might as well be," Blue answered, ignoring the last part of Zsak's statement. His eyes were on the weapon and rag in his hands, but in his mind he saw the slums of Polaris, his stomping grounds for the last couple of months.

Contrary to what Gem thought about his existence, he and Zsak had spent the last half year tracking the new designer drug, Nirvana, from dealers to suppliers on-world and off. They now knew it originated on Polaris, and there was only one spaceport from which it could come. However, on every suspected shipment they'd found products from The Spark and Cirrus Exports, Ltd., beer and exotic foodstuffs, but no drugs, even when they went through the crates with tweezers and microscopes. His people, the other officers in the IC's narcotics division, currently had an operative cozying up to Cirrus; he and Zsak had been sent after Gem.

Blue had been unsurprised at first by the relationship of the two suspects, but then they had gained some distance, which made him wonder who was truly guilty. Unfortunately, Cirrus's new girlfriend was losing her charm and he'd turned his sights back on Gem—whose equal desire to speak with Cirrus again was disturbing. Her effect on Blue himself was better left unspoken.

Zsak seemed determined to drag Gem's attraction for him into the light. "Maybe you should look up one of the ladies on base," he suggested. "You've got friends there, and you could use the distraction."

Blue just looked at him.

Zsak threw up his hands. "Okay! I didn't say anything. How about a game of cards instead? You're wound pretty tight. Can't be good for the ulcer."

"Fine." Blue snapped the pieces of his gun back together and set it on the table. The options were to either play or go crazy. "You deal."

Gem stepped out of the transport, keenly aware of the sultry night air. The half-sleeves of her gown were designed to start at her elbows, baring her upper arms, and a silver chain held the silk top of the outfit at her throat. Of pale orange brocade, with blue and gold dragons embroidered over her breasts and trailing down her navel, the dress had captured Blue's attention just as she'd intended. He'd frozen when he first saw her in it, visually tracing the embroidery with his eyes in horrified fascination. He hadn't said a word, but he'd shaken his head like a dog shakes off water and quickly looked away.

Gem smiled to herself. She wouldn't have to do the work of pretending he was her boyfriend now. She wouldn't need to say a word—not with over six feet of tense male hovering at her right shoulder, radiating lethal menace at any man who looked at her too long.

Seeing Cirrus's hostess, who stood on the threshold to greet guests, Gem was grateful she'd arranged for Blue to accompany her. The popular rumor was that Cirrus had dumped Gem for a rich heiress, but Gem's sources said differently. The leggy redhead in the doorway had been hired as

Cirrus's personal assistant, and she was currently providing the most personal assistance possible. Gem had learned the news from his former assistant, who'd been kicked out of Cirrus's bed without any severance, and who'd run straight to Gem and done some clever negotiating in exchange for a ticket off-planet. Gem managed a cynical smile, realizing the woman had done her a true favor by imparting the truth.

"Hello and welcome," the redhead said with a professional smile. "The other guests are gathering in the solarium to enjoy the buffet. My name is Jaqui, and I'll be happy to help with anything you need." A faint frown marred her expression when she looked at Blue.

Unsurprised by the reaction, considering Blue hadn't been extended an invitation, Gem said blithely, "He's with me."

"Ah. Welcome, then, Mr. . . . ?"

"Blue," Hyna said shortly, then ignored her as his eyes drifted to the hall beyond.

They walked inside. The foyer had been done in brown-veined, creamy marble. Arched niches were carved into the walls, displaying Cirrus's extensive collection of artwork, or at least part of it. Twin, curving staircases rose to the upper story, and an elegant balustrade of dark, polished wood matched the stair rail and complemented the cream and tan décor. Original oil paintings graced the walls, muted light gleaming off their gold frames.

Blue caught Gem's gaze with mocking eyes. "Looks like Mr. Money himself lives here. Nice pad, eh?"

She gave him a look of weary distaste. "He doesn't *live* here, Blue. He lives in his office. He's working all the time—when he's not fraternizing with his assistants. One or two rooms in this house he occasionally visits. Mostly it's a showcase."

"It could have been yours," Blue remarked. Gem didn't deign to reply.

They continued walking. Gem lowered her voice as they approached the solarium. "It might not be as expensively decorated, but The Spark could swallow this place whole, at least in terms of square footage. Plus, The Spark's not mortgaged to the hilt. We're expanding, while Cirrus has had to quietly sell off pieces of his beloved artwork to fund his flamboyant lifestyle. Business has not been good for him lately."

"Really?" Blue clearly was interested, but they were approaching the crowd and it was too late to ask more.

Cirrus noticed them almost immediately and oozed on over. Ignoring Blue's presence, he greeted Gem with warm appreciation. "As always, you look beautiful, my dear. What a wonderful gown!" He bowed over her hand and then gracefully released it. Looking at Blue, he said, "I don't think I'm familiar with your guest."

"My bodyguard," Gem said dismissively, quietly smiling to herself. "There have been some disturbing events lately and I felt the need for more protection."

Cirrus frowned, seemingly concerned. "Really? What sort of trouble? Perhaps I can help."

Gem smiled. "Don't concern yourself, Cir. I've taken care of it. Now, I assume you have some wine around here? I'm very thirsty."

"Of course." He summoned a waiter, who fetched a glass. "May I escort you to the buffet?" He looked distantly at Blue and suggested, "I'm sure you can amuse yourself. Feel free to sample the buffet, as well. I recommend the canapés."

Gem couldn't help giving a wicked little smile at Blue's expression. He wore a dark look, but it vanished when he saw her amusement. "I will," he replied.

Cirrus waited until he and Gem were alone at the quietest corner of the buffet table to murmur, "Your man is quite protective—for an employee."

"That's what bodyguards do," she replied, willing herself not to laugh.

She selected three small items for her plate and then moved away from the buffet table to take a glass of wine from a waiter. "Thank you, I'm not very hungry tonight," she remarked as Cirrus raised an eyebrow. Then she strolled to the other side of the room and a private little alcove where Cirrus held out a chair at a table for two.

"I was delighted to see you here tonight," he said as they sat down. "I was afraid you'd be unwilling to forgive me."

She smiled ironically and admitted, "I was curious at your sudden change of heart. You're not the sort to revisit past mistakes."

"You were never a mistake," he replied, looking at her from under his lashes. He leaned a fraction closer. "Allow me to convince you."

She smiled and raised her wineglass to her lips, effectively blocking his move. "Use words, Cirrus. I'm not in the mood to pretend anything foolish."

He sighed and sat back. "How dull."

She raised an eyebrow. "Sorry. But I can only assume some business concern has sent you in my direction."

He was silent for a moment, then seemed to throw in his cards. "Actually, you're right. I hoped you would introduce me to your brewmaster. He's proved, um, immune to my charms."

Gem sat back and savored the feeling of triumph. She'd been right! Not that this was very flattering, but she was glad she'd read him correctly. It gave her a bit more confidence regarding the world and her comprehension of it.

"Our brewmaster's rather reclusive," she admitted. "Very possessive of his knowledge. I don't think even Brandy knows his master recipe. I certainly don't, and I'm the most discreet person in my family."

"I believe that," Cirrus said, with an admiration that surprised her. "I only regret I was so late in discovering your business acumen. But . . . truly, I would appreciate an introduction."

Gem thought hard, but she couldn't fathom any motives other than the obvious. Unfortunately for Cirrus, she had no desire to further his interests, no matter how mundane they were. She smiled at the tabletop and then leaned forward.

"Cirrus?" she said.

He moved closer, his eyes shining with anticipation. "Yes?"

"Absolutely not." Then she stood up, forcing him to rise also.

He was slow to do so. "How cruel, my dear, to deny me such a simple request. But I suppose I deserve it."

"I suppose you do," she replied, maintaining a façade of calm, though her insides were sparking with nerves. "Now, if you'll excuse me? I'm afraid I have another engagement." Walking tall, she sauntered off without another word.

Blue joined her as she left the solarium, and he said, "Cirrus looks like a man who just caught his left nut in a jock strap. What'd you do to him?"

"Nothing," she said blithely.

"Okay, then what did you *say*?"

She smirked. "This and that." Busy savoring her revenge, tiny though it was, she didn't want to pause to answer questions.

Reading easily her desire to leave, Blue hustled her into a waiting transport and held his peace until they made it safely back into The Spark. But when she started to climb the stairs to her suite, he took her arm and steered her toward her office instead.

"Hey!" She frowned at him and rubbed her arm in protest, though his grip hadn't hurt.

"This might be important," he insisted. "Tell me what you talked about."

She rolled her eyes and flopped down on the couch. He'd installed new shutters that worked like blast shields, so she wasn't worried about being shot from behind anymore, but she missed the cool night air. "It wasn't anything profound, Blue!"

He sat down next to her. "So, tell me. No need to hide."

Feeling both relaxed and drunk with success, she eyed him playfully. "Or what? You'll kiss me again?"

"No. I'll arrest you," he said sternly. Then his expression relaxed and he put a hand on her knee. "Or maybe I will kiss you. And I might be diseased, you know. Better talk quick before I convince you not to care."

Gem remembered Brandy's words and laughed. "Fine. He simply wanted to be introduced to my brewmaster, so you can stop acting jealous. Apparently he's heard that our export business is doing well and wants in on it. Too bad for him Jean Luc doesn't like charm."

Blue's hand tightened on her knee. When she glanced at it, startled, he let go, stood up and paced a restless circuit of the room. "Maybe *that* has something to do with this whole mess. I've seen the brewery, but I'd like to take another look with you."

Gem frowned, confused. "Why? Cirrus is a worm, I've learned, but he wouldn't try to kill me over *beer*, for pity's sake."

"I still want to see it," Blue pressed.

Gem shrugged. "Fine. Go see."

"With you."

"Why?"

"I just do."

"Whatever." Suddenly peeved and not sure why, Gem brushed past him on her way to the door. There, she paused dramatically. "We'll look at it tomorrow. Will there be anything else tonight, or is that it?"

Blue stared at her. "That's it."

Shaking her head, she left him to his intrigue.

As Gem exited the room, tension churned in Blue's stomach. He was getting closer to the truth; he sensed it. Unfortunately, the evidence around Gem had just taken another damning turn.

He paced the office, feeling the pressure in his head mount. He'd gotten emotionally involved, and he knew better than to do that. He was dangerously close to screwing up his own investigation because he hadn't kept the distance he should have. It was unprofessional and unlike him. Of course, the bright spot was that he hadn't had sex with her. Contrary to Zsak's teasing, he was discriminating in his lovers. Gem had tested his resolve, but as of this evening he was back on track.

If Gem was guilty, she was going to pay.

Chapter Eight

Too keyed up to rest, Gem changed into more comfortable clothes and went to seek Brandy. Since her sister wasn't in the family suite, Gem figured she'd try the bar. No luck.

To her surprise, however, she saw Chief Blackwing settling into a corner table, the very table Blue used to haunt. Intrigued, she went over and smiled at him. "What can I get you, Chief?"

He smiled slightly. "I didn't expect you to be taking orders."

"Just yours," she admitted. "Though I'm not above fetching a drink or two. Spent many years doing just that before my father promoted me to accounts. So, what'll you have?"

"Just a beer. The Nebula is my favorite. Please."

Gem got them each a beer and settled down opposite him. "Found a night off, did you?"

"I have other responsibilities," the man said.

"I know how that goes," Gem admitted ruefully. "I wish I could hire an office assistant, but finding trustworthy help is hard. My sisters aren't interested." She laughed.

"Heard your younger sister joined the Galactic

Explorers," the chief remarked with faint interest. "Risky business, that."

Gem frowned. "She wouldn't be talked out of it. I guess I should be grateful that Brandy didn't want to follow."

"That one's spoiling for a fight, all right," the chief allowed. "Maybe the military would be a good fit for her."

Gem snorted. "They'd never survive her. I'm sorry she was so difficult the other day, though. She's like a bee-stung bear when she thinks her family is threatened."

The chief nodded. "Has anything else happened?"

"Nope. Maybe whoever it was got tired of taking potshots at me and moved on to better things."

"Or maybe your bodyguard is doing his job."

Gem grimaced in doubt, but offered, "Want to meet him?"

Blackwing looked to the side. Gem followed his gaze and saw Blue coming their way. She nodded and then looked back. "Chief Blackwing, meet Hyna Blue, my bodyguard and general pain in the butt. Have a seat, Blue."

Blue pulled out a chair, spun it backward and crossed his wrists over the back as he sat. "Chief."

Blackwing looked him over without expression. "Ms. Harrsidaughter tells me you're ex-special ops."

"You'd know," Blue replied.

"Just Gem," Gem interjected. "Nobody calls me Ms. unless they owe me money." She looked at Blue. "You never did tell me which unit you belonged to."

"I can't," he said. He didn't elaborate.

She scoffed. "Do I look like a reporter?"

"It's classified."

Blackwing smiled a little and said, "You're not going to get more out of him than that."

"What about you?" she asked lazily, flirting just a little. She was beginning to enjoy Blue's reactions when she did that, and she felt rather than saw him tense.

The chief's eyes slid toward her self-appointed bodyguard. "I don't have to tell him to be discreet. He already knows." Gem slanted a puzzled look at Blue, surprised, wondering what the man was saying.

"I know what I'm doing," Blue remarked.

"You two know each other," she realized slowly, reading the signals.

"By reputation," Blackwing admitted, giving her a warm smile. "Word gets around in our field."

He was handsome when he smiled, and she instinctively responded with teasing warmth. "And what's *your* reputation, Chief?"

"Call me Joe," he replied. "I hear Chief all day."

She nodded and made a decision. "Well, Joe, you seem to admire our beer. How would you like a tour of our brewery? Jean Luc has slunk off for the night, so I can promise he won't be growling over our shoulders the whole time." She glanced at Blue as she said this. He said nothing.

Blackwing grinned. "Dangerously possessive, is he?"

"Territorial," she allowed. "We built the brewery for him, never imagining he'd be like a junkyard dog with a bone. We barely get in there without passing some inspection first. He's a first-rate brewer, though, so we put up with his quirks."

She stood. "Bring the rest of your drink, Chief— you can work on it as we walk." She took her own half-finished bottle, giving Blue an absent look as she rose. "Oh, you wanted to see the place, too, didn't you? Might as well tag along."

They left the bar and headed for the back of the inn.

Uncharacteristically silent, Blue was a step behind them on the short walk. Aware of his subdued state and feeling unusually powerful, Gem smiled at Chief Blackwing as she unlocked the door to the basement and the brewery.

"I know the basic ingredients listed in his beers, of course," she said, "but even Brandy doesn't know his secret ingredient. The only thing he's ever told us was that it's a native herb." She snorted. "We could have figured out as much by reading the label! He keeps it in a locked, unmarked box down—"

She froze in mid-sentence as the door swung open, allowing out the sickly smell of blood and gore. All she could see were gleaming brass vats and pipes, but from somewhere arose something horrid.

"Get her out of here!" Blue whispered harshly, shoving her at Blackwing. "I'll call you when I know more." He ran into the brewery.

Gem had a sudden thought. "Brandy! She never came in. What if—?"

"Let Blue handle it," Blackwing interrupted. He almost had to drag her away, shocked into immobility as she was. "You and I have to call for backup. Medics. We might need them."

Having something to do broke her mental paralysis. "My office," she said. They bolted for the door.

Blue saw the man as soon as he opened the door, his cybernetic eyes instantly adjusting to the dimness within. The bastard stood poised with one hand on Jean Luc; the other hand held a knife.

A mask hid his expression, but the man froze when he saw Blue. He glanced at Jean Luc as if undecided, then took off running for the back exit.

"Call 1," Blue said, activating the code that sent his personal computer into action. It would automatically call for backup and paramedics. It would also alert Zsak, though that would be of little help. Zsak was running an errand far away from The Spark. He would be too late to help chase this guy.

Blue saw Brandy's condition as he ran past, and since he saw she was breathing, he was glad she looked unconscious. She was slumped against a copper pipe, her hands tied above her head. Her head was hanging down, her red hair matted and sticky with blood. She looked like she'd be in a lot of pain when she woke. Badly as he wanted to stop, paramedics were just minutes away. And if he didn't catch her assailant now, he might not get another chance.

The man was stocky and not very fast. Blue gained on him by doing a one-handed vault over a long workbench instead of running around it like the suspect.

The villain reached the back door and fumbled with the lock, but looked back over his shoulder and turned when he saw how close Blue was. He threw his knife. Blue barely deflected it from his face, and it left a long furrow over his cybernetic arm, exposing the metal within. It didn't slow him, though. He drew his gun and aimed for the suspect's back.

A sudden burst of light blinded him, and Blue cursed, suspecting a flash grenade. He reeled, listening to try and pinpoint his foe's movements. There!

It sounded as if he was opening the door. He must have disengaged the lock. Blue blinked as his cybernetic eyes compensated for the sudden burst of light, but it was too late. By the time he got out through the door and swept the grounds, the suspect had gotten away.

Damn.

Chief Blackwing had to take the key from her, Gem was trembling so badly, but they got inside her office and he took over the communicator after sweeping the room with his eyes. He called the medics, pushing her semi-gently into a chair, but she couldn't sit still. Other than an exasperated look, he gave no reaction to her occasional getting up and pacing. Long minutes ticked by as she sat and wondered what was going on.

Blue appeared in the doorway so suddenly that Gem jumped. He looked grave and said, "Jean Luc is in a bad way, but he's still alive."

"Brandy?" Fear clenched Gem's throat, making her words stick.

"She's . . . unconscious," he said slowly, cautiously. He caught Gem as she tried to dart by. "Whoa! The medics are working on her now. I let them in the back. Better wait, honey."

Honey? The endearment terrified her. Something was horribly wrong if he was being sweet. "I need to help!"

Blue drew a slow breath and backed her up toward the couch. "She's swarming with medics who are trying to save her life right now. If you get in their way . . ."

She fell backward more than sat. "What happened?"

Blue looked at Blackwing. "Someone broke in and—I'm guessing here; Jean Luc and Brandy obviously can't talk yet—interrogated them. They have a few broken bones, and some lost blood from strategic cuts. I think we might have interrupted things, but I have to check the surveillance tapes to be sure. The police are going to have loads of questions."

Gem put her face in her hands, unable to take everything in. Suddenly, a surge of strength surprised her. She looked at Blue and said, "I need to be with her now."

He started to shake his head, but she got up from the couch and said, "They'll have some forms for me at the hospital—or the medics will. There's always paperwork. And I'll . . . I'll have to arrange for more protection. Protection for them while they're recovering. . . ." It was so hard to think past the fog of shock, but she needed to keep busy.

"Already done," Chief Blackwing assured her. "The local police will be guarding your sister and Jean Luc twenty-four–seven, believe it. Gem, you need to think about going somewhere quiet until this settles down."

"Not now!" Gem snapped. "If I have to hire ten men like Blue, I will. Someone just hurt my family and I want to find out who. I'll do whatever it takes. I'm glad to be bait."

"You don't know what you're saying," Blue spoke up, his voice harsh. "You haven't seen Brandy."

"Then let's fix that," Gem snapped. "She needs me. Now."

"What she needs is a full medical team and a week of sleep," he growled, but he allowed her out of the room and followed.

Gem thought she was prepared, but her first glimpse of the stretcher holding Jean Luc was bad. Even surrounded by medics as he was, she caught sight of a deep slash that exposed bone down the bartender's cheek.

She closed her eyes and took a deep breath, then opened them in time to see her sister whisked by. Brandy's eyes were swollen shut, her nose was bloody—and that was just the damage Gem saw in a quick glimpse as her sister was rushed past. The rest was covered with blankets, so Gem's imagination started working overtime.

They traveled quickly to the hospital in a rented transport. Blue sat with Gem in the waiting room for hours. He didn't say much, but he brought her hot drinks whenever she ran out and a plate of food from the cafeteria. He ate most of it, actually, but she got a little down and it steadied her.

A doctor explained what they were facing. Brandy had a broken nose, a fractured jaw and several loose teeth. She'd been choked, and every finger and some of the bones in her hands were shattered. She had fractured ribs, internal injuries and both of her shinbones had been broken. Dawn came and went before a tired surgeon in burnt orange scrubs came out with more news. The scrubs clashed with his sparse green hair.

"She's heavily sedated," he said, obviously trying to be considerate in spite of his fatigue. "We've set all the bones, but there's going to be swelling, and you know that bruises get uglier as they get better. The important thing is that she's alive and you'll be able to talk with her, perhaps even tomorrow. Today you can have a short visit, but no staying in her room. The best thing you can do for her is to go home and get some rest. I promise you, she won't wake up before you do."

Gem shook her head, but the doctor was relentless. "Five minutes. Reassure yourself that she's fine and then come back tonight, or better yet, in the morning. I promise you'll have plenty of time to nurse her yourself when we send her home."

"Come on," Blue said gruffly, pulling her toward the ICU. "He's right, and we both need to sleep." He'd dozed in his chair off and on, but his voice still sounded scratchy with fatigue.

"I can't sleep," she said, though she felt awful from lack of rest.

"A few slugs of whiskey will solve that," Blue assured her. "And remember, it could have been worse. She could have been killed," he warned as he opened the door to her sister's room.

Brandy did look awful, beyond recognition. Though Gem wished she were awake and well, it was some comfort to know Brandy wasn't in pain. It was hard not to hold her hand. Her attacker hadn't left many places intact, so Gem stroked her hair.

Tears burned her eyes. "Oh, Bran. Who did this to you? And *why?*"

They stayed until a nurse shooed them out. Gem wasn't walking too straight, so Blue put a steadying arm around her waist. "Come on. We'll go home, take a nap and then come back. There's a lot to do tomorrow."

Gem rested her head on the transport's seat back

on the ride home, exhausted, but once at The Spark she had no interest in going to bed.

"We'll cure that," Blue promised, dragging her into the kitchen. He got her a glass of water, then handed her a pill. "It'll make you sleep," he promised.

She tried to hand it back. "I don't want—"

"Take it. Trust me," he said sternly, closing her hand. "Staying up worrying won't help right now. Get some sleep so you can be of use to your sister."

Gem narrowed her eyes. "Are *you* going to sleep?"

"Absolutely," he promised.

"Liar." She swallowed the pill anyway, knowing he wouldn't give in until she had.

It seemed she had just gone to bed when someone shook her awake.

"Eh? What?" she demanded, trying to roll back over and snuggle down.

"Gem, you need to get up," Blue's voice insisted. "There are some people who need to talk to you."

She could feel the bed dip as he sat down, so she rolled over and settled against the low point of gravity. "No." She snuggled against his thigh, hugging the warmth like a stuffed toy. Sleep came nearer.

"Gem, this is not the time to nap," he said, peeling her hands off his leg. He quickly stood up. "Remember Brandy?"

That woke her. In the odd moment before she drifted out of sleep, she also realized something else. "Why have you gone away?"

"What?" He frowned.

She rubbed a hand through her hair and groggily threw the covers back. "You know what I mean. You're here, but you're not like you were. You . . . you've changed."

There was a moment of silence. "What do you mean?"

"I *mean* . . . Oh, forget it." She was wearing a white sleep shirt. Nothing fancy, but it only came to mid-thigh. She waved him out of her room. "Go. I need to change. Was there anything good in the kitchen? I'm starving."

She frowned at the door as it closed behind him. He *had* changed. Not long ago he would have kissed her senseless if he'd caught her abed, half-dressed, and she'd have been lucky if he stopped there. Wistfully, she revised her thoughts: "Lucky" might have been if he pushed a bit further. These days he didn't even flirt with enthusiasm. Either he was taking his job way too seriously, or she'd lost her appeal.

Not that she could blame him. She closed her eyes, fighting despair, which she didn't have time for. Brandy needed her, and she still had an inn to run.

Blue hadn't enjoyed waking Gem up. Sleeping, she was almost irresistible. Heavy-lidded and with tousled hair, with her nightshirt riding up her thighs, the vision had been almost more than he could handle. Professional or not, he didn't know how much more he could take. His attraction to the woman was messing with his head.

He closed his eyes and rubbed his face. Maybe Zsak was right. Maybe he did need to find a woman. A different woman. But then he shook his head, knowing it was no cure. If it were that easy, he wouldn't be suffering right now.

He sighed and shook the idea out of his head, finger-combing his hair back off his face. He had work to do.

Gem was dry-eyed when she emerged from her room, but her face felt stiff. The first thing she was going to do was eat; then she'd go see her sister. Feeling better for having a plan, she headed toward the kitchen . . . and found Blue at the bottom of her stairs, looking carefully neutral.

"The *police* are here," he said, imparting information he'd clearly held back when first waking her. "They want to ask you some questions."

She closed her eyes and let herself slump for a moment, then rallied. Blue and Blackwing had kept the local police out of her hair last night, but now the piper had come to call and be paid. Drawing a strengthening breath, she said, "Okay, it's got to be done. Have to eat first, though. Would you send them to the dining room and offer them coffee? I'll be with them as soon as I can. Are they in the kitchen? Tell me when they've cleared out, please."

She waited until Blue gave her the all-clear, then entered, sat down at one of the worktables and let Jamir smother her with sympathy and pastries. Being around her own people was just what she needed, and she drew strength from their company.

Finally, fortified, she retreated to her office and let Blue bring in the cops.

Chapter Nine

Gem's first glimpse of the tall, lanky detective in the black narcotics uniform threw her. Long green hair tied back in a ponytail framed a cold face marked by an old knife wound that ran from forehead to temple. He was missing the tip of one ear, and a crystal stud winked from the lobe, as if drawing attention to the mutilation. Obviously the man's main occupation wasn't riding an office chair.

Blue took up a station against the wall. Arms crossed, he directed a cool look at the Narc's two intimidating comrades.

Gem rose automatically from her desk and extended her hand, extending common courtesy. The Narc looked at it, but made no move to take it. Puzzled and a little insulted, Gem let her hand fall.

"I'm Captain Azor, and I've been assigned to your case," the man said in the deep, raspy tones of someone who spent his days inhaling hellfire. "I have some questions for you."

"Okay." Gem gestured for him to take a seat and resumed hers. Reminding herself he was there to help, she looked at Azor attentively. "Do you have any idea who might have hurt my sister and Jean Luc?" In all the excitement, she'd almost forgotten Jean, but she planned to visit him, too. She blinked as she added the trip to her mental schedule. This was turning out to be a jam-packed day, and it wasn't even noon!

"We spoke with Jean Luc this morning," Captain Azor said coldly. "While he claims he didn't know his assailant, he gave us a general physical description. Short, masked, with an unidentified accent. He was trying to get information out of Jean by interrogating your sister. However . . . Jean would not specify what the man wanted."

Gem frowned. "Why not?"

Azor cocked a brow. "Perhaps because he would implicate himself."

Gem shook her head, still puzzled. "In what?"

Azor leaned back and assessed her. "Are you aware that there's a drug investigation centered around your inn, Ms. Harrisdaughter?"

Gem's eyes bugged. "A what? That's not possible. I'm aware of everything that goes on around here!"

Blue snorted.

Gem glared at him, then turned the look on the captain. "That's not possible. You've got to be wrong," she added.

Azor gave her a cold stare. "Are you aware that your sister is taking antidepressant drugs, Ms. Harrisdaughter? You didn't list them on her medical records last night while filling out her paperwork. Her surgeons would have found the information useful. Fortunately, they were in touch with her current doctor. Thank goodness for small communities."

Gem blinked, floored. She'd never heard of such a thing, never suspected it.

Azor continued in a conversational tone that still cut like a whip. "You're a busy woman, Ms. Harris-daughter, that's obvious, but maybe you should have looked into the background of the man you chose to affiliate with. Your brewer has a record of past narcotics violations as wide as your desk. Distributing, suspected manufacturing—someone didn't do their job on that one—fraud . . . The list goes on. You did claim to know everything that happens around here, didn't you?"

The blood had drained from her face as he'd recited the list. Now Gem stared at her desk, blinking in disbelief. This cop was investigating The Spark, and she was smart enough to know what that meant. If they thought she had anything to do with this, she could lose her livelihood, her self-respect and her home, all in one blow.

Azor inclined his head. "You should also know that your sister Brandy is one of our main suspects."

"No!" The word exploded from her in a burst of rage and fear. Gem stood up. "You're mistaken, Captain. My sister would *never* sell drugs."

Azor rose slowly to his feet. "You didn't know she was taking them, either."

"Legal drugs," she ground out. "And I can understand why she wouldn't tell me that."

"Can you?" He handed her a slip of paper. "This is a warrant to search the brewery and anything else on the premises we deem necessary. I trust we have your full cooperation?"

She couldn't speak, could only stare at him, hollow-eyed with shock. He tilted his head at her and left the room.

Gem looked at Blue. "How could I not know? And

Brandy is taking medicine? How could I not know that?"

She shook her head. "You snorted when I said I knew everything that's going on around here. What else am I missing?" She moved around her desk, then jerked to a halt when a plan came to her. "Jean Luc! I have to talk to him."

"He's in custody, Gem. He wasn't hurt *that* badly." Almost reading her mind, he added, "And Brandy's got a fractured jaw. No talking. Broken hands—she can't write, either."

Like a hornet in a jar, she paced, seeking a way out. "This doesn't make sense! Why Brandy? Why not me?" Suddenly a thought hit her, and she froze. "Why not me? They were shooting at me before. Why move to Brandy and Luc now? What's different?"

Blue moved toward her, looking concerned. Maybe he thought she was losing her mind. "I don't know, but settle down. Once Brandy is able to talk, we'll sort it out. She's not going to withhold information about someone who hurt her like that. You know Brandy—she'll want to see him fry."

"Unless he kills her first." She looked at Blue in horror. "She's not safe in that hospital!"

Blue took a deep breath. "Woman, that place is swarming with cops. Nothing's getting past them. Now calm down before you blow a gasket! Look at yourself." He grasped her shoulders and turned her toward a mirror on the wall. She didn't recognize the tormented woman who stared back.

She shuddered and looked away. "I have to get out of here. I have to see Brandy, then try to see Jean Luc and make him talk. Then I'll—"

He shook his head. "Still making lists? I think this

thing has gone beyond something you can organize."

"I have to try!" she exploded, using fury at him to boil off her frustration. "I can't even walk outside without a shadow these days, my sister might have been killed, and you want me to calm down? I know I can't do it all! I know I can't . . ." She broke off as a sob tore from her throat. Horrified, she turned her back on Blue. "Get out. I need a couple of minutes."

Hesitant hands touched her shoulders. She shrugged them off. "Get out!"

Instead, he turned her around and pulled her into a kiss. Cautious, restrained, the embrace grew into an emotional exchange of tension, fear and a buried tenderness. Blue kissed her hard and held nothing back—nothing except his heart, she was certain.

She pulled away with a small moan of pain and buried her face against his chest. He was killing her. He'd made her want him, made her want to have him in her life. When she felt him holding back, it made her realize how limited his offer was. The loss of hope hurt worse than the wanting. "I can't take this."

"Shh." He rocked her a little, stroked her hair, kissed the top of her head and rested his cheek against it. "Shh, little one. Just hush."

Blue wanted Gem to be innocent, wanted it desperately but didn't dare trust his instincts. His personal feelings were no guarantee she wasn't involved. It would be almost as bad if she weren't but her sister was. He knew where those kinds of situations went. The only possible way things could work out was probably the most unlikely outcome. How typical of his life.

Gem pulled away again and sniffed. "I need to go see Brandy," she said.

"Okay."

There was a guard outside Brandy's hospital door, but Blue wasn't necessarily reassured. A rent-a-cop was hardly a threat to the type of guy who'd been responsible for all the recent attacks.

To his surprise, Brandy was able to talk, though it cost her. She looked at Gem and said mushily, "Sis." Her eyes dulled with agony, and her lids half closed as she drew in deep breaths.

"Oh, Bran. Don't try to talk," Gem began, reaching for her hand. She stopped in mid-motion, remembering in time that it was broken.

Brandy's eyes flashed under the bruises. "Sh! M-man was short. A-accent."

"We know. Jean told us," Gem said hastily. "Blue caught him on video, too."

"Drrrrugs," Brandy struggled on. "Wanted know. Jean wouldn't talk." Furious tears ran down her face, but she flinched when Gem gently dabbed at them. "Ugh! Stop," she managed to say, her voice semi-garbled.

Blue stepped in. If Brandy was going to talk, he was going to help her. "Did you know Jean was making drugs, Brandy?" he asked.

She nodded. Gem's lips parted, and she pulled away a little.

Blue hurried on before Gem could interrupt. "Were you involved?"

A slight head shake: *No.*

"Then when did you find out? Recently?"

Brandy sighed and sent a guilty look at Gem. She shook her head. "Last year."

Blue's eyes narrowed as he considered the possibilities. "Was he blackmailing you for silence?"

Another gusty sigh and a nod. "Gem, sor-sorry."

Gem swallowed and looked to the side. "Girl . . . Bran, you should have told me. We would have worked it out."

"You . . . need . . . S-spark," Brandy gasped and closed her eyes in pain. More tears leaked out.

Gem wiped them away, careful as she did. She said, "Stop, now. I'd rather throw the match on The Spark and watch it burn to the ground than lose you. Sleep. Rest. There'll be time later to talk."

Brandy frantically shook her head. "He'll try kill. W-won't testify."

"You won't, or Jean won't want you to?" Blue asked.

"Won't . . . He won't—"

"Want you to," Blue finished grimly. "I understand. I'll take care of it."

Amazingly, her eyes closed and her body relaxed.

Gem looked sharply at him. "What are you going to do?"

"Move you both," he replied. "Whoever was hired to knock you off might not quit just because Jean's going to jail. Until we figure out who the other party in the game is, you'll be better off somewhere else."

"I have a business to run. My one sister is beaten almost to death, the other is off with the Galactic Explorers! I can't just—"

"As of now, your business is worthless to you," Blue interrupted ruthlessly. "It's in the middle of an investigation, and you're going to run for your life. We'll get you a manager and talk to your banker. I don't want you walking back in there until whoever did this is dead."

"But—"

Blue shot a frustrated look at Brandy's bed and dragged Gem out of the room. He didn't stop until they found a clear chunk of hallway. "Think, Gem! Jean Luc has a motive to kill your sister, but we still don't know if he was the one trying to snipe you. Someone else was after him. What if that same someone was the one who tried to kill you?"

She squeezed her eyes shut, trying to follow his logic. "This is too complicated."

"Agreed. Let's settle you somewhere we can sort it out."

"No."

"I have somewhere in mind. I'll take care of it," he promised.

"You're not listening, Blue! I said no."

Fury flashed in his eyes. "You're in the middle of a drug war, and you want to stay here and play house like nothing can touch you."

"Stop it! I'm not the guilty one here, so stop trying to belittle me. Nor am I so naïve that I think I can't be hurt. I have a reminder right there." She pointed back down the hall to Brandy's door with a trembling hand. She forced herself to steady and looked him in the eye. "My family needs me."

The need to cry was choking Gem, from fear and rage and worry for her sister. She wanted to stomp up and down, throw fragile things, watch the splintered fragments slide down the wall. Protect and defend? The cops had no idea what that meant.

"You're a fool, lady," Blue said. "This thing is going to tear you apart."

She looked at him so hard her eyes burned. "Maybe you don't know me like you think you do." She held his gaze for a long moment, then said, "I'm going to talk to Jean Luc. Are you coming?"

She had to do some fast-talking to get the cops to let her see him. Jean Luc wasn't being allowed visitors, but she convinced them she might be helpful. On the slim chance she might, they let her visit with him through a Plexiglas screen. It took an effort to clear the anger from her throat enough to speak. "Luc. You let my sister get hurt."

He stared at her, the stitched-up knife wound fresh and ugly on his cheek. "My apologies. It was regrettable."

"You led the wolves to her."

His expression was cool. "Your sister is an adult. She's responsible for her own actions."

Gem's smile was ugly. She took a moment to stare at this man whom she'd thought she knew, who had been running drugs out of her establishment without her permission or approval. She said, "You realize the cops have my full cooperation."

Jean Luc sat back and looked at her in consideration. "Did you come just to chat, then?" He shrugged. "I suppose it's a change of pace from my cell."

She smiled again without humor. "A small thing: I had a question about Cirrus." She noted the distaste on Jean Luc's face, and was pleased by it. She hoped it would help with the questions to come.

"I know you like him as little as I do," she said. Jean Luc remained quiet, so she added, "He approached me at the wake for that miner. He invited me to his house, which surprised me. It surprised me even more that he wanted me to recommend him to you."

Jean Luc's lip curled with disdain, but he said nothing.

"That was my reaction, too. I told him to piss off." She let the faint satisfaction in Jean Luc's face settle in before she said, "I have a clue what he wanted now, but what I don't understand is why *you* dislike him. He's a . . . persistent man. Is there something about him I should know?"

Jean was silent. It was clear he wasn't willing to give up any information. Gem wondered if he was nervous about damning himself further.

She stared at him for a moment. "Well, if he wanted to get me to promote his cause with you, he's going to be disappointed, isn't he? I expect he'll back off now. And with you out of the way, nobody will try to hurt my family again. I can chase Blue off, cooperate with the cops. Everything will go back to normal. Everything seems to work out for the law-abiding . . ." She stood up as if to go.

"Gem."

She hesitated but didn't turn.

"Don't let Cirrus near you."

Gem gave in, looked back over her shoulder. Jean Luc looked deadly serious.

"As for the other . . . keep him close. It's not over yet."

Blue dialed from his encrypted communicator and paced Gem's office as he waited for someone to pick up. They'd just gotten back from the local police station, and he was in a foul mood. He kicked the flowered couch as he passed, cursing for good measure.

Gem Harrisdaughter was ruining him; he'd seen Azor the other day and known it. He himself used to be the one with the cold smile, the cool head when everything around him went south. Now look at him: he'd tried to remove a suspect from an active investigation because he was afraid of her getting hurt—and because he was afraid she might be guilty. She might be guilty and he was trying to protect her! When had a woman become more important than justice? Snarling, he mentally flayed himself.

Blackwing's voice came on the phone. He wasn't Blue's commander, but he was support on this end for the underfunded and unappreciated Galactic Narcotics office for which Blue worked. "What have you got?"

Blue kept a wary eye on the door. Gem had gone to her room with her laptop computer, so she could look through online listings to try to choose a temporary manager for the inn. He was delighted, because her agreement at hiring the stand-in would make it easier to relocate her for security reasons until the assassin was caught. She wasn't doing it for his convenience, however. She'd determined that Brandy needed her right now, and she wanted to make sure The Spark continued to run smoothly while she was preoccupied. She still had no current intention of hiding, of running. He decided to skip the conversation with Brandy, and Blackwing already knew about the one with Jean Luc. He decided to simply report: "Gem refuses to leave The Spark."

"Interesting." Chief Blackwing sighed on the other end of the line. "Do we think she's innocent?"

"Well, with her sister as involved as she is . . ." Blue couldn't quite vindicate her. "Gem's part in this is still unknown. Personally, I think she's scared for Brandy, and I believe that she didn't know Jean Luc was blackmailing her." He thought the situation over carefully, reviewing all the details in his mind. Was Gem capable of dealing with Jean but leaving her sister unaware? Were the sisters so double-dealing as to lie to each other?

There was a beep as a new participant was added to the communicator frequency. "I think Gem's innocent," Zsak remarked, coming in late to the meeting. He walked through the door to Gem's office and glanced at Blue, who adjusted his earpiece. "She's too uptight, too straitlaced to get involved in something like this. Her sister? That's less surprising. She's wired pretty tight."

Blackwing pondered Zsak's remark. "That's a big difference of opinion between you two. Why are you convinced Gem's still a possibility if Zsak isn't, Blue? At this point, for her to be involved would require an enormous amount of deception and a convoluted scheme that—"

"I've seen it happen, sir," Blue interrupted, tense with warring emotions. He couldn't let this go until he was sure, didn't want to be wrong about Gem. He *couldn't* be wrong about her. He didn't want to look into why.

"Did we get a match on those surveillance photos?" he asked, changing the subject. Brandy and Jean Luc's assailant had been uncommonly stupid. Though the man had worn a mask, preventing Blue from identifying him, he'd avoided none of the cameras while entering and leaving the brewery, and the police had computer programs that could reconstruct his face under the cloth. It wouldn't be a perfect picture they created, but it was a great start. As soon as they could match that against another photo, they'd have the man dead to rights.

"Hamish Nasser," the chief said. "He's got a record and is suspected in several other cases where we lacked enough evidence to convict. He's a local miner, had been using an alias to lie low. This time we have him. The only trouble will be finding the bastard."

"Finding him? How hard can that be in a settlement this size?" Blue shook his head, surprised.

The chief sounded grim. "Harder than you think, if he's got friends. Until we find him, keep Gem under wraps. We've moved her sister to a more secure facility, and there's no telling whom he'll go after next."

"Gem's not going to like this."

"It's your job to keep her pacified," Blackwing said. His tone brooked no argument. "You ought to have enough emotional cash to do that by now. Her tender feelings are secondary to keeping her alive. Remind her that she should be grateful she's not being hauled in for questioning. No need to treat her like she's a suspect, of course."

"Not yet." The words were bitter in Blue's mouth.

Zsak stared at him in silence after they hung up.

"What?" Blue asked.

"Why are you doing that?"

"What?" Blue turned to look at the monitor. From what he saw, Gem had found a couple of candidates.

"You're making her out to be guilty when we both know she's not."

"We *don't* know that. Besides, why not prepare for the worst? If I go soft on her just because . . ." He couldn't finish the thought. Instead he said, "Her sister is going to be charged with conspiracy. Think she'll appreciate me then? Might as well give her a reason to hate me right away."

The silence stretched. Blue realized Zsak was a terrifying interrogator.

He shook his head, rubbed the bridge of his nose and finally looked at his partner. "What's the difference who I suggest is involved in this? Unless you have another agenda . . . It'll never work between us, though. I'm not stupid enough to get tangled up with this girl. You know that, so why are you pushing?"

Zsak shrugged and got up from the couch. "I just think you're throwing away something good. There's a way to work this out, man."

What was Zsak's problem? Why was he so fixated on setting the two of them up? Sure, Gem was one of the most attractive women Blue had ever seen, and he respected what she'd accomplished on this planet, with this inn, assuming she wasn't involved in the drug trade—but how could he assume that? A real relationship just wasn't possible. Didn't his partner realize that?

"'A way to work this out.' Really. What would you suggest?" Blue turned abruptly on his friend, unaccustomed pain making his sarcasm thick.

Zsak met his gaze, unflinching. "Tell her the truth. Tell her *before* you bed her—you know how emotional women get about these things. But as soon as she calms down from what you tell her, bed her. On this planet, possession is nine-tenths of the law. She can't accuse you of false pretenses if you tell her the full and unfettered truth, and she'll get over the rest."

"'She'll get over the rest,'" Blue repeated incredulously. "And we'll live happily ever after, right?" He laughed without humor. In fact, his friend's plan was so stupid that he laughed again.

"I didn't say you wouldn't have to work for it. Hell, man. And don't take it out on me. You're the one who's gone and gotten himself so smitten by a woman connected to his assignment that he can't think straight." Zsak walked out with one final parting shot: "But you should do *something*. You never used to be such a wuss."

Gem arranged for interviews of office manager candidates, did a few final chores and then called it a day. She hadn't been so tired in years. In fact, she hadn't been so tired since her father died. It was amazing how much she relied on her sisters. With them no longer around, she was shouldering the bulk of the work to keep up the inn. It was no longer fun, either. It had been a family thing, and now her family was gone.

Shaking off her feeling of emptiness—The Spark was full up, wasn't it?—Gem returned to her office, settled down on her couch and drew up a blanket, something she rarely did during the day. Eyes closed, she tried to rest. But . . . there was musk on the pillow.

Her eyes flew open. She'd conveniently forgotten that Blue slept here now. He still hadn't moved his equipment, and he still hadn't moved the place where he crashed at night. Which meant, in essence, she was sleeping in his bed.

She scowled and firmly closed her eyes. None of that, now! She didn't need to be fantasizing about another man who'd cooled to her. In fact, he'd cooled to her the moment her life had gone into the toilet. What sort of taste did she have in men, to keep choosing ones who were so unreliable? What was she thinking?

But . . . Her eyes slid back open. She'd already spent too much time thinking about him for her mind not to wander down its favorite track. Blue wasn't all bad. He'd been there for her at the hospital, and he'd remained in her life after things got rough. In fact, hadn't he been trying to protect her and her family all along? Hadn't he remained by her side, protecting her from assailants and lawmen alike? And he'd kissed her, and she wanted more. This might not be exactly love, but she was dangling over the abyss. One more kiss and she'd be free-falling.

Did she want him? Yes. She couldn't deny that. Did she want him to stay? That was harder to answer.

Another question was, would he want to?

She thought about things for a while and decided it was impossible to know Hyna Blue's mind. What she did know was that he was jealous when she flirted with other men. No, he didn't handle it at all well when she dressed up and went public. That had to mean something.

Chapter Ten

Preparing the new office manager she hired, Tam Rasheed, ate up a huge chunk of the following days. Of Lupish decent, Tam was stout, taciturn and had a resume to be proud of, along with an excellent recommendation from his former employer, a man Gem had actually met: It seemed prudent to be particularly careful regarding any new hires at this juncture. Tam also had the face of a wolf—if a dignified one—and a full pelt of white hair. There'd be no end to the shedding, but she couldn't afford to be prejudiced.

While Tam was experienced, there were a thousand details to cover. An amiable sort, he clearly had a different way of tackling problems than Gem, so she decided to let him know the most important aspects of the business and let him ask questions about the rest. There was also the headache of moving her private things to her father's old room, where she'd decided to make her new, non-working office.

Blue helped. A far cry from the irreverent drifter he'd once been, he now exuded an attitude she would call "professionally aloof." He didn't flirt; his eyes didn't linger on her body. He was everything she would hope for in a man hired to protect her.

She hated it.

She climbed the stairs behind him, carrying a box of books. At first she tried not to stare at the picture those snug pants made of his behind, then decided she didn't care. He was a good-looking guy. It wasn't as if he had a wife, and there was no law against looking.

As she reached the room, instead of gently setting the box on the bed, she dropped it to the floor with a satisfying thump. Then, with a grim smile, she turned to leave.

Blue had been on his way out, but as the box fell to the floor he stopped and stared at her, clearly surprised by her abandon. "Are you all right?"

His eyes were so blue. Combined with his beard shadow and the black knit shirt hugging his chest, there was only so much a girl could take.

Gem bared her teeth in a parody of a smile. "I'm getting married."

He stiffened as if she'd thrown ice water on him. *"What?"*

"You heard me." She made a move to pass him.

He refused to move. "What do you mean, you're getting married? To whom? Why wasn't I told?"

"You're my bodyguard, not my brother," she snapped. When he still wouldn't get out of her way, she put a hand on her hip and canted her head. "Are you going to stand there all day?"

He stepped aside but was hot on her heels as she headed back to her office. "Explain yourself. Who are you marrying?"

She shrugged, grabbed the first box she could lay hands on and spun to make the return trip.

Blue didn't grab a box. He just followed, nearly stepping on her heels as he pursued her.

Exasperated—but, yes, enjoying his reaction— Gem swung around and glowered at him. "The person I'm marrying shouldn't matter to you. As soon as this is all cleared up, you'll be gone and I'll get on with my life."

Blue's eyes narrowed. "You haven't picked anybody yet."

She smiled, a little self-deprecatingly. "I don't think I'll have any problem finding a willing partner. Everyone thinks I'm rich, right? The Harrisdaughter fortune. Who wouldn't want a piece of that?" She turned and headed back toward the family suite.

Blue looked upset. He let her get as far as her living room before demanding, "Why would you even say that? And you can do better than someone trying to marry you for your money."

She tried to make her eyes hard, though she was afraid she failed. "How would you know what I can or can't do better than? With my father dead, one sister in the hospital and the other off with the Galactic Explorers, what do I really have to look forward to? I'm not getting any younger, certainly. And . . . what is it you men are always saying? Oh, yes: 'I have needs.'"

"Wait a minute!" He stopped her as she tried to pass, wearing a horrified look.

Anger and an unfamiliar grief made her grit her teeth and push away. She didn't want to look at him now, didn't want to see his reaction. Not unless . . . "This is getting old, Blue," she warned.

He leaned forward, trying to move past her, trying

to see her face. "You don't have to marry some idiot just to take care of *that*. There are other ways." There was a note in his voice she couldn't quite place, and he put a hand on her shoulder.

She scoffed, realizing she should have expected this response. She shook off his hand. "Yeah, for you. For a *man*. If I took a lover out of wedlock the news would be all over town by nightfall. Polaris society is intolerant of such shenanigans. I'd be ruined; my business would never be the same. Then where would Brandy be? Where's she going to get the money for her medical care?"

"No one would have to know," Blue argued. "Believe me, there are people in this town—"

"What exactly are you suggesting, Blue?" she asked coldly. When he hesitated, she gave him a mocking smile. "Yeah, I didn't think so."

This time when she tried to move away, he stopped her with two hands. There was a heat in his voice that hadn't been there since before the incident with Brandy and Jean Luc. "What are *you* asking *me* for, sweetheart?"

A trembling started at his touch, and it spread through Gem, causing a shaky hollow in her belly. She couldn't meet his eyes. "Nothing," she said. "I don't want anything from you."

One large, callused hand slid into her hair, cupped the back of her skull. His thumb rubbed gently behind her ear, making her weak, and he stared into her eyes. He seemed to come to a decision and said, "Well . . . I want something from you. I've wanted it for a long time."

He caressed her temple with his lips, gently nuzzled in front of her ear, but she drew a tight breath and said, "You can't have anything you want."

She'd meant to say *everything*, but maybe the other was true, too.

He laughed. "Maybe not 'anything,' sweetheart, but I think we can come to an arrangement."

His kiss was seductive, possessive. He took her mouth like a man who'd thought about the act and savored its fulfillment. If kisses could be drugs, his were the very essence of ecstasy. One hit wasn't enough. She'd never have enough.

Lightning shocks started at her knees and shivered through her bones. A fire began low in her belly. She wanted to breathe Blue in, to lose all control. And she did precisely that. Gem, who'd never kissed a man the way she now kissed Blue, slid her hands under his shirt and tugged, trying mindlessly to get it off.

Blue didn't laugh, as Gem might once have feared he would. Instead, he ripped his shirt over his head and sent it flying, then tumbled her horizontal.

He was so hot. Hard, heavy muscle pressed Gem into the couch, his heated mouth scorching. Her own body blazed as if she'd run miles under the noonday sun, and Blue's back flexed under Gem's hands like living steel, his hair brushing like silk against her jaw as he kissed his way down her neck. The very different sensations melded in a ceaseless duet played by steel guitar and drum.

He ripped open her shirt, making her gasp. There was nothing but air between his mouth and her breasts, then not even that. The fire of lust devoured all restraint. She'd waited too long, wanted this too much. She couldn't stop him. Didn't want to stop him.

Blue growled something urgent and then pulled down her pants. He didn't bother working them off her knees, just flipped her over on her stomach, raised her hips with a pillow and set his lips to her center. Gem's first touch from a man was the invasion of Blue's tongue. Her first climax came seconds later.

His hungry, desperate growl vibrated tissues slick and swollen with passion, triggering aftershocks. She twisted on the couch, gasping as he tongued deeper, as the tapestry fabric abraded nipples new to such stimulation. She sought it, rubbed against it. Her body continued to burn.

He laved her flesh until her body grew weak from her screaming into the couch; then he pulled back with a curse. Through a curtain of hair she saw him shed his clothes, leaving him wearing nothing more than a braided hemp necklace.

She sat up, her wide eyes riveted on his body as he sat beside her. He lifted her legs and took her pants fully off; then he lifted her onto his lap and kissed her. She felt the prodding of his sex. After a moment he slid her down between his legs so that she was kneeling on the carpet, facing him. His eyes on hers, he scooted to the edge of the couch and cradled her to him, her face against his hard abdomen.

Her breasts rested in his lap. Between them rose . . . She shuddered, her damp thighs a reminder of how much pleasure he'd given her.

How much he *still* gave her. Blue leaned down and kissed the top of her head, her temple. He threaded his fingers through her hair and stroked. Both soothing and provocative, his touch made her ache again, made her squeeze her legs together to try and soothe her desire.

Her first kiss to his stomach was almost involuntary: she had to touch him. But as his hands stroked her hair in tender encouragement, caressed her spine, she scattered shy kisses all around on his hips and thighs, gently touched the dark hair that grew there. Then, when he leaned back against the couch, his head falling back and his hands going slack, then stroking her shoulders, she carefully kissed swollen flesh covered by silky skin. He was so hard! How?

His whisper sounded like a benediction as she explored him with her fingers, all sensual curiosity. His head moved from side to side as she stroked, found a rhythm.

"Harder," he gasped. His hand closed over hers, showed her what he liked, both harder and faster than what she'd assumed. When his hand fell away, she kept up the rhythm, watched his face, his breathing. Then he climaxed in her hand, arching back and shouting with release.

Gem drew back, shaken and dazed. What had just happened? What did it mean? Unsure what to do with the wetness on her hand, she murmured something apologetic and headed for the bathroom.

In a fog she washed her hands, trying not to notice her naked chest even as spray from the faucet dampened it. She still wore her torn shirt. The face in the bathroom mirror was scared. She'd never done this before, but the smell of sex was an unmistakable reminder that it had really happened.

Her eyes wide, she pulled the ragged edges of her shirt closed as Blue came in. He was naked. He dampened a washcloth and cleaned himself up. His eyes were brighter than ever.

"Are you all right?" he asked.

"Uh, yeah." She didn't know what to say, where to look.

"Hm." He tossed the washcloth he'd used toward the tub. "Do you want a shower?"

Confused, she shook her head.

His smile was lopsided. "I mean, with me. It'll be fun."

Fun? Somehow, that had been the wrong word to use. It sounded too . . . nonchalant. She shook her head again and scuttled away, hurrying to her bedroom. There, with the door locked, she discarded her torn shirt and quickly grabbed another. She was unraveling and didn't understand it.

A knock sounded at the door. "Gem? Are you all right?"

"Yes. I'm fine. Go away."

She bit her lip. She shouldn't have added the last part. It would only make matters worse.

Sure enough, he failed to leave. The silence on the other side of the door was damning. A full minute went by.

Then, "Open the door, Gem." It was an order: calm, but not to be ignored.

Gem knew the door wouldn't last if he decided to take it down. She didn't want to have to repair it.

She didn't meet his eyes as she let him in. At least she'd had time to dress. Unwilling to sit on the bed, she stood on unsteady legs and inspected her fingernails.

"You're ashamed of this," he said. It wasn't a question.

She took a deep breath. "I might have been hasty. I apologize for—"

"I don't."

Her head whipped up. She saw that he'd re-donned his jeans, but his shirt was bunched in one hand and his feet were bare. His eyes glittered with the memory of what they'd just shared. Gem closed her eyes against the fire it lit in her.

"Just so we're clear," he added, "I intend to do it again. Don't bother saying you didn't like it—I was there. A man doesn't like to give up what's already been given to him, and you've given yourself. You should've thought twice, darlin', but now your thinking's done."

His eyes flicked possessively over her; then he turned and left.

Gem wrapped her arms around herself after he'd gone. Shivers wracked her body, but it wasn't from cold.

Blue was a man of his word.

Xera was coming home! Gem was torn between relief at having her sister back and worry over the circumstances. She'd been summoned by the police, both the local cops and the IC's narcotics division. Though Xera would be a source of personal support, Gem also didn't want her involved. She couldn't imagine that Xera knew anything relevant to the case.

Regardless of Gem's fears, Xera would arrive in three days. And their single conversation hadn't gone well:

"What did you think you were doing, waiting *days* before you told me Brandy was in the hospital? All it

would have taken was a simple pin beam. Three minutes, Gem! Don't you think I deserve to know that
people beat the hell out of my sister?"

Gem held the communicator away from her ear
and winced. "Xera, you were in the middle of a flight
to—"

"I don't care! Get that through your head, Gem. If
my family is harmed, I need to know. Why would any
amount of distance change how much I care? And
this would never have happened while I was home."

Wondering what Xera thought she would have
done, Gem rolled her eyes. Her sister had always had
this Amazonian protective streak. Still, she tried to
reassure her. "Look, Jaq and Blue—"

"Blue! That worthless drifter? As if he could do
anything I'd be remotely reassured by. All he does is
eat and try to crawl into your bed."

Guilt strangled Gem. Thank God her sister couldn't
see her face.

Xera took her silence in stride. "Look, this is what
I want to you to do. Stay close to home, close to Jaq. I
talked with him, and it sounds like he has the bar
and the staff under control. Keep Blue in the gardens, working on something there—you don't need
him for a distraction. You've got the local police and
that Narc guy—Azul? Azor?—on quick connect,
right?"

Gem ground her teeth. This was an aspect of Xera
she hadn't missed: her bossiness. "I've got things under control, sis. Just get yourself home."

"As fast as this ship can fly," Xera agreed. "But before I get there, is there anything else I should
know?"

The urge to lie and deal with her sister later was

strong, but Gem knew she'd rather have Xera a solar system away when she exploded. Yes, better the people on the other end had to deal with Xera than Gem suffering her rage in person. So, quickly she gave Xera the full scope of what they were dealing with, including the background on Blue, Chief Blackwing's assessment of him, and the fact that he was now her bodyguard. She could almost hear her sibling's fury quivering over the communicator's pinbeam.

Surprisingly, Xera's voice, when it came, was tight and controlled. "Gem, I will be home in three days. When I get there, we are going to make some serious changes. Until then, don't do a thing. I'm afraid of what you might screw up next."

As soon as the communicator clicked dead, Gem got a stomachache that wouldn't go away.

Blue didn't help. He wasn't subtle about the change between them, and the way he looked at her—all smoky heat—made her weak.

Jaq noticed. The first time he saw, he raised his brows, considered her, and smiled. Then he went back to polishing shot glasses.

Gem knew her new manager noticed, too. Mr. Rasheed often sent both her and Blue faintly suspicious looks, but since they were never making out directly under his nose, he seemed to reserve judgment. Gem did her best to remain professional around him, and that seemed to settle his mind. She hired an assistant whom she let Mr. Rasheed train. The time this saved was freed up for her to visit and help out Brandy.

Brandy. Gem's sister was a situation of her own. The swelling was going down, but she still looked terrible. Talking hurt, so they did little of that. Mostly Gem kept silent company while Brandy watched comedy broadcasts.

Worry hounded Gem. Not only because Brandy was so badly hurt, but because there was still the matter of her involvement in the drug smuggling operation. That problem wouldn't go away simply because the girl was recuperating from assault. And yes, she'd been blackmailed, but Gem could hardly believe the lengths to which Brandy had gone in trying to protect her partners in crime. It just wasn't in character.

The unhappy thought occurred to Gem that Jean Luc held something else over her sister's head. Could the two have been lovers? Gem grimaced. She couldn't see it, herself, but she also hadn't seen this drug operation. Her sister was a passionate person. Perhaps she'd been lonely. Maybe she'd thought she'd never do better.

Gem didn't want to bring it up, didn't want to deal with the pain and deception, but she also was never the kind to let things fester. The only choice was to ask Brandy about it.

Her sister's eyes bugged out when the question was posed. "No! How could you even . . . ? *No!*" She winced, for her healing jaw protested. Even with healing accelerators, wounds didn't vanish overnight.

Quickly raising her hands in defeat, Gem tried to appease her sister before she hurt herself. "I'm sorry! Really. I'm just trying to figure things out. It seems so incredible to me that you'd let Jean Luc blackmail you for so long. You're not a weak person, Bran. I *know* that. Was there something else he used against you? We need to get it out in the open if there was. These secrets are killing us."

A cynical look came into Brandy's eyes. She looked

away for a long moment, as if thinking. When she met Gem's eyes again, it was with bitter self-disgust. Nonetheless, she admitted: "Xera. I covered for her."

Gem just stared.

"I walked in on her and a guy in bed together last year. Jean Luc overheard us arguing about it."

It was lucky Gem was sitting down. She hadn't had a clue.

A good thing, too, that she'd been unaware. If word of this kind of indiscretion had leaked out, Xera would have *had* to move off-planet. As all three sisters knew, Polaris society didn't tolerate people bedding down outside of wedlock. Sure, if she'd married the guy, the furor would have eventually settled down, but it didn't sound as if it had been that kind of alliance. Of course, Xera's plan had always been to join the Galactic Explorers, and Gem knew how stubborn she could be.

What burned most was, Gem had never met the man. Had she? "Who . . . ?"

Brandy shrugged. "Some drifter."

A drifter? Oh, Xera had some gall, throwing Blue in Gem's face. At least Blue had proved he would . . . She frowned. What? What had he proven? That he would stick around? Maybe for a while. She didn't know anything more than she had before he'd taken her body so thoroughly and—

She wrenched her thoughts back to Xera. "Were there . . . any complications?"

Brandy sighed. "She says they didn't get that far; she just wanted to explore. They looked pretty naked to me, so I don't know if she was telling the truth."

"Naked?" Gem repeated.

Brandy glared at her. "What do you want, a book

on it? Here's what happened: They were in bed with the covers over them. They were kissing. How graphic do you want me to get? He wasn't on top of her." Brandy colored suddenly, obviously feeling she'd gone too far.

Gem felt her own face burn and wanted to get away from the topic. "Okay. That's that. But about the other situation: I assume she didn't know you were covering for her? Dumb question—of course she didn't. She would never have allowed that. So, how about I stop asking you questions? Your jaw must be sore."

She needed to think. No wonder Xera had wanted off-planet so badly. She'd made an indiscreet choice and it was haunting her. Not that Gem could point fingers. It seemed all three of the Harrisdaughters were long overdue to settle down and therefore making rash decisions.

Which circled her around to Blue. What was his deal? She clearly believed that she needed to settle down to be happy, needed to create her own little family. But making that family wouldn't be done with him. He wasn't going to stay and she knew that. That whole thing with him was an aberration she needed to squelch. She'd been so controlled her whole life, and so maybe she'd been due for a crack in the dike. She'd been under a lot of pressure lately, and she'd chosen a dangerous release. She wasn't the only one to have done so.

No, she decided, she had to work on making herself happy in her life. Until then, she'd just have to find a better way to relieve the stress.

She had to remind herself that a healthy release just couldn't happen in Blue's arms.

Chapter Eleven

"What are you doing?"

Gem pulled another weed before she looked up into Blue's furious face. "I'm reclaiming my sanity."

"Is it worth dying over?"

It was late afternoon and she was in the gardens behind the inn, hidden from casual observers by the tall hedges. The flowering berry plants released sweet perfume into the breeze. It had been a relaxing ten minutes until he'd stormed up, breathing fire.

"Perhaps not, but it's an improvement over going crazy, pacing inside my room. I don't take confinement well."

"Yeah? Then you're going to love a coffin. Come on." He reached for her arm.

She calmly whacked his hand with the flat of her trowel. "Thank you for your concern. Why don't you spend your time protecting instead of badgering me?" She'd decided working in the garden was one of the ingredients of normalcy she'd been missing. Since the whole thing with the sniper had begun, she'd barely had access to her own front yard. Kept from the regular release of tension that gardening gave, she'd slid into something explosive with Blue. If she wanted to regain control, she needed this.

His eyes narrowed as he shook his stinging hand. "Do you have any idea how easy it would be to shoot you in the open like this?"

"No. That's your job. Well, to protect my family is your job. If you'd been doing it the night Brandy and Jean Luc were attacked, my sister wouldn't be in the hospital." All feeling of relaxation had begun to vanish from Gem: Blue had a talent for stealing it.

"Thank you for the reminder. Yes, I think I will do my job," he said. Then he stooped and gathered her up in an armful, then began striding for the inn.

She'd just opened her mouth to lambaste him when she felt his body jerk. Blue staggered as if struck by a club, then dodged right, left and pitched through the open kitchen door and into the inn.

Gem landed heavily on her hip, the wind knocked out of her. Tears sprang to her eyes, blurring the rising chaos. Someone dragged her away from the door, bumping her cheek on a chair leg as he did. She didn't realize it was Blue, or that he was bleeding all over the floor, until they both staggered into the taproom.

"Jaq, help him!" she gasped as Blue collapsed into a chair. He listed forward, and she tried to steady him.

Ignoring everyone and everything else, Blue summoned all his strength to raise his head and meet Zsak's shocked gaze; his friend had been prowling the bar.

"Get him," he commanded hoarsely. There was grim purpose in his eyes.

Zsak nodded, grabbed a gun from under the bar and took off.

Gem didn't have time to wonder. Blue had been shot in the left shoulder and was bleeding buckets. She and several waitresses formed compresses out of bar towels and laid him on the floor, but Gem didn't like his pallor.

"The ambulance is on the way," Jaq said, alerting her to the fact that he'd made a quick call. Then he muttered, "They ought to have the route memorized by now."

"Stay with me, Blue," Gem warned. Nothing felt real right then, nothing except her fear.

Blue's lips curved in a weak grin. "Bossy," he rasped.

"Scared," she whispered into his ear, resting her temple against his as she corrected him. It was a moment of honesty brought out by terror. "I don't want you to leave me."

"I won't," he said softly. Then he could say no more.

Gem was learning to hate hospitals. Worse was the knowledge that this visit was entirely her fault. Blue wouldn't be here if she hadn't irrationally acted on impulse, told herself the danger had passed and gone into the garden. It wasn't like her to be so fluff-brained, but apparently her common sense had taken a permanent vacation. First she'd had that intimate interlude with Blue; then she'd almost killed him trying to avoid another indiscretion. Maybe it would have been better if she'd just hopped into bed with him and stowed her fears—at least then he wouldn't have been shot. No matter what he believed, the man would be better off if he put a few light-years between them.

She put her head in her hands and silently groaned. This thing was bringing her to her knees and there was no comfort anywhere. Xera would bring strength but not comfort. Jaq could run the inn, but she was sure he knew nothing about the care and feeding of a heart. She hadn't realized before how dry her life had become. She had no friends outside of the family, no girlfriends to calm and boost her spirits. Had work really consumed the last few years? Had she become so good at shutting out her feelings, hiding her loneliness?

She'd wanted her father to be proud of her, so she'd thrown everything she had into his baby, this inn. Once she'd attained excellence, she knew she was expected to maintain it. After he died, she'd used work as a distraction from the grief—and her sisters had needed her. Only now did she realize what carrying all those burdens had done for her: Nothing. She had nothing in her life of any value, save her family, who were leaving one by one. The only thing that might stay and be hers was bleeding somewhere in the bowels of this hellhole of a hospital.

The tears came, and she didn't try to stop them. She did move from the waiting room to the chapel, though. Tears were expected there, even if no one was present to see them.

She went through half a box of tissues and had to find another. The very act of looking sobered her. Bawling her eyes out wasn't going to help Blue.

Maybe it helped a little, though, because she was a lot calmer when she rose to leave the room. But that calm vanished the moment she opened the chapel door and saw Zsak.

"What are you doing wandering around without

someone watching over you?" he demanded when he saw her. He stood right in front of the door, his hand outstretched as if he'd been ready to walk in.

She scanned his disheveled hair. It always looked ruffled, but now there was a bandage taped to his brow just under his hairline. He had a scrape on his chin and there was a fleck of dried blood in his mustache. The rest of him looked all right, but she couldn't tell for sure through his clothes.

"What happened?" she asked.

He looked around at the hallway, which was busy with traffic. "Not here. Come on." He first glanced into the chapel, then seemed to decide against it and led her to an empty conference room. When they were both inside, he shut the door. "You want the good news first? Your sniper is dead."

Gem stopped breathing. "Dead?" It took a moment, but her next thought was: "It's over?"

He propped a hip on a table. "That's the bad news."

Captain Azor suddenly walked into the room. Gem wasn't certain whether he'd been summoned by Zsak or found them on his own. "Ms. Harrisdaughter," the policeman greeted her. "You've had an interesting day."

She frowned and sat on the edge of the table, wincing as her bruised hip protested. Azor's dark eyes flashed to her expression, but he didn't comment. If her eyes were still red from crying, he didn't mention that, either.

"I'd like to hear your statement," he said.

She sighed. "I was tired of being in the house, so I went out into the gardens. I deliberately ducked Blue so he wouldn't notice. He paid for my mistake." Her eyes dropped and lost focus. She fought tears; she would *not* cry in front of this man.

He didn't act impressed. "I hope you're not prone to repeating mistakes or you'll solve all our problems for us. We've identified the people who hired the sniper—they're not the kind of men you should make enemies of." Her eyes snapped up to his, and he smiled without humor. "Are you familiar with the drug trafficking problems they've been having on Enjor?"

She glowered at him. "Why wouldn't I be? It's all over the galactic news, and I run both an inn and a shipping company." She immediately regretted saying the last bit; there was little question her family's foray into exports was on everyone's mind.

Azor didn't comment; he simply looked grim. "One of the major smuggling operations has put out a contract on your life. The Spark was a profit-eating upstart, they decided—one they're determined to rub out."

She blinked. Blinked again. Her mind just wouldn't form coherent thought.

Azor continued. "Let me just be upfront with you about our perspective on your situation. In Jean Luc's quarters we found a box full of Pax, an herb native to Polaris. It seems to be one of the main ingredients in his beer—the beer you've been exporting. In its original state, it's mildly addictive, like coffee or chocolate. Once illegal chem labs get their hands on it, the stuff can be refined down to some pretty potent pills. Some of your recent exports contained a very high percentage of Pax, cleverly hidden among bottles with a lower percentage. This failed to tip off the narcotics teams. If you hadn't particularly mentioned your brewmaster's attitude toward his recipes to Blackwing that night, we might never have checked this out. This is one point in your favor.

"On the other hand, your master brewer is being charged with drug manufacturing and trafficking. It seems he was involved in discovering Pax, and also the process to enhance it. Your own role in this whole operation is quite unclear. Public knowledge of it could be very bad for your business, don't you think? At least among the law-abiding set."

He was threatening her. After all she'd done to keep her family's inn respectable, he was threatening her. And what could she do? She simply crossed her arms and waited. What could she say? He knew more than she did.

"I'll cut you a deal, Gem. You fill in the blanks. Tell us everything we don't know yet. In return, we'll save your life. You've had a taste of what these men who want to kill you can do. Next time, they're not going to miss."

She shook herself back to life. "Wait a minute. You've already decided I'm guilty! These people think I'm . . . !" She shook herself again. "No."

Azor looked at her carefully. "No?"

"No, to everything." Rage welled in her, rage at the whole situation. "I'm not guilty! Whatever Jean Luc—or even my sister—might have done, I had no knowledge of it. I'm not going to play your game. But I'm also not going to let these gangsters do me in."

He looked amused. "You have a plan to stop them? Intergalactic smugglers? After your bodyguard was shot? These aren't local hoods, you know."

She looked away to get a rein on her temper, then fixed him with a glare. "I guess if I can't get you people to do your job, then yes, I *will* think of something.

In the meantime, if you have nothing useful to add, I have a waiting room chair with my name on it. Thanks so much."

She gave an insincere smile and brushed past, trying ignore his flunkies at the door. They stepped into her path.

"Gem?" Azor said mildly.

She made a slow turn, her temper simmering. "You have something to say?"

His smile was faint. "As of now, you're in my custody. You're a witness, darlin'. You get protection. I insist."

She drew a breath, fighting fury. "Am I under arrest?"

He shrugged. "Not yet."

"Mind if I'm in your protective custody in the waiting room?"

He sighed. "I do, as it's not very secure. We can arrange a private waiting room for you, though. Least I can do."

"How kind."

One of Azor's goons motioned that he would lead the way. Another fell into step behind her. Gem saw Zsak grimace, and could feel Azor's eyes on her back as she walked away.

The doctor finally came out and briefed her about Blue. His soberness scared her.

"First of all, let me assure you that Mr. Blue is now stable. Unfortunately, his recovery is going to be slow and painful. The bullet entered his back through the left-hand side and created a messy exit wound in his chest. On the way through, it grazed his heart and perforated his lung. Fortunately, we got to him in time, and he's a naturally healthy individual. If he tolerates the healing accelerators well, he should be able to leave in as little as two weeks—provided he has someone to look after him and plenty of rest."

"Absolutely," Gem assured him. "Whatever my family can do. Can I see him now?"

The doctor shook his head. "I'm afraid not. He's still sedated, and he'll be in the ICU until we're certain he's out of danger."

"Out of danger?" she echoed. She was tired, but she didn't like the sound of that—especially not when the doctor had just assured her Blue was stable.

The surgeon sighed. "We had to restart his heart more than once, and he lost a lot of blood. Fortunately, he has a very strong will to live. Don't worry; he'll be receiving 'round-the-clock care. The best thing you can do for him now is to go home and get some rest so you can keep him company when he recovers."

Gem nodded, but she felt just as terrible as she had when leaving Brandy's sickbed. Except this time it was all her fault. A—she felt the blood draining from her face—nicked heart? A perforated lung? Her stupidity had nearly killed him.

Zsak, who'd been present for the briefing on his friend's health, put a supporting hand under her elbow. "Let's get you home," he said. "You're dead on your feet."

Dead? She laughed without humor.

She didn't remember the drive home. She would have been too tired to sleep, except that Zsak made her down several shots of eighty-proof. He and Blue apparently had a lot in common regarding their medicinal prescriptions, but the alcohol worked. Gem passed out cold and didn't rise until late afternoon.

She wasn't really up to her chores when she did wake, but lying around gave her too much time to think. Instead, she wandered into the kitchen and let Jamir fuss over her.

It was a wonder he hadn't quit—they'd already had three resignations. Ironically, business was up as curious visitors from both Polaris and space came out to see what all the fuss was at The Spark.

"Cheer up," Zsak said as he joined her at the kitchen table, a monstrously heaped plate in one hand. Apparently Jamir was being kind to him. "Blue's survived worse."

She looked at Zsak tiredly. "Really? How long have you known him?"

The man thought about it. "Four years? No, five. He saved my life more than once."

Head propped on one hand, she studied him. "You were in the service with him?"

"I've been in the service, yeah." He took a bite of sausage. "These are good. You know, he's far gone on you."

Gem blinked. "What?"

Zsak smiled. "I've never seen him carry on the way he does about you. If he's not in love yet, he's tipping."

She didn't know what to say to that. Hyna Blue was a hard man to read. Yes, they'd shared something very special and intimate, but that didn't mean it was special to him. Men didn't always equate intimacy and love. His best friend thought he knew what Blue felt. She knew what she herself felt, but . . .

"I don't think he sees himself as the 'settle down, raise a family' type," she thought aloud.

Zsak shrugged. "Men change."

Gem sighed impatiently. "Have you ever seen him in love?"

Blue's friend was silent for a long moment. "Yes," he finally said. "I've seen him in love." Sadness shadowed his eyes.

Gem needed to know: "How did it end?"

Zsak answered in a brisk voice. "She was involved in some ugly things. Blue wanted to believe in her innocence, and she let him. When her friends went down, when the police finally got them, she went down with them. Worse, he was cast under suspicion for a while. He's never gotten over that. He might not look like it, but justice and integrity matter."

"And here I am, in the middle of an investigation. I'm surprised he's stuck around."

"I'm not," Zsak replied. "You're quite a woman." He flashed Gem a wolfish grin.

She felt herself color even as she smiled. She could see why Blue liked Zsak.

Before she could say as much, however, one of the newer barmaids walked up. "Ma'am? There's a Mr. Cirrus to see you."

Gem sighed. Closing her eyes, she debated whether or not to see him. She glanced at Zsak, who wore a guarded expression.

"Very well. Send him to my . . ." She frowned. The old office was no longer hers, and she wasn't about to meet with Cirrus in her private rooms. "Send him to Jaq's office," she decided. After watching the barmaid walk off, Gem glanced at Zsak and said, "Might as well hang out in the bar while you wait—since I know you will."

He gave her a small smile.

Gem rose from her seat. Azor's agents watched

her from across the room, but they gave her space as long as she was with Zsak. She wondered if they would be okay waiting outside while she spoke to Cirrus.

She headed for Jaq's office. Located at the far end of the bar, the man's lair looked nothing like her own neat workspace. The desk was piled haphazardly with stacks of paper. Odds and ends, old gun magazines and cracking, jam-packed binders filled the shelves. If those arsonist kids had started a fire in here, The Spark would be cinders by now.

She left the door open—both for Azor's agents and herself.

Cirrus turned from his survey of the room as she walked in. "Gem. I was so sorry to hear of your recent troubles." He took her hand and pressed it, looking earnest.

"Thank you. It's been a long week," Gem admitted tiredly, extracting her hand as she moved behind Jaq's desk and took a seat. "Forgive the mess. Since I hired my new manager, I've moved myself out of my usual office. When things calm down, I'll remedy that."

"That's quite all right," he soothed. "I'm only concerned that your family isn't available to comfort you in this trying time."

"Actually, Xera will be home tonight," Gem corrected. "If we can bring her here without incident, things should start to look up."

"And your bodyguard, Blue? I'd heard he's not doing well." Cirrus's eyes were searching.

"As well as can be expected. The doctors say he can come home in a week or two, if all goes well. I imagine he'll be indisposed for a while, though."

Cirrus looked thoughtful. "Home. So you'll be bringing him back here?"

"It's where he was staying beforehand," she pointed out, a little annoyed. Had he come here just to gossip? If so, he was going to find his welcome would be short-lived.

He nodded. "Bear with me a moment—your charity is not in doubt. This is what concerns me." He opened his briefcase and drew out a few papers. His gaze on hers, he handed them over.

Gem looked at the first page and froze. It was a picture of a younger Blue in a narcotics officer's uniform. The article was a scathing commentary on police brutality on Enjor. It went on to allege certain things Blue had done. He wasn't referred to as Hyna Blue, however. This man was called Officer Indigo Santana. "Blue Satan" the reporter had dubbed him, going for a dramatic splash.

A little unsteady, Gem slowly set that page aside and looked at the next. This article was dated a little later. It gleefully reported that Officer Santana had received a dishonorable discharge for conduct unbecoming.

"The discharge was just a ruse. It helped him to go undercover," Cirrus explained.

She let her eyes meet his, unhappy that her shock was evident.

"Look at the next one," he suggested gently.

It was a class photo of a military group, probably a graduating class. Blue and Captain Azor were both there.

Gem dropped the photo on the desk.

Cirrus looked sympathetic. "I know. I was outraged when I realized this supposed 'drifter' who was taking advantage of your kindness was actually an investigating officer with the IC's Galactic Narcotics office. They used a very real danger to get as close to you as humanly possible—to exploit you. I'm sorry."

She nodded, numb. She'd been giving room and board to a Narc? Not that she resented his job, but his treatment of her was abhorrent. Blue Satan, indeed!

Cirrus's mouth tightened, and he left the room, returning shortly with a tumbler. He pressed this into her hands. "You need a drink."

For once she didn't argue. "I'm going to kick him out," she was muttering. Him and his sweet-talking, lying friend. Zsak had to be part of the equation. No doubt he had a badge hidden somewhere, too.

Cirrus nodded. "I've been thinking about that. The trouble is, there really is someone trying to hurt you. I didn't want to bring you this mess without offering some solution. If you'd accept him, I'd like to offer you the services of one of *my* bodyguards. He's agreeable, if you're willing. This is his resume." Cirrus laid a folder on the desk in front of her.

She closed her eyes and bit her lip, despising that he witnessed her weakness but unable to get a grip. Blue was a traitor! A liar, too, if she wanted to think about that. And what he'd done to her body . . . What she'd done to his!

"Give me some time, Cirrus. I . . . appreciate what you're trying to do for me."

Taking his cue, the businessman nodded and stood. "Again, if you need me, Gem, I'm available day or night. Please, call me and tell me how you are once you've caught your breath."

She nodded, then sat and stared at the door, horrified. She'd fallen in love with a traitor.

Love? she thought, closing her eyes in anguish. What a time to find a name for her feelings!

Zsak chose that moment to look in on her. If she'd been a cougar, Gem's ears would have lain flat back on her head. She bared her teeth. "Get out!" He opened his mouth to speak, but she grabbed the gun Jaq kept stashed under his desk and aimed it at Blue's friend. "I said, *move it.*"

The liar wisely ducked back out.

Gem set the gun aside and massaged the bridge of her nose. It was hard to remember a time before trouble had perched on her shoulder. Much more of this and she might actually think of selling The Spark.

Jaq looked in on her less than a minute later. One glance at her face and his own became set like stone. "What did he do?"

She stared at him for a moment, trying to figure out how to answer, how to plan for and overcome this disaster. At last, bested, she handed him the incriminating papers.

Jaq looked them over and grunted. His jaw worked as if he were chewing on a thought.

Tired of waiting, Gem threw out, "Obviously, we won't bring him back here."

Jaq tossed the papers on the desk, seeming unconcerned. "Don't see why not. You've got nothing to hide. Me, I'd confront him with what I know and work some of my spleen off. Keep him here, where you can keep an eye on him. Better to know what the man is doing rather than send him off and wonder."

She stared the old man down. "You *want* me to bring him back?"

He shrugged. "Man did save your life. You're a big

girl. Keep him around until you get your feelings worked out, then give him the boot if you like. Myself, I'd prefer the extra eyes watching out for you . . . even if he is a cripple."

She scowled. "He's not a cripple, just wounded."

Jaq was making sense, though. She'd never run from a fight, and she did have fury she'd like to dump all over Blue's head—if that was really his name. Dump it out and rub it in. Yeah, that sounded like just the thing.

It was either that or let her head explode.

Jaq saw her evil, calculating expression and shook his head. "Let him come out of ICU before you rip into him, girl. No sense in killing him twice."

She grunted an agreement, despite her misgivings. The sympathy card didn't play well with her at the moment, of course; she wasn't feeling too torn up about his condition. But, okay. No revenge now. Maybe later. Not too much later, though.

Certain of Zsak's true profession, and that he would search the office later, she folded the papers incriminating Blue and stuck them in her pocket. "Don't suppose you have a handy line to feed Zsak, do you?"

Jaq grinned. "I'll tell him you're having man troubles."

With a growl for his efforts, she led the way from the room.

Chapter Twelve

One minute Gem was going over what to say to Xera; the next she was grabbed by Azor's flunkies and hustled out the door to a transport.

"What's going on?" she demanded as the two men flanked her.

"Captain Azor has ordered you to be secured somewhere safe," one of the officers replied. "You'll be briefed as soon as we get there."

"My sister is coming in—" she started to protest.

"We'll take care of her," one cop promised.

She didn't know how to take that. What if these men meant to hurt Xera?

She looked around, but all the windows of the transport were black. She could get no idea where they were going. "Where are you taking me?"

"To a safe location," was all they would say.

It took twenty-five minutes by her watch until they stopped, and then she was hustled out with the same speed in which she'd been collected. Captain Azor wasn't present, but he was waiting on a teleconference in the hotel-like room to which she was escorted.

"Hello, Ms. Harrisdaughter. Comfortable?" He had a wicked gleam in his eye.

She didn't appreciate any humor in the situation. She glared at the laptop sitting on the hotel table. "What's going on?"

"We had to put you in a safe house. An explosive was found on your sister Xera's ship—it was dismantled with no loss of life," he hastened to say, cutting off any expostulation of concern. "However, your friend Cirrus's current girlfriend was found dead about two hours ago. I understand he came to see you today?"

Gem's mouth worked, but no sound came out for a moment. "He . . . he didn't say anything about . . ." Had he known that the redhead was dead?

"He had some interesting things to say about Blue, though, didn't he?" Azor remarked softly.

Gem just stared at the policeman's image. How had Azor gotten this information? Jaq wouldn't rat on her, would he?

Seeing her expression, the Narc explained. "I'm afraid we listened in. We can't afford to have any more screwups like the one that brought down Blue. Cirrus is in custody. I'm afraid you'll have to wait to find out the details of his case. Meanwhile, perhaps you could entertain me with any other details you might have remembered about your sister's case? What was Jean Luc blackmailing her with?"

She was not ready to let go of that bit of information, so she clung to what she'd heard. "You said my sister Xera is all right?" Worry swamped her. She'd come close to losing Xera and hadn't even known she was in danger.

"You'll see her tonight, probably late. Now, what do you know about the blackmail?"

In desperation, she asked, "Brandy didn't say anything?"

Azor didn't blink. "You know it's a federal crime to obstruct justice, don't you, Ms. Harrisdaughter?"

He got a glare for that, but she knew this was one piece of sisterly confidence she couldn't hide. It would eventually come out, and hiding it from the authorities could help nothing. "Brandy was covering for Xera. She saw her in a compromising situation. Jean Luc found out about it and held it over my sister's head."

"What sort of compromising situation?" Azor wouldn't release her from his stare.

Gem told him.

His lips quirked. "And *that* was worth covering drug trafficking?"

Gem's eyes narrowed. "Something like that could ruin Xera, could keep her from being respected or accepted on Polaris."

"Better to ruin all of your lives, eh?" The policeman didn't look impressed. "Who was the lover?"

Gem shrugged. "I don't know. Some drifter."

Azor considered for a moment. "Very well. I'll look into it. Enjoy your stay under our protection. Try to stay out of trouble, won't you? I'll be in touch." His image vanished off the laptop.

Gem's head throbbed. She sat on the bed with a groan and ran her fingers through her hair. One of her guards collected the laptop and left.

Now what?

Xera was brought to Gem late that evening. With the bad luck that had become Gem's lot, she wanted to talk.

"I leave for a little while, and this is what I come home to," she grouched as she walked in. She looked around the hotel room. Unimpressed, she dumped her bags on the floor.

Gem gave her sister a weary smile. "I'm glad you're home. Are you okay?"

"I'm tired and I've been interrogated half the day. Why haven't you hired a lawyer? How did we get mixed up in *drugs*? The cops explained, but I still don't believe it."

"Tomorrow would be better, sis. We're both tired, and I have the mother of all headaches."

Xera's eyes narrowed. "As if I could sleep."

Her sister's fierce glare amused Gem. Of course, after the two shots of scotch she'd had, everything was looking rosier. It was a sad thing, to be a tavern owner and such a cheap drunk. Nonetheless, that was the case.

She poured some more scotch into a glass and slid it across the table. She'd had the bottle fetched from The Spark. "This'll help."

Xera eyed it suspiciously. "You're drinking the good stuff?"

Gem grinned. "Why shouldn't we drink the good stuff if we want? I'd say the occasion calls for it."

Xera looked nonplussed. "You hate scotch."

"Never say it." Gem took another drink to prove how wrong her sister was. The more she had, the better it tasted—probably because her taste buds were going numb.

Lips pursed, Xera fiddled with her glass but didn't drink. "Where's Blue?"

Gem smiled without humor. "Where's Blue? Who's Blue? We all have questions for him. Your answer is: in the hospital. He got shot."

"Shot? What happened?"

Eyebrows raised, Gem sighed fatalistically. "He took a bullet for me. Sad, isn't it?"

Xera looked at her funny. "Okaaay. I think it's time you went to bed. Come on."

Even drowning in fifty-year-old scotch, Gem recognized the expertise Xera used as she smoothly rounded the table and helped her upright. Friendly, unobtrusive. The girl knew a thing or two about handling drunks. How could she not, after all the time they'd spent together in The Spark?

Gem giggled in self-mockery. "Aren't we a pair? I sell the booze to drunks and you've got to deal with them. No wonder you left."

Xera grunted. "Good thing you don't drink often. You're crazy as a squirrel on crackweed when you do."

"What's a squirrel?"

"Never mind. Watch your feet—I don't feel like carrying you."

"Why not? You should put all those push-up muscles to good use. I think Mama was on steroids when she carried you."

"Jealous, aren't you?"

"You bet. Sure you don't want a drink?"

While a little hazy on the details of how she had gotten to bed, Gem woke up the next morning feeling every one of the shots she'd drunk pounding in her brain. The swirling in her stomach took care of itself. As she hung over the rim of the commode, Gem promised herself she'd find a healthier outlet for her anger.

Xera came in as Gem was brushing her teeth. Crisply dressed and groomed, she set a glass of red tonic on the bathroom counter, along with a white pill.

Gem rinsed her toothbrush and popped the pill, grimacing at the taste of the tonic she used to wash it down. "Thanks," she murmured.

"Hm." Xera sipped from a steaming mug of tea. Arms crossed, cup resting against her arm, she said casually, "I had an informative conversation with Zsak this morning. Amazing, what the man will say when dragged out of bed at five AM." She paused for a moment to study Gem's bloodshot eyes. "I assume you're going to visit Blue today? He's been moved out of the ICU."

Gem nodded. "Well, if they let us out of protective custody. If they do, I also have to check in with our manager—I want him to give bonuses to those staff members who've stayed with us. And I want to visit Brandy. When we're done with her we can tackle Blue." She brushed past Xera and headed for the dresser, eager to grab some clean clothes and take a shower—and also to end the conversation.

Xera followed. "Does he need tackling? Where did I lose track? Between you falling in love and him getting shot protecting you, at what point did he become an enemy?"

Pricked by the annoyance in Xera's voice, Gem looked at her sibling. "He's a cop, sis. He and Zsak and who knows who else, they're all cops who've been investigating The Spark. They've been lying to us. This whole time he's been working his way closer, lying every step of the way." Faintly satisfied by the shock on Xera's face, she gathered a pile of clothes and headed for the shower.

"What do you mean they're cops? Blue was just a drifter . . ."

Xera trailed off in confusion as Gem climbed into the shower. Over the sound of running water, Gem called, "Cirrus brought by some papers that show the evidence. I'll get them for you when I get out of here. For now, just know that I'm mad at Blue for a good reason."

"Well, yeah! I can't believe Blue used you like that. I *knew* I didn't like him."

"Just don't pick a fight with Zsak yet. Not until I confront Blue."

"Definitely. We're going to tear him a new—"

"Ah, no. Not we. I own this one, Xera. Say what you like to Zsak, but Blue is mine."

Xera frowned. "Possessive, are we?"

Gem took her time to answer carefully. Her emotions were a hornets' nest, but angry as she was, there were unresolved issues between them. Logic even argued that the man was doing his job, and she'd benefited from it twice, if not more. The key now was to discover just how much of Blue's actions had been business.

She decided to simply say: "I'm just not finished with him yet."

Blue hurt. They'd taken the breathing tube out of his throat, but there was still a mechanical leech attached to a tube in his chest that sucked fluids into a quart-sized plastic bag, which the nurse changed regularly. There was an IV in his left wrist and various tubes and wires he didn't like thinking about, but that wasn't the worst thing.

Gem hadn't come.

Zsak had visited, and Blackwing and Azor, though

the latter's visit had been official. He and Azor didn't like each other much. The important thing, however, was that Gem hadn't come.

Maybe he was worried for nothing. Zsak said she'd been pretty torn up. People reacted funnily to things like this. Maybe she was the type who couldn't bear to see someone she cared about hurt.

But that hadn't stopped her from seeing Brandy.

Restless, he shifted and paid for it with a stab of pain. Stupid painkillers weren't doing their job.

Just as his mind started to cycle through its loop of worries again, Gem walked in. Blue lit up, until he saw the guarded expression on her face.

"What's wrong?" he asked.

A cynical smile curled her mouth. "I was just wondering whether to address you as Blue or Officer Santana."

He stilled. Tension squeezed down on his chest, making already painful breathing harder. Fighting it, he concentrated on each breath as it came, his eyes glued to hers.

A shadow of worry darkened her eyes as she glanced over the tubes and wires poked into him, but she crossed her arms stubbornly. "I was wondering when you were going to tell me. After you bedded me? After you *arrested* me?" Her voice grew harsh. "Just how close are you supposed to get to your subject, Indigo?"

A horrible crashing started inside him, the fall of all his recent fantasies about happily-ever-afters. Wounded, he fell back on sarcasm. "Is there something to arrest you for?"

"You know there's not," she shot back. "I'm not sure exactly what information you thought you could trick me into revealing. When all this is over, I'd love to see you fry in court. I have a feeling you passed the bounds of acceptability, even for an undercover agent like yourself. Scum."

"Scum?" he growled. "You let this scum do some pretty remarkable things to you, baby. Are you willing to have those details passed around in court?" Just the memory of their escapade made him want to relive it, especially now that it was too late: She was never going to let him touch her again.

Fury lit her eyes, but her voice never rose beyond a normal pitch. "Jaq thinks I should let you come back to the inn—keep an eye on your enemy, and all that. Me, I'm not willing to make that mistake. Your cover is blown, Officer. There's no point in continuing the ruse, and I'm not letting anyone else get close to me, so you can forget that tack. As soon as I get home, Zsak is getting the boot, too." And with one last poisonous smile, she turned to leave.

"Forgetting something, girl?" he called out, desperate to make her stay. Pain lanced his chest, but this fight needed to happen. He couldn't let her walk away. "I'm lying here because I took a bullet for you. Zsak took out the sniper. We saved your life. Doesn't that count for something? And what are you going to do with us gone? You think that sniper was the only one after you? Your little sister is home again, isn't she? You think you can protect the both of you by yourself?"

Gem froze with her hand on the door. Her eyes upon it, she ground out, "Didn't you know? We're in protective custody now."

Blue sighed in relief. "Thank God for small favors. You can't solve your problems by yourself, Gem. Not this time." He let that soak in for a moment, then added, "No more games. You know who we are. Fine. It'll be easier with the truth between us."

Slowly, she turned and gave him a brittle smile. "What will be easier? You think I'm going to trust you again?"

He ignored the question. "I won't be here forever."

Her eyebrows rose. "In the hospital? So what? What do you think you're going to do when you get out? You're going to be too weak to even take care of yourself for some time to come, let alone try to interfere with me again."

"Then you shouldn't feel threatened by me coming home."

A vulnerable flash in her eyes gave him hope, but then she looked away. "The Spark is not your home."

He played on what he'd seen, praying it would work. Quietly he said, "It's more home than anywhere else. Please." He would have held his breath, but pain made that impossible.

She wouldn't look at him. Keeping her eyes trained on the wall, she finally said, "I'm not even home right now—at least, I'm not living there. I'm not even sure where they're keeping me, or for how long. You'd only complicate things."

"We'll see," he replied.

She stalked out of the room, sparing him only one last dark look.

Blue went limp. After a lifetime of avoiding romantic entanglements, he'd finally fallen in love with a gorgon. God had a wicked sense of humor.

"How'd it go?"

Gem kept her eyes forward. Xera had been waiting outside the door, eager to hear the results. Maybe the lack of shouting had worried her.

It worried Gem, to be honest. She hadn't liked how hollow she'd felt, seeing Blue so pale and tethered to a bed by wires. He'd almost died for her. Seeing him today . . . Well, it had been too close.

"Gem," Xera said warningly.

Frustrated, Gem glanced at her sister, forced a smile. "Zsak is all yours."

An evil smile lit Xera's face. "I can hardly wait."

Unfortunately, Gem's sister's enthusiasm was blunted by the urgent expression on Blue's friend's face. Zsak pulled them both into an empty room and shut the door. "They've found Hamish Nasser's body," he said.

"Who?" Xera demanded.

Gem took a cautious breath. "The man who beat up Brandy. I think I'm getting a little behind, Zsak. I thought the sniper you caught *was* Hamish Nasser."

He frowned. "No. Why did you think that?"

"Well . . . it seemed too improbable that they would be two different people."

Xera held up a hand. "Hold it. You're saying two different groups are attacking our family? How likely is that?"

"Very, since they both link back to the drug case," Zsak replied.

"I see. And how close are you to solving that case, Officer?" Xera asked. Her tone was caustic.

Zsak stiffened. "I can't say."

"Typical."

Blue's friend drew a calming breath. "There are things in progress."

"You can do better than that," Gem snapped.

"I'm sorry. Some of it's restricted information. I wish I could tell you more but I can't."

Xera moved forward. "Let me hit him. Just once."

Gem grabbed her biceps. "Don't."

Xera shrugged, rolled her shoulders. She shook her head and told Zsak, "Well, I guess we should hear about this Nasser guy. Where does this take our case? Where was he found?"

"That's need-to-know right now. But I can tell you that the body was quite decomposed by the time it was found."

Gem winced, but Xera pushed for more gruesome details. "How long ago did the murder happen? Any suspects?"

"We imagine the man who sent Nasser after Brandy was the one to kill him. Perhaps police presence was too high, and maybe he feared discovery."

"Who do you suspect?" Xera asked again, watching Zsak intently.

Blue's friend glanced one way and then another, as if considering his options. Finally he sighed and admitted: "Cirrus."

There was a beat of silence. The two sisters exchanged glances.

"Cirrus? Why?" Gem asked.

Zsak looked around again. "Look, not here, okay? Let's go somewhere more secure before we discuss this."

He waited until they were back in the hotel room where Azor had put them up. Then he shrugged and said, "Here's what we think is going on. Cirrus has been living big, beyond his income. He needs money. He's already got his fingers in the illegal exports gig, and would like to break into drugs."

"He does?" Gem interrupted, shocked.

Zsak frowned. Maybe he ought to have kept that nugget for himself.

"*Anyway,* he gets word that Jean Luc is making a bundle selling spiked beer, beer used to export an illegal substance. He tries to get Jean to come work for him, but Luc is cautious, doesn't want to draw attention to himself. He refuses, in fact, so Cirrus tries to beat the recipe out of him through Hamish Nasser. Later he kills Hamish to cover his tracks."

Gem shook her head. "Is any of this possible? Is it all conjecture—or fantasy? And are you supposed to be telling us?" She stared at him in incredulity. "I'd think you'd get in trouble with someone."

Zsak shook his head. "I'm only sharing the barest details. The important thing for your safety is that the big boys, the heavy drug runners, see you as competition. Jean Luc may have been the manufacturer, but you distributed the beer, ran the actual business. Naturally they think you're involved. They want to eliminate the competition, so they sent a sniper. Luckily for you, Blue was in place and saved your life."

"He was investigating us," Gem muttered.

"He was trying to find the source of the drugs, yes. You've got to understand the misery this stuff is causing—people have died from it, and even if you live . . . well, it ruins lives. Blue and I want to stop that from happening, and he's got more incentive than most."

"How is that?" Gem snapped. She wondered if it had anything to do with her, and if she should be worried.

Zsak considered, as if he could guess her thoughts.

He took his time about replying. "Blue grew up in the slums of Enjor. His father was an addict. It made life at home pretty rough."

Gem digested that. "He told me he was kicked out pretty young."

"He told you that?"

"Why are you surprised?"

"He's usually so quiet about his past. I wouldn't have thought he'd open up to you."

Zsak looked so speculative that she couldn't hold his gaze, not with Xera sharing the same expression. Gem studied the table. She didn't really want to think about this now, not with witnesses.

Brandy grunted and swung the conversation back on track. "So, what about these 'big boys'? These smugglers. How do we convince them we're not competition?"

Zsak smiled grimly. "We put you on trial."

Chapter Thirteen

Xera stared at Zsak silently for a moment. "You know, Officer, so far I'm not liking your solution."

"Hear me out," he implored. "If they think you're going down, they might pull back the assassins. Why waste manpower and money when the law will take care of their problems for them? And with luck, the law will decide you're harmless and back off."

"And without luck?"

Zsak shook his finger at her. "Don't be a jinx."

"She has a point," Gem spoke up. "You're talking about a lot of bad publicity. It will be hard on business." More to the point, she didn't want her family's name sullied like that.

Zsak shook his head. "You'll have to testify at trial, anyway—or are you forgetting that it's your brewmaster who's up on charges? Right now the investigation's centered around him and your sister Brandy, but—"

"Brandy is innocent," Xera interrupted hotly. "Why does she have to go through this?"

He pinned her with his eyes. "We have to prove she's innocent—or at least that she was working under duress. That's the way the law works. At least, that's how it works when you've been covering for a drug smuggler."

Xera muttered under her breath and turned away.

Gem wasn't happy, either, but there wasn't much choice. She tried to look at the bright side: "At least we'll have time to catch our breath. The trial is probably months away."

"Weeks," Zsak corrected. "Strings were pulled."

Gem stared at him. "Weeks? That's not possible!"

"Anything is possible under the right circumstances. We have all the information we need to prosecute, and HQ decided it would be less expensive to move the case up the docket than spend money and manpower guarding you. Some minor cases were rescheduled. You've got three weeks to choose a lawyer and prepare for the trial."

Gem hissed. Three weeks of broiling pressure? Now? What else would she have to take?

Xera put a steadying hand on her shoulder. Her silent strength was surprisingly soothing. "We'll get through this, sis," she promised.

"Yes, you will," Zsak assured them. Maybe he didn't care for the tense atmosphere, for he added, "I have a feeling you'll do all right. Meanwhile, we're moving you and your sister Brandy to another location. Somewhere more secure. You'll be safe there until the trial."

"Moving us? Where?" Gem asked. She was tired of surprises.

Xera smiled, but there was mockery in her eyes. "You mean you can do better than a hotel room?"

"This isn't a hotel," Zsak said, with a sweet smile of his own. "Why do you think you haven't been allowed to see where we are, why you've been escorted in and out whenever you want to leave? But yes, we do have something else in mind."

"Bring it," Xera said. "Preferably before I die of boredom."

Gem would have cause to remind her of that.

"I can't believe we're stuck on *his* ship."

Gem looked at Xera in resignation. If it wasn't Brandy saying it, her other sister was chiming in. Nobody was happy about being stuck on a starship with Captain Azor. Even though it was a large vessel, they saw far too much of the man.

"He's like a cold, dead fish," Brandy chimed in. "One with teeth, of course. Big, sharp, pointy ones." Denigrating Azor was one of her favorite pastimes.

"Grim," Xera agreed. "I don't know why they couldn't have sent Zsak instead."

"Zsak wanted to stay near Blue," Brandy pointed out, giving a sideways glance at Gem.

Gem looked away. She hadn't spoken to or about Blue in days, not since she'd seen him in the hospital and given him grief. It was starting to wear on her conscience, the way she'd treated him. He was right that he'd saved her life, no matter what lies he'd told. He'd taken a bullet for her. Cooling anger had a way of leaving regrets.

"It's not as if Blue could leave the hospital yet," Brandy continued, blithely rubbing it in. She'd decided to take up the cop's cause, having cast him as the hapless hero in this drama. It was unclear why she championed him but despised Azor. Then again, for a villain, Azor was a pretty good choice. He had the bedside manner of a stick. As far as Gem could see, he had absolutely no redeeming personality traits. If she wasn't so sick of her sister's complaining, she'd have been tempted to join in maligning him.

Brandy stared at Gem, asking, "How long until our next teleconference with our lawyer?" She was understandably obsessed with the woman's progress.

"Not for a while. But you read the last e-mail. She seems to be doing well," Gem soothed. The woman was expensive, but she'd come highly recommended. Hiring her had been one of their last actions before leaving Polaris.

"You need to get your mind off it," Xera said. She stood up and grabbed her sister's wheelchair, then pushed it over to Brandy's bed. "Why don't we go for a walk?"

Brandy groaned. "There's nothing to see here. Besides, we've already gone for a walk today—twice."

Xera flipped the covers off Brandy's legs. "Then we'll go a third time. Sitting around moping won't help you any. Besides, we haven't toured the bridge yet, and the captain said I could take you around it today. After that I'll take you down to the flight simulators and teach you how to fly."

"My hands are broken," Brandy said tersely, as if Xera hadn't noticed.

"Your head is going to be broken, too, if you don't stop feeling sorry for yourself." Xera calmly helped her sullen sister into her chair. She then wheeled her out of the room. "Coming?" she called to Gem from the hallway.

Gem trailed along, feeling oddly as if she were on vacation. Other than trial preparations, which were largely out of her hands, she had nothing pressing.

She'd spent some of the time working out with Xera, some playing games with her sisters and some watching movies. While there were moments of boredom, she had to admit the free time was rather nice.

The rough, rubberized surface under her feet dulled any echoes in the ship. The craft was large, military in design, built for function. There were precious few frills onboard, though Gem did enjoy the occasional glimpse of stars out the port windows. Sometimes she just stood and admired those points of icy fire, imagined that they were diamonds of light on a coverlet of black velvet. It was soothing to let her mind wander in such ways.

Even though the circumstances were not ideal, she enjoyed the recaptured time with her sisters. Knowing that they would again go their separate ways—assuming everything went according to plan—made their interaction even more precious. Xera would again leave with the Galactic Explorers, and Brandy would eventually vanish, too. Gem had realized this over the past few weeks. She'd also discovered that what made The Spark precious was her family. When her family was gone . . .

She shook her head. She didn't think she'd toss the inn aside, but maybe this was a wake-up call. It was surely time she made room in her life for more.

It was a little embarrassing to find that she wasn't sure how to go about building a social life. How did people make friends? Real friends, and not employees? There was a big difference when you weren't focused on efficiency and expedience. She wasn't sure she was prepared for it.

She thought about Blue and sighed. It was the

fourth time in the past hour. She was going to have to do something about that man. Did she owe him an apology? It was hard to reconcile her anger over his deceit with her concern for his injury. There was no question she owed him gratitude for the latter.

Why had he seduced her, though? She was confused and hurt over that. Had he really desired her, or had he been cold enough to manipulate her to further his investigation? She couldn't see how it would have helped him. From her point of view, she'd have thought it would have complicated his life.

Zsak had hinted that Blue was in love with her. Maybe she was softhearted, but she couldn't see him leading her on. If Blue loved her . . . She shook her head. She was going to have to confront him sometime. Later, though. After she'd considered the situation for a while.

Honestly, what could she say to the man?

"Man, you've got to snap out of it," Zsak remarked with concern. "The doctors say you're setting back your recovery with all this tension."

Blue looked silently at his partner. He didn't want to talk about it.

Zsak shifted uncomfortably. He'd always hated being the go-between, but he viewed this as a necessary evil. "Xera says Gem is depressed. She says that whenever she tries to be upbeat, she gets a smackdown. Even Brandy is trying to cheer Gem up, which is really saying something. I can't imagine what that looks like."

Blue glanced at him sideways.

Zsak sighed. There was nothing for it but to be

honest, especially since he'd been equally honest with Gem. "I think she loves you. This thing with her . . . I think it will pass."

Blue grunted. "Not one lousy call. She chews me out and then leaves. She's cutting her losses and not looking back."

"Or she's nursing a wounded heart. Look, why don't *you* call *her?*"

Blue's jaw tightened. He wasn't into begging. He'd never done it in his life. "She won't talk to me."

"But you haven't even tried to call her!"

"I've thought about it," Blue remarked.

Zsak scratched the back of his neck. He let his gaze travel around the barren room. "Maybe you could send a gesture of some kind. You know, something she can't return. Something to make her feel guilty for ignoring you . . . soften her up. Women always like feeling wooed." He grinned.

"She's on a starship. What could I send? And how?" Blue was tired of doing nothing, however. Maybe it couldn't hurt.

Zsak thought a moment, then grinned. "I have the perfect idea."

Gem stared incredulously at the quartet of singing crewmen. They'd come up to her in the mess hall and told her they had a message from someone who was thinking of her. And then, just like that, they'd burst into a love song.

Xera looked at them before glancing at her sister with unholy glee. "Betcha I know who that's from." She laughed.

Gem shook her head in disbelief. "He wouldn't."

The lads finished their song and bowed to the thunderous applause of the crew; live entertainment was always welcome aboard ship. "Blue says hello. This is from him," their leader explained with a grin. He handed her a greeting card and left to get his dinner.

Gem drew a sharp breath. She stared down at the card, almost afraid to see what it might say. When Xera reached for it, however, she blocked her sister's hand and slowly opened the envelope. It said simply, "We're not done."

Xera read over her shoulder. "Well!"

Gem flushed and folded the card closed. "I guess I should call him."

Brandy had watched the scene with interest. She awkwardly put a potato chip in her mouth. "Yeah. No telling what he'll have the crew do next if you ignore him. Maybe it will be acrobats."

The thought was enough to galvanize Gem. She found herself at a message center a few minutes later. She stared at the communication device, but couldn't think of what she would say if she spoke to Blue in real time. It'd be so awkward, and fighting for words didn't appeal to her. Besides, there was always that horrible lag when talking from a ship . . .

She bit her lip in anxiety. She really wasn't any good at this. Squabbling with her sisters and making up really hadn't prepared her for dealing with a man. Would he expect her to be straightforward? That was how she usually solved problems. How would he react if she just launched into their issues? It might be best to establish communication first, a connection, and gradually lead up to it.

She groaned in frustration. Dithering wasn't helping. Fine! She'd just send him a message. Nothing too personal, though. Polite. How could that possibly go wrong?

Blue looked at the electronic tablet, unsure how to interpret Gem's message. It said, "I don't know what to say. Thank you, I guess."

Zsak looked over his shoulder. "Well, it's something." He laughed.

Blue exhaled in frustration and then grunted in pain. The woman was stubborn, but at least she was talking to him now. He thought about sending another message but decided to wait her out instead. How long would it take before she wrote again?

Like all such plans of patience, this one sounded better in theory than it worked in practice. Days went by and nothing else came to him. The girl was as silent as a distant star.

At last, after a lot of dithering, he talked himself into not sending any more messages, not even thinking about it. He was tired of feeling guilty about his inaction. It frustrated him to be stuck in a hospital bed with no way to get to Gem. This was a situation that called for a delicate touch, and the kind of touch he would use worked best in person. Two short days and he'd be out of here. He'd put that time to good use and plan his siege. After all she'd put him through, he wasn't planning to be nice. He'd use every weapon he had—seduction, persuasion and Gem's sisters—to get this woman to admit she needed him.

To that end, he decided to seduce the sisters. Oh, he didn't intend them as romantic conquests, of course, but as potential allies. After all, no one could be as sneaky and underhanded as a sibling.

He just had to convince them to help.

* * *

"I hear the nurses are all over him," Xera said conversationally.

Gem chewed doggedly on her bland breakfast. She refused to comment. Lately her sisters had taken to discussing Blue's life as if it were a soap opera. Being stuck on the ship with little to do but torment their sister was driving them to new heights of mischief.

They talked over her head, of course, as if the conversation weren't specifically chosen to tickle her ears. It was driving her mad, but she was determined to ignore them. If she wanted to talk to Blue, she'd call him. She just hadn't decided what she should say. Bad enough that she couldn't get him out of her head, but her sisters kept grinding away on the subject, torturing her further.

She'd spent a lot of time thinking after she sent that first message, and she'd come up with another good reason why she shouldn't contact him now. Blue was part of the investigation. He'd have to testify at the trial. She had no doubt he'd be honest in all of his assessments, but his testimony could really hurt her family. She didn't know how she'd handle that if it came to pass, so she'd backed off.

She felt unwilling to share her concerns with her sisters, though. They were trying valiantly to forget their own stress over the approaching trial, and they used matchmaking to take their minds off the subject. If she brought up her concerns, it would only bring them down. They were making it difficult to stay silent, though.

"Zsak says the healing accelerators are doing a

great job. Blue's been working hard in physical therapy. Things are looking good for his release in two days."

Gem's heart skipped a beat. Two days. Suddenly that seemed too short a time. She wasn't ready to see him yet. Unfortunately, her pounding heart didn't share her reservations.

Xera glanced at her sister, her face blank. "Zsak says the therapist has a crush on Blue." She raised her brows in innocent inquiry when Gem shot a look her way. "You can't blame her. It is kind of romantic, him risking his life for you."

A muscle twitched near Gem's eye. She was tired of being cast as the villain. Maybe it was time she opened up.

"Remember that night you were so worried, Xera? Well, since then he did a lot more than kiss me." She watched then, as her conversational rock splashed violently into the pond of their conversation.

Her sisters chewed on that information. Brandy asked tentatively, "How much more?"

A hot blush crept up Gem's cheeks, even though this was her own ploy. "Enough."

Xera raised an eyebrow. She didn't look upset, however. In fact, a certain glow lit her eyes. It might have been glee.

"Are we going to have a shotgun wedding?"

Gem sucked in a breath. She hadn't wanted their minds going *there*. "He didn't do enough to warrant that!" she snapped.

Xera's lips twitched. "But he did 'enough.'"

Gem's face grew hotter. "Yeah."

Her sisters exchanged glances. Brandy looked at

Gem sternly, but her lips fought to remain straight. "I think we need details. You know, to determine how best to punish him."

Gem's temperature soared like a nuclear meltdown. She shifted in her chair, pondering. Her sisters had no idea what they asked. The things she'd done with Blue were going to the grave with her. Just thinking about them made her uncomfortable—uncomfortable and aroused.

"Look, he was in the middle of investigating me. He shouldn't have done it," was her point.

"His heart must have tripped him up," Brandy said.

His heart? Gem and Xera stared at each other. Where had that thought come from?

Brandy's expression turned stubborn. "He's not the kind of guy to do something like that if his feelings weren't involved," she explained. "I know it's against what I once believed, but . . . Well, didn't he risk his life for you? Isn't he trying to win you back?"

Pain made Gem's throat tighten. "He's not," she forced herself to say. No, he was flirting with his nurses, for all she knew, just like he'd once flirted with her. The table grew blurry.

Xera put a soothing hand on her shoulder. "Just call him, sis. You'll see."

"I don't know what to say."

Brandy shook her head. "We'll coach you. Come on, let's go find a communicator."

Unfortunately, Gem got an answering service when she tried to put through the call. She hung up without leaving a message.

"You could have at least said hello!" Brandy admonished.

"The data pad will tell him he got a call from the ship," Gem explained.

"But not who called."

Gem hesitated, then decided, "I'll send an electronic message." That was really the safest thing. It would be easier to guard what she said.

She ended up sending him a very formal message, thanking him again for saving her life and for his services. It didn't take long for him to reply, which surprised and pleased her, though she fought the emotion. His reply was a warm, "You're welcome. How is everybody holding up?"

The message started a series of cautious exchanges. Cautious for her, at least. Blue never failed to be kind, though he didn't push or flirt. He simply wrote to her as a friend.

Gem started to feel wistful. Was friendship all he wanted? As the feeling grew, she began to forget her anger. She began to consider his side, and to give it the weight it was likely due. He hadn't known them when he'd taken the job. Except for his relationship with her, it had been nothing personal. Maybe something had grown from it. Maybe he was as unhappy with the situation as she was.

If he'd been able to see inside her head, Blue would have smiled, but she was too uncertain to send her tender thoughts to him. Instead, she sent him reports about her days.

"You might as well be sending him a news sheet," Xera said in disgust as she read over Gem's shoulder one afternoon. "I've seen tax reports with more passion." This earned Xera a dirty look for her trouble. Undaunted, she suggested, "Just tell him you love him and be done. It can't be that hard."

"So speaks the voice of experience," Gem muttered. She ran a spell-check, trying to ignore Xera's hovering.

"Well, you do love him, right?" It wasn't really a question.

Gem's hands froze on the keyboard. Her feelings of . . . *affection* weren't in question, not if her sisters could see them; but was it love? A better question was: what did Blue feel? If it was love, could it survive this kind of tension? What kind of life could she have with him?

A good one, her conscience whispered. As for love? What else could be breaking her heart?

Chapter Fourteen

"All rise."

Gem rose with the others as the court was called to session, but her mind wasn't on the trial. She'd spotted Blue. She hadn't seen him in weeks. Their only communication had been through the stilted electronic messaging she'd instituted. Now she regretted the silence.

He looked good in his police uniform, maybe a little pale. He'd lost weight.

She'd watched him walk slowly down the aisle to claim his seat next to Zsak, and it felt as though a live wire connected her gut to every move he made. She couldn't breathe. Her stomach hurt with tension. She'd kept her gaze on him as she moved down the aisle and took her own seat, avoiding his eyes at the last possible moment. Now they were at the trial, and her fears would be proved or slain. Today she would learn what his testimony was, what the man really thought. Her stomach burned at the thought.

He turned his head and caught her staring. His expression didn't change and his gaze never wavered; Gem closed her eyes and looked away.

Brandy had cut a deal with the cops to spill everything she knew about Jean Luc. Their lawyer hit the pain and suffering angle hard, detailing all Brandy had gone through— her beating, her many injuries. They wanted the jury to see her as a victim. Misguided, perhaps, but protective of her family. And, after all, her father had died at a young age . . .

The prosecution butted in then. "Irrelevant, Your Honor. Her father's death has no bearing on the trial."

Their lawyer gracefully conceded, but hoped the positive work was done.

It was a lovely innovation of the local galactic court system that the case against The Spark's owners and their brewmaster could be dealt with all at once. But this also meant Jean Luc retaliated by spilling the terms of the blackmail. His recounting of details was lurid enough to cause Xera to stiffen in her seat. Her eyes narrowed and her jaw hardened as she stared the scum down. Single-handedly, he was destroying her reputation on Polaris. If she'd ever dreamed of marriage here, those dreams were dead. By evening, people she'd known all her life would shun her. There was no future left for her on Polaris.

Gem placed her hand on Xera's and squeezed. They'd been prepared for this, but the reality hurt.

Xera turned her palm up and clasped Gem's hand. Her face held sorrow and resolve, but no fear. "No tears, sis. My future was never here."

"Objection, Your Honor," their lawyer said calmly, as details became even more candid. "We will cede that the blackmail is legitimate. The details of my client's sister's assignation are of no consequence."

"Agreed," said the judge. "Have you anything further for the defendant?" he asked the prosecutor.

For Gem, the worst moment of the day had been her sister's public humiliation. In a way Xera had sacrificed her reputation, making her sisters look good in comparison, by showing that they were willing to go to such lengths to protect her. Their strategy hadn't planned for that, but it worked, and the facts would have come out anyway.

Gem finally had reason to be grateful for her sister's determination to join the Galactic Explorers: Her reputation wouldn't matter there. On a planet far from home, Xera could find happiness. She would have to.

If Xera's reckoning had been the worst part of the day, then Blue's testimony was the best. Along with Zsak, he told the court he believed the sisters were innocent of drug trafficking. No hint of their relationship was mentioned, since Blue had always behaved fairly reputably in public. Even if there were rumors, it would have done Jean Luc's lawyer little good to mention them. Blue would have simply said he was undercover, using romance to get closer to Gem. Polaris law also allowed prior convictions to be brought up in court on a case-by-case basis, and that helped the Harrisdaughters' side, as Jean Luc's history was a witness against him.

The jury heard the case and then went into deliberation. By noon the next day, they delivered the verdict. Jean Luc was found guilty of drug trafficking. Xera and Gem were found innocent. For her involvement, Brandy received six months of house arrest. She was fitted with an electronic bracelet to track her whereabouts, but because of her injuries she would be allowed to travel to the hospital for continued therapy.

Gem wilted with relief when she heard the news. She hugged her sisters in exultation, but something was missing. She wanted to see Blue.

He'd met and held her eyes after his testimony, as if assuring her silently that, yes, he believed in her. It had been terrifying, but it also felt so good. Her doubts seemed so ludicrous when she looked at him. He really had been just doing his job.

They hadn't had a chance to talk. He'd disappeared after the trial. She presumed he'd gone back to the hospital, but when she'd called his room that night, she'd been told he'd checked out. He could be anywhere.

Azor's men still surrounded them with protection, but Gem dismissed the assassins, assuming they'd be called off at any moment. It was the media who were their enemy now. They camped outside The Spark, barely held at bay by security. And while they shoved their microphones at neighbors and customers alike, it was Xera they were most in a frenzy to question. Every time she walked out of the inn, they swarmed. She couldn't go anywhere without being stalked by a photographer or reporter.

She bore it well, but the strain showed.

The family lawyer instructed her to greet the press with, "Good morning" or "Good afternoon" or "Good evening," and to say "Farewell" when she left the gauntlet; that was it. The lawyer had also hooked them up with an image consultant. Things would eventually settle down, but it was important for the family to earn back the community's respect. It would take time, but everything would settle . . . especially after Xera left. Unfortunately, that wouldn't happen for some weeks. Even though Gem didn't want to see her sister leave, she was also anxious for Xera to get her life back. No one would bother her at the academy. Gem couldn't offer her sister a refuge here.

That was when Blue came back. He simply walked in the kitchen door the day after the trial, as comfortable as if he'd never been away. He saw Gem and smiled as if he were her lover returned from an overnight trip. "I've heard you ladies could use a vacation."

Gem froze, struck by sudden shyness. She couldn't get any words out.

"Blue!" Xera came up and gripped his forearm in pleasure. "Where've you been?"

His eyes moved to Gem. "I've found a place for you to get away for a while, if you can convince your sister. I had an idea things would get ugly here."

Gem swallowed. *"That's* why you left?"

He didn't move, but the space shrank between them. "Yes. I can give you your privacy back . . . if you'll accept." He glanced shyly at her from beneath his lashes.

"Yes!" Xera answered firmly for both of them. "I'll go pack. Come on, sis—or do you want to stay here and feed the media sharks?"

"No," Gem answered softly. "I'll go." Suddenly she had a lot to say, but Xera's presence forestalled it. "But what about Brandy?"

"I've taken care of it," Blue assured her. "Do you need any help getting ready?"

"Uh, no. Let me just tell our manager what's going

on and then I'll pack." She hesitated then asked, "How long will we be gone? Do I need to bring some cash? I can stop by the bank . . ."

Blue shook his head, a small smile on his face. "Pack for a week. You'll be able to wash your clothes if we stay longer. Bring something you'll feel comfortable in. And don't make this complicated, sweetheart. If you don't control every detail, it will still be okay."

His attitude won a smile from her. Suddenly, Gem's heart felt light. "I'll be quick."

She was disappointed to learn that Blue wouldn't be joining them right away on their supposed vacation, though.

"I'm sending you and Xera on ahead with Zsak. Brandy and I will follow after we've worked everything out with her doctor. They may want to send along a nurse or therapist—or a parole officer for her. If so, I'll take care of it."

"But where are we going?" Xera asked. Blue had arranged to sneak them out with the morning deliverymen, to avoid being followed.

Blue winked. "Trust me. It'll be an adventure." Some of his amusement faded as he looked at Gem, and her sister moved to the opposite side of the kitchen to give them privacy. "We need to have a long talk," he said.

She looked down at the tile. "I know." There was a lot to be said, but this probably wasn't the place.

He seemed to agree. "There'll be time and privacy where we're going. We'll work this out. It'll be all right." He studied her for an awkward moment, then reached over and drew his fingers along the side of her face. "See you soon."

He walked away.

* * *

Two days later, Xera stared out the beat-up window of their shuttlecraft with dismay. They were rapidly approaching a barren hunk of asteroid whose sole possibility of comfort was a biosphere spanning a third of its pocked surface.

"This is your answer to our security and stress relief?" she asked.

Zsak grinned. "It has underground living quarters and an oxygen generator. What else do you need?"

"It's a mining claim!" she snapped.

"Sure, and a lousy one. We got it cheap and had it zoned for farming. You ever done farming, Xera? I can just see you running a tractor!"

Gem sighed. She tried not to be disappointed, but with all of Blue's talk she'd held out hope for something a little more luxurious. Even another jaunt on a starship would have held more comforts than this.

It didn't help that she was suffering some major mood swings. Stress had been doing crazy things to her. As much as she appreciated what was being done for her and her sisters, it was hard to keep her emotions under control.

It was no wonder she was upset, either. Blue hadn't called. Was the man allergic to the communicator? Did he want her to stew? Did he want her to worry? What exactly *did* he want?

After a moment, her frustration found release. She turned and hissed at Zsak. "This is the big plan, eh? You're serious. What do we know about farming? You've seen our garden. Why do you think we hire gardeners? Blue probably knows more about farming than I do." She thought about him working in the family gardens and felt a stab of nostalgia. Things had been so much easier when he was just the hired hand. She missed their time in the gardens, watching him work in those ragged, provocative shorts, teasing her . . .

Zsak smirked. "Good thing. He'll be joining us in a couple of days when the doctors release him. He'll have to advise *you* how to use the hoe, though, 'cause the doctors said it would be a bit before he'll be allowed to do hard labor. That bullet came close to his heart, you know." He'd been dropping little burrs like that. She wasn't sure what he was trying to accomplish, unless it was to point out how hard-hearted she'd been.

"*When* they release him? I thought they already had."

"No," Zsak replied. "He sort of checked himself out over their protests. I imagine they're giving him grief over that now."

She could see him doing that: checking himself out against professional advice. She just hoped he hadn't hurt himself with his stubbornness.

Ever practical, Xera drew the conversation back to the barren rock that would be their temporary home. "How do you figure this is a good place to hide out?" she asked. "There's nobody out here to blend in with! Of course, there's also no one to rat us out . . ."

Zsak didn't respond at first, just silently watched the pilot guide the ship down.

There were seven other "farmers" in the security team, all of them male. Zsak was in charge. He finally nodded and said, "There should be very few people here to report back to your enemies. Besides, it's not unusual to get an influx of new blood out here, not with new mines opening up all the time. Add a couple of green-haired Kiuyian lasses to that, and we make the perfect picture."

Gem and Xera glared at him. They knew what miners in the area would assume they were there for. He'd made them dye their hair and chrome their lips dark green before they'd left home. Only hookers made it a point to dye their lips with the slick, shiny dye; it was a calling card of the profession, especially among Kiuyian girls. Also, Xera and Gem's otherwise utilitarian jumpsuits were nipped in.

Gem hadn't even been aware she had all the curves the suit now revealed. She'd never felt so exposed in her life. And when Blue came and saw her in it . . . She shivered. Isolated, dressed provocatively, with seven other men as competition—this was the kind of situation that gave a man ideas. In her present frame of mind, she wasn't sure she could fight him off. More to the point, maybe she didn't want to. She wondered if Zsak had done it on purpose.

The moment her feet hit the gritty surface of the asteroid, she felt a wave of distaste. It surprised her. She hadn't realized she felt so disdainful of miners and land developers. After all, her father himself had been like them, settling his land and starting The Spark, right when that relocated asteroid was practically trailing vapor. Had other people looked down on him as an immigrant? She'd been born there, grown up the daughter of a successful businessman; she'd never known what it was like to come to a new place, to make a living as a stranger. It was humbling.

Yes, people came here to scratch a living from the bare rock. She'd always felt distrustful of such desperate people—and still did. She'd seen too many of the dregs of the galaxy come through her tavern. Of course, she had to admit a few of the Kiuyians had done well, even though they'd recently appeared. Still, she didn't feel comfortable assuming the role of an immigrant. Even less so, posing as a prostitute.

"Nice digs," Xera said ironically next to her. Gem's sister's expression, her posture, her voice were about as un-hookerlike as it was possible to get. She looked like a young Galactic Marines sergeant surveying an unruly group of cadets as she glanced around the pockmarked surface. "Can't wait to see what the living quarters look like."

They walked a short distance to a stone knoll that had been hollowed out with lasers. The rooms were nothing but small, spare chambers with tarps covering the doors. Depressing. There was an area large enough to be used as a gathering chamber and not much else.

Both sisters leveled unimpressed stares on Zsak as he walked in, carrying equipment. He grinned at them. "Not what you're used to, ladies? Can't be much worse than a Galactic Explorers barracks. Right, Xera? You even have a room to yourself."

"We could always sleep in the ship," Gem suggested.

"Wouldn't send the right image for true farmers, now would it?" Zsak replied. She could tell he enjoyed teasing them. "Don't worry, we'll at least make sure you have comfortable beds. Gotta keep up appearances."

Xera grunted and brushed by him to go get her stuff. She was unquestionably put out by their disguise—which likely had something to do with the embarrassment she'd suffered at the trial. Who would enjoy having her reputation smeared further?

With a sigh, Gem joined her. Even if it was only a week they stayed here, it was going to feel like a year.

Then again, there was no media here. That alone helped.

Gem said as much to Xera, and added, "Just think of it as camping. You know, like those squalid little cabins dad used to rent so we could go fishing. Well, he fished, anyway. I used to bring a stack of books." She smiled fondly at the memory.

Xera grinned faintly. "And I stomped around the woods, pretending to stalk our dinner through the stinkweed." She wrinkled her nose in memory. "Don't mind my moods, sis. I'm just . . . decompressing. I really am glad to be away from those blasted cameras."

Gem nodded. "I know. Things were rough for me, too—still are. It's like all the stress is suddenly bleeding out. I wouldn't be surprised if we both go a little crazy for a while."

"That could be fun," Xera said, laughing. "Maybe we should concentrate on acting as crazy as we can for a while. If we go nuts on purpose, maybe we won't do it for real."

"That's a pretty wacky philosophy." Gem chuckled.

"Do you have a better one?"

"Nope. Let's run with it."

So they did. Xera took up wearing her hair in pigtails and Gem painted her nails green to match her lips. They wasted hours doodling, chatting and playing cards with the guys. They also took up practical jokes, playing pranks on each other with a vengeance. It was wonderful taking on a second adolescence after being so mature about running the inn all those years.

Zsak didn't mind being included in the jokes, it

turned out. A wicked prankster himself, he took pleasure in gluing their boots to the floor, the ceiling, and once to the door of the fridge. The man was a monster with a tube of Lock-Tight. The sisters finally took revenge by gluing his pants closed. They turned the fabric inside out and smeared glue around the knees. It was only when Zsak pulled them out the next morning and tried to slide his feet in that he discovered what they'd done.

His revenge had been to spike their breakfasts with extra-hot pepper powder the following morning. It was fire going down and, later, coming out. They behaved for a while after that.

Though he hadn't arrived yet, Gem suddenly realized she had a lot to thank Blue for. In the years to come, these would be the days she'd smile about. She looked forward to telling him so.

It was easier to think of him now, in this atmosphere. Odd, how she hadn't realized how stressed she'd become. Looking back, she could see how that tension had colored so many of her perceptions, clouding her decisions. Coming to this place really had been a godsend. She hoped she could move forward with her old optimism.

If she could just settle things with Blue, the future could bring some of the best years of her life.

Chapter Fifteen

It took a couple of days for them to finish setting up camp. On the third day the lunar ice for the mist irrigation system was delivered. Gem and Xera set aside their cooking preparations to walk outside and watch. Gem shaded her eyes to better see the ice barge lumber through the biosphere like a beetle through a luminous bubble. It was lowered slowly to the far side of the asteroid, kicking up an enormous amount of dust. She actually felt the ground shift as the colossal block of ice settled in the crater bed. Situated on a raised bit of land, it would form a natural lake as it melted.

Cables hissed as the pilot retracted the grappling hooks. Normally a ship took off again after delivery, but to her surprise, the captain took the time to disembark. Curious, Gem followed Zsak and the others closer as a crewman and another man followed. Only as she got close did she recognize Blue.

She hadn't been warned he was coming today. Her pulse started to race. With fear or excitement? She couldn't tell, but the unfamiliar sensations made her stiff and awkward.

He seemed self-conscious, also. Like a teen with a

crush, his eyes flicked to her, but he focused his attention on Zsak, who gave him a one-armed hug and carefully slapped him on his good shoulder.

"Hey, man, didn't expect you so early! What did the doctor have to say?"

Blue gave his friend a half smile. He spoke as if playing to the audience of the pilot who'd flown him here: "You know how it is—guy gets a little scraped up and the docs want to bleed him dry with a long hospital stay. They gave me some healing accelerators and told me to take it easy. Truth be known, I'm itching to get to work."

The pilot and his fellow crewman seemed pleasantly distracted as they looked Gem and her sister up and down. "Hey, you guys got quite the entertainment here. They exclusive, or do you share?"

Zsak took Blue's bags. "You gotta be one of the club. Sorry."

The pilot shook his head. "We don't have time to stay, anyway. Speaking of which . . . we'd better get going." He gave Blue and Zsak a sketchy salute, and both he and the crewman headed back up the ramp.

As soon as everyone was clear, the barge took off. Blue waited until the ship was gone to look at his pal. "Hookers?"

Zsak shrugged. A small smile lurked around his mouth. "Seemed to work."

Blue looked at Gem. She eyed him carefully, saw that he was moving under his own power, if a bit stiffly, and said, "Hi. We were just having lunch. Are you hungry?" Struck by a sudden bout of self-consciousness, she didn't know what else to say. The man hadn't been in touch, and suddenly they were face-to-face, with lots of ground to cover. Maybe it was best to keep everything simple.

"Lunch would be nice," he agreed, studying her as if he expected more.

"Great! I'll see you inside," Gem replied, then quickly retreated to the caves. Her nerves were getting the best of her.

Blue sighed as he watched Gem flee.

Zsak hefted his luggage. "Cheer up, buddy. Even that iceberg over there will thaw, given enough time." He pointed at the ice that had been delivered, and laughed. "Now, let's go see what's cooking."

Xera hadn't fled, and she fell in readily next to the guys. "You'd have an easier time of it if you'd been in touch with her," she pointed out to Blue.

"I know. It's just that some things are easier said in person."

Xera looked skeptical, but she changed the subject. "What did you do with Brandy?" she asked.

"Her doctors weren't thrilled with her leaving the hospital, but she didn't want to stay home with all that mess outside. I told her what to expect out here and she wasn't excited at the idea, so we compromised. She elected to stay on a military ship for a short while with her nurse."

Xera shook her head, flabbergasted. "She did nothing but complain last time!"

Blue shrugged, then grimaced at the discomfort. "She claims it's quiet. Me, I think she likes the company."

Xera tilted her head in suspicion. "Who?"

Blue looked innocent. "Azor is there."

Xera stared, nonplussed. After a moment she chuckled. "I don't think so."

"He really is," Blue swore.

"Sure, but there's nothing to what you're implying. Brandy hates that guy's guts."

Blue started walking. "If you say so."

Xera opened her mouth and then shut it. After all, it was obvious he was teasing.

Blue didn't try to have a serious talk with Gem right away; instead, he smiled at her and made small talk over lunch. She found herself coloring for no reason whenever he looked her way, and he did that often.

She was glad to see him, but uneasy, too. It was almost as if they were starting over again, testing their boundaries. He'd violated her trust, however good his motives might have been. They couldn't just take up where they'd left off. He was going to have to prove himself.

Not that he was in a position to chase her around, she thought guiltily. He looked weary, and it was obvious that movement brought him pain. She had to wonder why the doctors had released him so early— or if he was still acting against orders.

As soon as she could get Zsak alone, she asked him about it.

"We've got a trained medic here," he assured her. "It's amazing what a healing accelerator and a good surgeon can do for a body," he promised.

"But he doesn't look good," she fretted, glancing covertly Blue's way. "You can tell he's tired."

"Look, darlin', if you want to fuss over him, I'm sure he'd welcome it. As for me, I've got to make like a farmer and go raise some grass. See you at dinner." Zsak took off.

Gem frowned after him, then looked back at Blue. He really did look weary.

Ignoring the sudden nervousness in the pit of her stomach, she squared her shoulders and marched up to him. "Come on, you need to lie down."

He glanced at her sideways but didn't make the obvious wisecrack. "I've been doing too much of that lately and my back is sore. I'd agree to sit down if we could find a comfortable chair, though."

Now here was something she could handle! Encouraged, she said briskly, "I'll find you something. We'll get you a place to recoup. You need any medicine?"

He groaned softly as she helped him walk. "Had it." But the meds seemed of minimal help, for his steps were slow as she steered him to a room he would share with Zsak for their stay here. She kept hold of his arm, afraid he'd falter.

He lowered himself to the edge of the bed with an expression of pain.

"I'll be right back with some pillows," she assured him, then hurried to rob the ones off her and Xera's beds.

They made a nice stack against the wall, keeping him propped upright. She adjusted them until he was comfortable, and then he looked at her for a moment.

"I wish I'd had you with me when I was trapped in that hospital," he said. "You would have made a good nurse."

She flushed. "I . . ." Was what? Angrier then? Hurt? Her excuses sounded petty to her own ears. "Do you need anything?"

He dropped the subject of his hospital stay, clearly willing to focus on the here and now. "No, not really. Although . . . you could get the viewer out of my bag. I think there's a book or two I haven't read yet."

"Right." She fetched the device, glad to think of him relaxing. "I'll be fixing dinner. Call me if you need anything else."

She was feeling guilty and unsure. If she stayed, he might bring up her not visiting him in the hospital, and what could she say? She'd felt justified at one time, but now she just felt bad. He really hadn't deserved her reaction.

She left, and he didn't call for her. A couple of hours went by before she gave in to her instincts and looked back in on him.

"What?" he asked, glancing up from his book.

"Just making sure you're okay," she murmured, and ducked quickly out.

A little while later he made his way into the common room and quietly sat at a table. The location had changed, but she almost felt as if they'd stepped back in time to the days when he hung out in her taproom. It made her feel a little more relaxed, and she brought him a fruity drink—the same kind with which she used to tease him.

"You hungry?" she asked.

"A little. We got anything good around here?" He looked at his drink in surprise. "Hey, you brought this to me cold."

Her smile was lopsided. "You always complained when it was warm."

He grinned. "That was just a ruse. I enjoyed showing off and you know it."

Her smile brightened for a moment then faded.

The silence in the room weighed on her. She'd put this off too long. "You . . . you should have told me you were a cop, Blue."

He considered her seriously. "At what point would it have been appropriate?"

She frowned at his lack of repentance. "If you didn't think you could share that information, you should have at least controlled yourself."

"Yes, I should have," he admitted. He looked her straight in the eye but didn't apologize. "I wanted you bad then, and I still do. I'm not going to say I'm sorry for that."

She didn't know what to say. She hadn't expected him to come out and admit something like this, but maybe she should have. He'd never been shy about expressing desire. "Being lovers would never be good enough for me. You know that."

"But you want me," he pressed. He considered her expression, waited to see if she'd deny it.

She sat back in her chair, challenged. Slowly she said, "I'm not going to compromise my honor, Blue. If that's all you're after, you'll be disappointed. All I can offer you is friendship."

"I'm not after friendship," he replied. But that was all.

After a moment, not sure what he was implying, Gem stood up. "Right. I'll bring you a snack." There were times when strategic retreat was the only option.

"You look pale," she told him after dinner. "Maybe you should go lie down." She was trying not to hover, without success.

Blue grunted. It seemed as if fatigue had robbed

him of any interest in further seductions. Now he looked just plain grumpy. "I told you, my back is sore from lying around. I'm sick of it."

She looked at him and sighed, wondering about the wisdom of her next offer: "I suppose I could massage it for you."

He considered her words without apparent enthusiasm. "You'd have a hard time, avoiding my shoulder and still doing good." He looked about as excited as a young child given an early bedtime.

His mulishness made Gem annoyed—and all the more fixated on performing the massage. "I'll be careful," she promised. "I don't think I need to worry about you getting ideas when you can barely sit up," she added for the benefit of all listeners. She was getting some very speculative looks from the security detail—the downside of looking like a hooker, she supposed.

Blue smiled slightly. "No ideas because I'm tired? You don't know men too well, do you? Lead on, however. You can just shoot me if I misbehave." He stood up stiffly and slung an arm around her shoulders.

"Very funny," she retorted as she let him use her for support. Then, avoiding Xera's watchful gaze, she took him to his room and helped ease him onto the bed.

He settled facedown on the quilt with a grateful sigh. Only when he was lying prone did she realize how much easier it would be without his shirt.

He made a muffled sound when she suggested he sit up so she could remove it. Then he said, "Not worth it."

She fought back annoyance. Nonetheless, she set to work on his back, careful to avoid his injury. She asked, "How long did they say it would take for a full recovery?"

"A month or more. Considering, that's not too bad," he said.

"Seems fast for all you went through."

"The nanotech the military put in me helps. Amazing, what a nanobot can do for a hole in the body."

"I thought that stuff was expensive."

"Depends. Sometimes it's cheaper than training a new soldier."

She worked on him in silence for a bit longer, until she caught herself wistfully wishing he could remove his shirt. But maybe it was wise to keep all that skin covered.

Another minute passed. She bit her lip, wondering if rubbing through his shirt might be chafing his back. She didn't want to hurt him, of course.

A few more minutes went by, and finally she worked up the nerve to slide her hands under the hem. Her pulse rose. His skin was so smooth!

He groaned and levered himself up. "I'd better get up before I fall asleep," he remarked. He caught her confused expression and smiled faintly. "Thanks for the massage." Then he left.

Gem simply stared after him, an unwanted yearning burning in her heart.

Zsak glanced sideways at Blue as he followed his friend into the pantry. "How's it going, lover boy?"

Blue gave Zsak a sardonic glance but otherwise ignored him. He searched for a snack as his pal leaned against the doorway.

"I can't help but notice that you seem spryer than you did earlier. Could it be you're playing on that poor girl's tender mercies?" Of course, for all his joking, Zsak didn't seem too distressed by the possibility.

"Whatever it takes," Blue replied. Seduction came in many forms, and he was playing for keeps.

"Just so you watch out for her sister. Xera's on your side, but she won't ignore it if you go too far."

"Don't worry—that's not part of my plan. I don't need *her* chasing after me." Blue allowed himself a slight smile. It felt good to have Gem doting on him, finally. Yes, he was annoyed she hadn't come around sooner, at least to talk to him, but he had loftier goals than just sponging up sympathy.

"I've finally got that girl figured out," he remarked. "The cooler the reception, the closer she slides. At this rate, we'll be married before she knows what hit her."

They'd had a lot of time to talk while Blue was laid up, so Zsak wasn't surprised to hear his friend's ultimate plan. He did question the method, though. "Are you sure playing hard to get is the way to go? Isn't that a girlish strategy?"

Blue's annoyed glance was quelling. "I know what I'm doing."

"Well, don't take too long about it. The betting pool isn't leaning in your favor, and I could use the money."

That made Blue smile. "You're betting on me?"

Zsak grinned back. "Couldn't resist a sure thing."

Chapter Sixteen

Xera cornered Blue the next day. She was waiting for him as he came out of his bedroom, leaning against the wall, her arms folded. He considered her and waved an arm back toward his room. "You want to talk in there?"

She gave him a look and led him to the empty commons. The rest of the supposed farmers, that is, the security team, had already eaten and were off working the rock.

She waited until they were seated and then said mildly, "What exactly are your intentions toward my sister?"

He raised an eyebrow, questioning her right to even ask.

She shrugged, realizing his intent. "Our father is dead. Somebody has to look out for her."

"Are you asking me if I'll marry her?"

Xera exhaled forcefully. "I already know you will. I've grilled Zsak—and I know about the betting pool. You'll ask."

"You don't like it."

Xera shrugged. "My sister's getting older, has her

future established in The Spark. She wants to get married and may think you're the best she'll get. Whether it's true or not . . . Well, I'd hate for her to settle."

He glowered at her. "Is that right?"

"Of course, it would all be all right if you loved her," Xera added, nonchalant. "So many men just care about her money, which is all tied up in the inn, you know. Not much in loose change."

Blue had to smile at such transparency. "I'm not after her money. I have my own."

"How's that?" Xera asked.

"Good investments, and I've saved some of my salary. That's the way we working-class types do it."

Her eyes narrowed. "So, you're saying you love her. She's not just another sort of investment?"

Blue leaned in. "I'm saying that's between Gem and me. I'm not about to tell you how I feel when I haven't even spoken to her. Now, if that's about it, I'm hungry. Care to get me something from the kitchen?"

Xera stood up and her eyes raked him. "You seem hale enough to me. Go find your own food." Then she flounced out.

"What's up with her?" Gem asked, looking over her shoulder at her departing sister as she entered the room. "Hey, are you hungry? I saved something for you." Almost shyly, her gaze skated over Blue's as she headed for the kitchen.

"Thank you!" He rose and followed, settling down at a table closer to the stove so he could watch. "Your sister doesn't like me."

Gem laughed. "What else is new? She likes to mow people over. It irks her when some of them don't lie down and take it, don't let her walk over them. She has her wonderful moments, for all that."

"Maybe she can go back to the academy soon," Blue suggested. He knew she was tired of being someplace other than where her career required.

"I think that will help." Gem slid a plate toward him. "Any chance of it happening soon?"

He savored a bite of what she'd given him, considering. "Depends on Azor's part of the operation. He's close to an arrest that will take out the player who sent the hit men after you, but they've got a few things to tie up first. Once that happens, you can go home. Even if the results of the trial didn't convince that smuggler to drop his grievance, your enemy will be too busy to trying to save his own sorry hide to worry about you. Most likely, the contract on you will be ignored once his assets are seized. No money, no service. Assassins don't work for free."

"Glad to hear it," Gem said dryly. "Who exactly is my enemy, anyway? Are we sure yet?"

"Can't tell you," Blue said. He tried to keep his tone conversational. "Could you pass the hot sauce?"

Gem sighed and slid it over. "So . . . are we talking a matter of weeks, or what?"

"Maybe. Got cabin fever already?"

"Yeah. I'm twitchy," she confided. "I don't know what to do with all this downtime."

He considered the immaculate kitchen. "Cooking and cleaning aren't enough?"

Her smile was wry. "Honestly, it's like a vacation. I was never good at vacation—not that I ever got much experience. I hardly know what to do with myself."

Blue gave her a sly look.

"No, Blue," she retorted.

He shrugged, gave an amused smile. "Can you blame me? I've got plenty of free time, too. And I desire you."

"Well, maybe you should learn something new to do in your free time. Why don't you help me cook today?" she suggested with a smile. But it was obvious she didn't expect him to say yes.

"Sounds good!" he replied. "Just don't get upset when I set myself on fire."

To Gem's surprise, she found Blue a good hand in the kitchen. His arm was stiff, but there were plenty of things he could still do, and he worked without complaint. She found herself actually enjoying his company.

When she stepped outside later to call the guys in for dinner, she was surprised to see Xera covered in grime and sweat, her short, dyed-green curls plastered to her head. She looked more like a field hand than a pampered seductress. It was obvious she'd been working beside the men. If they had visitors now, her condition might be hard to explain.

Xera just grunted when Gem pointed it out. "I'll go soft in that kitchen. I need to stay in shape for the academy."

Gem made a noncommittal hum as she gazed out over the farm. In the distance she could see the transport-sized rock-splitter robot they'd rented. It slowly rolled over the dirt closest to the iceberg, pausing to emit sonic waves that shivered the solid rock into smaller dirt particles. At a rate of 2,000 square feet an hour, the machine had its work cut out. This particular asteroid was roughly twenty-seven miles wide and forty-four miles long.

Not all of the rock would be turned to farm soil, of course. Buildings were already being "printed" with a giant construction arm. Also rented, the construction machine was very simple to use. Once a site was leveled and prepped, the machine and its crew of two got set up. All you had to do was select a design and keep the "printer cartridge" full of cement. Once started, the machine could print one three-dimensional house per day. On day two the hollow walls were fitted with prefab, wireless energy transmitters, snap-in light fixtures and plumbing. The third day would see the filling of the hollow walls with a type of spray insulation. After that the roof would go up, for the walls would have had time to cure. Super-efficient solar panels would be mounted on top.

Gem had to admit the process was amazing. She could see herself investing in a venture like this. But suddenly she wondered who was funding it. This kind of setup wasn't cheap. For that matter, who would knowingly allow a bunch of Narc officers to use this equipment?

Blue shrugged when she asked him. "Maybe Zsak knows."

"It's a private investor," his friend remarked. "He'd rather not have his affiliation with our office mouthed around, you know? I can tell you he has a few bucks, though. Constructing this type of digs isn't cheap."

Freshly showered, Xera set her supper plate down at their table of four. "I'll say. Have you seen the blueprints for this place, Gem? It's going to look like a private estate! Not sure what they're going to grow that will make enough profit to pay this place off before doomsday, though." She shook her head.

"Medicinal herbs," Blue supplied. He set his computer on the table and changed it to projection mode. A holographic map spread out before them.

"I've had time to read," he explained, answering their curious looks. "Once dried, some of these plants go for as much as illegal drugs would, but they are completely lawful." A series of plants, complete with captions, scrolled past. "They hope this will serve as a model for other farmers who want to pay off their land, too. A portion of this island will be set up for tenant farmers to grow their own food, both for themselves and their livestock. It should be a nice place once it's done."

Gem looked at Xera, both pleased and amazed. "We couldn't afford a whole rock, but this is genius. What about investing in something like this? Someone with some business sense could make a real go of it."

Xera shrugged. "It sounds rosy, but what are the risks? Crop failures, bad tenants . . . How many ventures have we seen go bankrupt? I say we keep all our money invested in The Spark. You have plans to expand, remember? It's not as exciting to stick with what you know, but it is practical."

Gem mulled that over, still tempted to diversify. "It would be nice to have a trustworthy financial advisor, someone who's already found the path, you know?" She relented at Xera's frown of concern. "Don't worry, I see your point, sis. I really don't want to risk our futures."

Zsak poked a vegetable with his fork, hesitated, then passed it up in favor of meat. "You seem to be doing well enough with what you've got," he remarked.

Blue shook his head slightly, but if he had any doubts, he didn't elaborate. "As soon as the rock bot gets done breaking up the soil, we're going to seed it with good microbes, bugs and fungi. When that's done we'll start the first green manure. In a couple of months it will be plowed under to enrich the soil. We'll do that a couple of times before the cash crops are started."

"Not that we'll be here. Seriously, why bother? Whatever our deal is with the owner, why not just throw some fertilizer down and get farming?" Xera asked.

"A person could do that, and wear out the soil," Blue explained. "This is the most economical way to build the soil up. An owner would want really good dirt to produce the best plants. The best plants get top dollar. To do otherwise just isn't good business sense."

"Huh," Xera said, and promptly lost interest.

Gem considered Blue with interest. She'd never seen this side of him, never known he cared anything for business. Now that he was being his true self, what else might they have in common? She asked more questions, and before she knew it they'd whiled away most of an hour just talking investments and commerce.

Xera had long ago wandered off in boredom when Blue finally excused himself to go take his meds. Gem nodded absently and watched him leave, then rose to go take a walk. He'd given her a lot to think about.

It was dusk outside, with the last rays of the sun sinking over the rim of the asteroid island. She imagined the belt of breathable air outside, and imagined farther still, to the unseen islands beyond, dotting the edges of sight. The area must be a beautiful view from a ship.

Her aimless roaming took her down into a crater where the sunshine quickly retreated, leaving only long shadows. There was a three-story ridge to her left, but the low walls on her right allowed her to glance over and see their craft and the entrance to their home caves.

It was cooling off as night fell. She'd go back in a little bit, but she wanted to think about Blue a little more.

A sudden faint noise to her left made Gem turn her head. She glanced up, but there was nothing to see but a rock wall. Then a following shout made her look back and to the right. A crushing weight immediately dropped onto her left shoulder. Something cracked, and then the weight rolled off her arm, hit the ground and settled hard against her ankle.

Gem howled in pain and dropped helplessly, barely registering that it was a huge rock that had felled her. She gritted her teeth against the waves of pain, each beat of her heart bringing a new agony.

Footsteps sounded as someone ran up. Blue snatched her hand, lifted her up and ran with her, never giving her a chance to protest, not saying a word even if he could have been heard over her shrieks. He was hurting her, and she raged against the pain, not understanding why. She was so agonized by the time he set her down in their home cave that she couldn't make out what he was saying.

He left her and someone else took his place. It was Xera, and her sister was trying to soothe her, but her body *hurt*. She couldn't breathe.

There was a tiny sting against her good arm, so insignificant it barely registered. In moments the pain receded, became manageable. Gem began to curse Blue.

"He saved your life," Xera told her fiercely, breaking in against her rant. She helped the group medic cut off Gem's shirt. "Someone dropped a rock on you. He's gone out hunting the man who did it."

"What?" Even with the meds, Gem whimpered as the medic probed her shoulder.

Someone new skidded in with a medical kit and handed the medic a scanner. He stopped probing to wave the device over Gem's injury. At the view of her bones on the display, he grimaced. "Nasty break there."

"Do we need to get her to a doctor?" Xera asked anxiously.

The medic frowned. "I *am* a doctor."

"Okay, but can you fix this without a hospital, I mean. Does she need surgery?"

He shook his head. "I can fix her up on the ship—it's got everything I need. We'll have to move her, though, and we'll need a stretcher. Looks like her ankle is banged up, too, though that's only a bad bruise. See?" He held the scanner over the ankle in question.

Xera winced. "I'll go see what's keeping the stretcher."

"Just don't go anywhere alone," the medic warned.

He covered Gem with a blanket. Grateful, she closed her eyes and tried not to think too hard.

They hadn't found the attacker.

Blue studied the ground as the rest of his team

fanned out. There were a few tracks in the dust, then nothing. It was as if the man had suddenly vanished.

Zsak was up on the canyon wall, too, trying to find out who'd breached their security. He held up a scanning device and remarked, "I'm getting traces of Kiuyian DNA."

Blue looked sharply up. If a shape-shifter were involved, it would answer a lot of questions. "Do we have any match on record?" he asked.

"It'll take a bit to check against all we have, but this explains the sudden lack of tracks."

"He flew out," Blue agreed. "He probably got on this island the same way. Who ever notices a bird? Our surveillance equipment wouldn't register it as a threat, either. We'll have to reprogram. Meanwhile, we'll regroup around the women. Half our men watching them isn't enough now. We'll update them, and I want to talk to Azor. He'll need to know what we're dealing with."

Blue felt a stab of guilt. There'd always been a risk in bringing the women to such a desolate place, but he'd felt it was worth it—for many reasons. Military ships were patrolling the general area, and his men here were experienced. If there'd been any lingering threat, they should have nullified it.

Of course, none of his plans had factored in a Kiuyian. That oversight could bring major complications. He'd never had to deal with an adversary who could change form at will. Not in his work as a policeman, at any rate.

And, nobody knew all the capabilities of the shifters. There was speculation, of course, but they were a tight-lipped race who guarded their own secrets. He knew not all of them could shift. Fewer could take the guise of another humanoid, though nobody understood why. Perhaps it was too difficult for their bodies to overcome their instinctual, natural form. Maybe it was taboo.

Regardless, he had to warn his men to be wary of the possibility. They didn't know what this enemy could do. Even if they found a file on him, it was doubtful it would list all his abilities.

Blue gazed speculatively at the sky. At the very least, their enemy could fly. That advantage was dangerous enough, although a good homing rocket could overcome it. Not that he had one of those at hand.

His hand brushed the grip of his gun and he thanked his lucky stars that he could make his enemy bleed.

"Let's get moving," he ordered his men. They didn't have time to linger here; his women were in danger.

Chapter Seventeen

"Nobody goes anywhere alone." Blue stared Xera down, and for once she had nothing to say.

They were on the ship they'd flown here, in the cabin she shared with her sister. Gem was too medicated and tired to care much what rules Blue was laying down. For that matter, she agreed with him; she wasn't in a hurry to collect more injuries.

"We think we're dealing with a shape-shifter. We're not sure yet, but we think he flew in at the same time as one of the delivery ships, either in a small craft or as some type of avian. Since we can't find any trace of a ship, my money's on the bird form. We know it's possible for such creatures to fly between the islands—imported flocks do it all the time."

"But why do you think it's a Kiuyian?" Xera asked.

"DNA traces found at the scene," he said. "We haven't found any matches in our crime database yet, so we don't know who he is, but based on his actions, we suspect he's got a record. You don't just jump up one day and decide to become a killer for hire."

"We know a little more than that," Zsak said as he walked through the open door. "Intel has finally found a match. Our friend's name is Kiyl. You were right about the record, though——he's a wanted felon with an addiction to drugs. Our sources are saying he's the bastard son of the drug lord who was targeting Gem."

Xera was listening closely. *"Was* targeting her?"

The men exchanged glances. "We just found out this morning that he was arrested. And he was killed in the process. We were waiting to see how the complications played out before telling you."

"I see," Xera said coldly. It was plain she was unhappy with the delay. Not that she could have done anything. "Go on."

Zsak tilted his head to crack his neck. "Unfortunately, our would-be assassin seems to blame Gem for his father's death. Why he arrived at that conclusion, we can't be sure. He was apparently on the fringes of his father's operation, never very well connected. Someone must have leaked it that she was responsible for pinpointing him. There are a lot of rumors going around about Gem and Blue, and the wrong people now know he's a cop. A lot of them would like getting revenge on a snitch and 'her boyfriend, the Narc.'"

Xera's murderous glare tore into Blue. It was obvious she felt like killing him herself, for putting her sister in more danger.

Gem finally spoke up. "How are we going to stop him?" she asked. She made an effort to sit up but quit immediately. Her face was creased with lines of pain.

"We aren't," Blue told her firmly. He sat down on her bunk, facing her. "You are going to heal up and let me and Zsak take care of this. This guy is motivated

by family, so he's not going to quit when the money dries up, like other hunters would."

"Then why are we staying here? Shouldn't we be headed somewhere else?" Xera demanded.

Zsak shook his head. "You're not listening. He's patient, and good at hiding. There's little point in running unless you want to do it for the rest of your life. If we can nail him here, the threat is over. We've got backup on the way, and holing up in the ship seems the best strategy. You really don't want to be looking over your shoulder for the rest of your life, do you?"

"What's to stop him from just flying away? If he sees a bunch of ships arriving . . ." She trailed off as the answer came to her. Even if he could fly, he couldn't outrun a starship. And of course there was always his desire for revenge. "Oh."

"Right. He's not going to run."

"It's late. We should get some sleep." Blue chose the bunk opposite Gem's. Even if he'd have liked to curl up with her, the bunks were too narrow, and he didn't want to jar her shoulder.

Xera frowned at him. "What do you think you're doing?" she grunted.

Blue regarded her calmly. "I told you that someone would be with you and your sister at all times."

"Are you planning to join us in the bathroom, too?" Xera asked acidly.

He ignored her. "You can stay here or leave with Zsak. This ship should be secure, but always stay within hearing range of a friend."

Xera looked at him sternly, then glanced at her sister, who was in no shape to feel amorous. She exhaled heavily and finally left them to their rest.

Gem waited until the door was closed. "Thank you, Blue," she said softly.

There was a long pause, in which he could have said many things. In the end, he said quietly, "You're welcome, darlin'. Sweet dreams."

Xera couldn't sleep. She prowled the bridge until Zsak started giving her annoyed glances. He was working on the computers and talking into the communicator perched on his ear. Apparently, her restless energy was distracting.

It had never been a problem back home. In the inn, an extra body prowling the night had been an asset. Sometimes she'd helped out in the bar, occasionally ousting an angry drunk. Bar fights did damage and cost money, so she'd taken martial arts training early on to help keep damage to a minimum. She'd become an expert on disabling the unruly with a minimum of fuss, and she didn't take chances. A drunk might be apologetic later, but that wouldn't stop him from lashing out when he was first getting going.

She wished the changeling would throw a fist at her: he wouldn't be the first Kiuyian she'd taken down. Unfortunately, rocks in the dark seemed more his thing. Growling to herself, she took pity on Zsak and headed to the galley for some water.

The deck echoed dully under her feet, the sound of metal decking barely muted by the rubberized coating underfoot. The ship felt empty, cold. She was used to voices, even in the dead of the night.

She never knew what triggered the impulse. Maybe it was a smell, a sound. All she knew was that she rounded the corner into the galley and adrenaline surged through her blood. A shadow moved, and instinctively she struck out, her fist connecting with a hard stomach that whooshed with deflating air. She saw green hair as the man bent, and she didn't pause to study the face—just punched him hard in the temple. Stunned, he wavered a second, which was all she needed to knock him down and get him in an armlock. She didn't depend on the arm, though; a doped-up fighter could get out of that. The knife she drew and pressed to his throat was another matter.

"Who are you?" she demanded, her breathing harsh.

His answer was muffled, but it sounded like a curse.

She wrenched his arm up a little higher. Much more and it would break. "Speak up!"

"Captain Azor!" he hissed.

She studied his face but didn't see any of the things she remembered. She eased up a fraction on his arm. "Turn your head." Sure enough, there was the mutilated ear with the stud earring, the old knife wound and the angry, cold eyes.

"You can let go now," he said frigidly.

She settled more comfortably. "I don't think so. Zsak!" she bellowed, summoning help. It arrived at a run.

Zsak skidded to a stop, blaster in hand, and stared with horror at Azor. "What are *you* doing here?"

Azor curled his lip.

"I found him sneaking around the galley," Xera replied. "You said we were looking for a Kiuyian—I bagged one."

Zsak reached down and practically dragged her

off the other cop. "He's the backup, you twit! We were expecting him."

She glowered suspiciously as Azor peeled himself off the floor. He stood and flexed his arm, then sent a killing look her way. "Are all the women in your family this bloodthirsty?"

Blue arrived on the heels of that comment. "What happened?" he asked.

Azor sent him a chilly look. "I was testing the security of the ship. This shrew walked in and punched me."

Blue looked astonished. "You let her?"

Zsak turned his snort of laughter into a cough, then muttered for Blue's benefit, "She had him on the floor when I ran in. I had to drag her off him."

There was a hint of bronze around Azor's cheeks. "I didn't expect her to lash out like that."

Xera folded her arms. "Tough luck. You might want to fix your hair, by the way—it's coming out of its ponytail."

His nostrils flared but he didn't move to tidy himself up. "Who's with Gem?" he asked instead.

Blue nodded, took the hint and headed back to the bedroom. But not before Xera noticed the laughter in his eyes.

Azor tugged his uniform down, straightened it. "Your security seems to be in order," he muttered.

Zsak choked.

Azor's eyes narrowed. "Now that I've arrived, we can transfer the women to my ship until we have the killer. Their sister Brandy is anxious to see them."

Xera lit up. "Brandy's here?" She'd talked to her sister that morning, but had had no idea of her location.

Azor nodded. "I have a shuttle outside. Go wake Gem and we can leave."

Xera was eager to go, yet she noticed that, while Zsak let her pass, he didn't immediately follow. She paused and looked back at him, something in his manner making her uncertain.

He was staring thoughtfully at Azor. "How come you didn't call in? I would have met you at the door."

Azor shrugged. "Call a shifter to catch a shifter. I was checking to make sure our friend couldn't make it on board."

"And you got in."

"I had the door codes."

Zsak slowly smiled and raised his gun. "No, you didn't."

Azor's expression seemed to darken. "Don't threaten me, Zsak. You won't like the brig."

Zsak gave him a predatory smile. "Azor doesn't believe in brigs, and he wouldn't let a girl—no matter how skilled—whip his butt."

Azor slowly blinked. His eyes shifted, became long reptilian slits in place of the round human eyes he'd sported before. Scales sprouted on his face, covered his visible body like a suit of chain mail. Even his voice changed, became lighter, cocky. "Don't take on a fight you can't win, cop. You know about dragon-skin? Your blaster can't hurt me now. Give me the girl and I'll let you live."

Shocked, Xera fought hard not to step back. She'd heard about Kiuyians who could grow scales that even a blaster couldn't penetrate. It was a rare talent, but it seemed this man had it. These Kiuyians were often physically faster, as well, and tougher. You practically had to hit them with a mace to even leave a bruise. She couldn't understand why Zsak seemed so calm.

"Xera, go warn Blue," he said.

Xera blinked at the order, but she backed up and did as she was told. It was tough to turn her back on the Kiuyian, but she knew she had no choice. The sound of hissing filled the hall. She ran.

When she reached him, Blue took one look at her face and demanded, "What?"

"A Kiuyian with dragonskin! Zsak's fighting him."

Blue cursed and slammed a hand down on the door latch, locking them inside the room. He aimed his gun at the door, thrust out his hand. "Back off. Get by your sister."

"Aren't you going to help him?" Xera cried. She pulled her knife and waited by Gem, who was alert but didn't ask questions.

"He's doing his job," Blue said, but his eyes were hard. He stared at the door even as he took his communicator from his belt and tossed it to Xera. "Dial one. Tell them what's up and tell them the situation's urgent."

Xera did as she was told, then jumped as something clanked off the door. Fumbling with the communicator, she hurried to explain the situation to the person who answered on the other end. Another blow to the door caused it to bulge slightly. The metal wouldn't take much more abuse.

Suddenly a new voice came over the com. "Xera, tell Blue we'll be on the ground in five minutes."

Xera glanced at the buckling door. "We don't have five minutes!"

"Tell him I copy," Blue said grimly. He must have

inferred the information from her side of the conversation.

The door was warped off its hinges, barely hanging on. After a moment's pause on the other side, silence. There was a gap nearly wide enough to admit a man's fist . . . and something started flowing through it.

Blue fired his blaster, but the tentacle slithering through the crack seemed to simply absorb the shots. Actually, it avoided them: Its substance parted, only to ooze back together. And the Kiuyian was getting in.

Blue snarled and grabbed the tentacle with his bare hand. It writhed, clearly in pain, and Xera realized what was going on: it was being hit with intense cold. Blue was freezing it with his bionic arm.

A screaming noise came from the other side of the door. The tentacle turned white with frost, stiffened and broke. The shattered fragment dropped to the floor with a *clack*. Its inside was pink with ice and frozen solid. The shifter howled.

Xera didn't know how injuries affected Kiuyians, but she hoped their enemy had just lost his hand. There was the sound of running, which quickly faded away. She wasn't eager to chase after it, no matter what.

A voice came from the communicator, and Xera recognized it now: Azor. "We're on the ground," he said. "We're tracking him."

"What about our guys outside? Can they get to him?" Blue asked.

"They're dead," came the reply. "He got to them."

Xera's mouth dropped open. She stared at Blue.

He took the communicator from her. "We clearly underestimated our opponent."

"You think?" Xera muttered.

Blue gave her a hard glare. "I need to open the door. Zsak might need me," he said.

If Zsak wasn't dead. Xera was more than aware of the possibility.

Blue tried pulling on the door but the steel was hopelessly warped. Thankfully, his augmented fist was stronger than the shifter's flesh, and Blue managed to punch through. But neither the door nor his hand looked too good afterward.

"Bring your sister," he grunted when he was finished and they could pass through. "Easy with her shoulder."

Xera and Gem followed closely behind Blue and could only see his back, but it was clear when his footsteps slowed that he'd come upon something. Xera glanced forward and saw blood sprayed all over the walls.

Blue stopped and turned, his face white. "Wait here," he said, his voice strained. "You don't need to see this."

Gem placed her good hand on his shoulder. "Blue?"

"It's okay," he said gruffly.

But it wasn't. Xera's throat hurt as she watched him walk to Zsak's fallen body. His right arm had been ripped off at the shoulder. Zsak wasn't moving. There was so much damage, and for what? Was any revenge worth this kind of carnage?

Blue knelt and felt his friend's neck. A look of surprise and impossible hope crossed his face. "He's alive!"

Azor might have been late to the party, but his medics had impeccable timing. They were suddenly there, in the ship and helping, and they took over, shoving everyone else out of the way. Grateful for their help and smart enough to leave them to it, Blue escorted the women outside to where Azor was working.

He didn't waste time with pleasantries. "Azor? I want the women out of here now. Someplace safe."

"Yes. They're going to my ship." Azor gestured to two men. "Yiu, Pelig, take five men and escort these women to my ship. Their sister is eager to see them."

"Brandy's here?" Gem asked, perking up. She still seemed a bit groggy.

"I'd like to help," Xera put in.

"No," Azor snapped. His voice rang with authority. He turned his attention to Blue then, and it was obvious by the look the men shared that he'd heard about Zsak. Azor looked grim. "Let's get him," he said.

"Brandy!" Gem lit up when she saw her sister. Brandy looked a hundred times better than she had the last time they'd visited. There was color in her skin and her bones were knitting nicely. She still couldn't walk easily, however, and used a wheelchair to help her travel.

In spite of this, she was well able to give them grief over their disguises. "Hookers?" she demanded, and there was a sparkle in her eye as she spoke. "You let them disguise you as prostitutes?"

"It was Zsak's idea," Gem said, but her smile faded almost immediately. "He's been hurt."

"Looks like you have, too," Brandy noted, glancing at Gem's left arm and shoulder. "What's happening?"

Xera quickly filled her in. "And now they're out hunting for the Kiuyian." She glanced toward the big window in the galley, as if it could offer any kind of useful view.

Gem could practically read her sister's thoughts. Xera wanted to be one of the hunters.

To distract her, she said, "Why don't we go down to the sick bay and see if they can tell us anything about Zsak? I'm sure they're still working on him, but I'd like to be there when he wakes up. We owe him."

"Yeah," Xera agreed. "Besides, we can catch up there as easily as here. I just wish they'd let us know what was happening!"

"Don't worry," Gem assured her. "Blue's not going to let this creep get away. First he attacked me and now he's seriously hurt Zsak. The man can't run forever—but he'll wish he had."

Blue glanced at the blood trace on the rocks. The Kiuyian was hurt badly, but he hadn't collapsed yet. They were using infrared to track his movements, and he was proving slippery. The bastard.

"It would help if he'd stop shifting," Blue muttered.

Azor studied their equipment's readouts. "He can't keep this up forever. He's been shifting too much, too fast; he's probably panicked. Even if he's tripping on drugs he'll run out of energy soon. When that happens, he'll be trapped in his natural form."

"You don't think he'll try to fly out?"

"He's smart enough to know he can't leave this rock by wing unless he wants to be shot out of the air. If I didn't want to bring him in alive, he would have been fried long ago. We're stationed in just the right spot."

The Kiuyian alternated between flying as a reptile

and running on four legs to evade them. So far they haven't gotten close enough for a stun shot, but they would soon. They'd herded him close to the rim of the island and cut off his escape from the edge. He was now dead center in their circle, and that circle was growing smaller.

"There." Blue's bionic eyes zoomed in and found the Kiuyian's location. In the form of a hunting cat, the killer had stopped running and now just stood there panting. He stared back at Blue as if defying anyone to get closer. Slowly, reluctantly, his form shifted back. He was again a humanoid—and exhausted, visibly shaking.

Azor smiled. "Stun him."

Blue was happy to oblige. One shot, and the shifter was on the ground, beamed into unconsciousness. "Pity," Blue commented. "I'd hoped he'd put up more of a fight."

Azor watched his men move forward with restraints. Specially designed, they'd mold themselves to any form this prisoner tried to take. There would be no escape, not even for a Kiuyian. "He killed your team and ripped off Zsak's arm. I'm not about to chance anyone else's life," Azor vowed.

Unfortunately, his oath was impotent. As his men reached the body there was a sudden flash of light. The blaze grew in intensity until it was too brilliant to look at, then gradually faded away. In seconds, both the Kiuyian's body and those of three of Azor's men were dust.

Blue blinked as his eyes adjusted, then stared at the empty space. The Kiuyian had been wearing a bomb.

Azor cursed and wiped his own watering eyes. "I

should have expected that," he muttered. Frustration darkened his face, but there was nothing he could do; his men were dead. He stared a moment; then his jaw tightened. "Well, it's finished. There's nothing more we can do."

His remaining men gave him unhappy looks but didn't protest. They all knew the risks of the job.

Suddenly, Blue was very tired. His shoulder ached more than ever. "At least I can tell the women they're safe. They're finally free to return home."

"Yes. They can go back to business as usual." Azor seemed pensive, a rare thing for him, at least in Blue's experience. He glanced over at Blue and realized he was being watched, and all trace of emotion disappeared. "Let's go tell them."

Chapter Eighteen

"Finally," Gem said wearily. She seemed as spent as Blue looked. "We can go home."

"No more hooker hair," Xera agreed with relief. "I can finally get back to the academy."

Brandy didn't say anything. She slanted a look at Azor, then glanced away. She was the first to leave the waiting room.

Zsak was still sleeping. He was alive. The surgeons had reattached his arm and treated him for a mild concussion as well. With time he'd be just fine, but maybe not so quick to take on a Kiuyian solo. The whole incident made Blue wonder what Azor would be like if he ever used his ability on the job.

Azor was very private about his heritage. To Blue's knowledge, he'd never shifted while on duty. After seeing the possibilities, he wondered why. The man's abilities could be a real asset in the right setting. Then again, they all had hang-ups.

Blue hadn't thought twice about freezing the Kiuyian assassin and punching through the door, but now he looked at his battered hand and wondered what Gem thought of his robotic arm. She'd known about it, of course, but it was one thing to know someone had mechanical parts and another to see the proof. He hoped it didn't negatively affect her opinion of him.

It *felt* like a real hand. He flexed, marveling that the sensations were every bit as good as those of true flesh and bone. It had hurt to hammer away at the door, but instead of a bloodied hand his false skin had now curled back to expose a metal skeleton, gears and wire. Even now, the nanotechnology of his hand was repairing the "tissue." In a couple of days he would be good as new.

He'd seen Gem glance at it, but she hadn't said anything and her face gave nothing away. No, he hoped she wasn't repulsed, and he would give her the benefit of the doubt. And he couldn't wait to show her how functional the hand was when they first made love.

He was going to marry her, he'd decided. This was no time to ask, of course. Everything was still unsettled, and she was still in pain from her shoulder wound. He'd like to make sure the pain meds weren't interfering with her reasoning when they talked. And they could use a little more courting time. She'd just begun to thaw when all this had hit.

Also, there was her family and their situation. Brandy had cut a deal with the cops to spill everything she knew about Jean Luc, but she still needed to serve her sentence. He couldn't see Gem planning a wedding while she was still growing accustomed to that situation. And then there was Xera. She'd want to leave for the academy ASAP, which would be a problem if Gem wanted her to be at the marriage ceremony in person. It had taken a court order to get the girl home last time. Once they had complete hold of her, the GE wouldn't give her any leave for at least six months.

Blue's impatience built just thinking about things. He'd have to talk with Xera, see what her priorities were. It would be awkward, sharing his intentions when he hadn't spoken with Gem, but sometimes a man had to bend the rules.

There was no time tonight, sadly. They all needed sleep, and he still had a report to write. The ship was heading back to Gem's home island, and in the morning they would be at The Spark. He hoped he'd think of a way to stay by then, because he didn't want to leave Gem again.

Ever.

"Xera, can I talk to you for a moment?"

It was early in the morning and they'd just filed into The Spark. Xera nodded and followed him curiously into the garden. Blue glanced around, then studied her as they walked the path. "I'm going to ask your sister to marry me."

She halted, clearly surprised by his abrupt announcement. "Now?" she said cautiously, but she didn't look upset.

He crossed his arms and, out of habit, scanned the dirt paths with his eyes. "I haven't asked yet. I wouldn't mention it to you first, but you're gung ho to leave."

She gave him a confused look.

"She might want you here for the wedding."

"Oh." Xera blew out a breath and looked out over the garden. "How long do you think it will take?"

"You tell me. Think she'll say yes?"

Xera narrowed her eyes, thinking. "Eventually, sure. You'll wear her down. She won't want to say yes right away, though, when she's still unsettled. This is a lot to throw at her."

"I know. I'd rather not wait if I can help it, though."

Xera grinned. "Afraid she'll find something better?"

"Something like that," he admitted ruefully.

"Ah, the eager suitor," she mocked, but it was good-natured. "I'll help, but it's going to cost you."

"How much?" he asked. She could rake him over the coals with this and probably knew it, and he would likely pay any sum, but he doubted she'd ask for money. More likely, she'd extract blood.

She considered him. "I've noticed you working out—you're good. Of course, I'd expect that from someone who was special ops. I'd like to learn whatever you have to teach. It's bound to come in handy with the Galactic Explorers. In return, I'll do whatever I can to speed my sister to the chapel."

Ah, the girl was merciful after all! And now he knew she approved of him.

"Deal," he said. "We can even start right now if you like. The far side of the garden makes a good place to work out."

Xera grinned. "A man after my own heart. This is going to be fun!"

But an hour later, Xera wasn't looking so perky. Sweaty and disheveled, she hunched over with her hands on her knees and desperately sucked in a breath.

Blue raised a brow. "You're out of shape."

She said something uncomplimentary. It was hard to make out the exact adjective over her gasping.

Blue *tsk*ed. "An hour or two a day of working out

won't put you in the same shape as men who train for this. On the job it was dawn 'til dark of push, push, push. A month of training ought to see some improvement, though."

She straightened up. "Fine. We can hit it again after lunch."

"If it's any consolation, you've got natural talent." He waved his hand toward the path for her to precede him.

"I'm consoled, all right," she joked. "But just don't tell me how long it took you to learn all you know or I might be tempted to stay."

"You'll be on a ship cruising the galaxy before you know it," he assured her. "It won't hurt to take these extra routines with you."

"Yeah," she agreed.

Gem met them as they walked in the kitchen door. She eyed Xera's stringy, sweaty hair and asked, "What have you been up to?"

Xera swung an arm around her shoulders. "Blue's teaching me his martial arts, sis. You should join us."

Gem grimaced and pushed Xera's arm away. "Yuck. You're covered in sweat."

"It feels great. Nothing like a workout to get the endorphins flowing."

Blue looked sideways at Gem and winked. He knew a few other ways, and all of them were flitting through his head.

Gem's cheeks flushed, as she clearly saw what he was thinking. "Glad you're having fun," she said. Her eyes fell to Blue's bandaged hand. "How is it?" she asked.

"Healing. The nanobots will have it good as new very soon. I'm just covering it to keep from grossing you out."

She smiled. "I'm not grossed out, just worried. And . . . thank you for what you did for us."

Xera discreetly left.

Seeing an opportunity, Blue took a step closer. "My pleasure. I'm just glad I was there and able to help."

"I meant to ask you, what about your heart? Have your injuries been bothering you? What with all that exertion, I'm surprised you didn't have any issues."

Blue shrugged his good shoulder. "The patches must have grafted in there pretty good, because I haven't dropped dead or anything. The medics looked me over and chewed me out, but they didn't order bed rest." They had warned him to take it easy, and his shoulder burned some, but the healing accelerators had done an amazing job of speeding his recovery. It didn't hurt that the medical nanobots he'd had implanted in the navy were still hard at work, too. As the military had finally discovered, it was a lot cheaper to heal a wounded soldier than to train a new one.

"Just in case, maybe you should take it easy," Gem was saying. "There's no reason for you to push yourself now. I was thinking that it would be more comfortable for you to move into the spare room. Like we offered a long time ago. I don't think my manager wants to share his office anyway," she added with a wry smile. "Now that you're back."

"So, you're letting me stay?" he asked casually, but his heart and happiness were riding on the answer.

"I'd say I owe you. You have free room and board until you're fully healed. That is, if you want to stay, I mean."

"I want to," he was hasty to admit. "In fact, I'd like

to talk to you in private, if you have a moment." It was time to strike, while the iron was hot.

"Sure." She let him place a hand on her lower back and guide her out into the garden, to where he and Xera had just been. He'd have to suggest she build a gazebo out here, maybe add some more flowers. It would be nice if couples had a place to be private— couples such as the two of them. In lieu of that, he sat with her on a crude plank bench under the shade of a fruit tree.

He gave her a serious look and took her hand in his. "Gem . . . I want to marry you." The words were blurted out before he could think twice.

She blinked. Her mouth worked but no sound came out.

He held up a hand. "I know it's soon, and there's a lot going on right now. I'm just telling you my intentions up front. I plan to court you, to give you time to get used to the idea. I also want you to know that money has nothing to do with my feelings. That asteroid we were farming? Well, *I* own it. Don't look so surprised! I told you I'd made some good investments in my life. I've prepared a spreadsheet of my assets to go over with you so that—"

She waved her hand, embarrassed. "You don't have to do that!"

He captured her hand again, held it gently. "Yes, I do. I want you to be sure that what I want is you, not your money or your business. You deserve no less." He took a deep breath. "I've seen a lot to admire in you—"

"I nearly got you killed!"

He gave her a stern look. "Don't interrupt. I've seen a lot of good in you, right from the beginning.

You took an interest in me when you thought I was nothing, took a chance and gave me a job. You put up with my behaving like a tramp, though I have to admit not all of it was acting. I do love irritating your cook and eating his food." He grinned wickedly before slowly sobering. "We still have a lot to learn about each other, too, but I'm willing to give us time. I hope you'll consider my request for what it is: an offer of partnership. I want a wife and a lover. I want you."

Gem's eyes were misty. She swallowed hard. "I . . . it's so unsettled now."

He grazed his fingers under her chin in a caress. "But you favor me?"

She smiled and looked away. "You know I do."

"Then it's settled. We're courting," he said softly, and sealed the deal.

It had been so long since their last kiss that Gem had almost forgotten how he made her feel. She moaned into his mouth, obsessed with his taste, his feel. Here was a man to drown in. All her pain faded in his arms, and her fear melted under the force of passion. It wasn't passion only, though. What she felt for him had grown until she ached with it, wanted nothing more than to curl inside him and heal. His kiss promised rest and joy and peace. She'd longed for those things without knowing what she wanted. Now he was here and she needed nothing else.

He broke their kiss and grazed his lips across the plane of her cheek. His breathing was harsh in her ear. "Much more of this and I'm going to go up in flames."

She laughed, feeling dizzy. It felt good to rest in his arms. "Mmmmm."

He held her a moment, then sat up. "We should go inside."

"Should we?" she protested mildly when he stood and gave her a hand up. "I can't remember anything pressing I have to do."

He chuckled and wrapped an arm around her. "We could announce our courtship."

"I think it'll be obvious," she said dryly. It would be hard to miss their besotted looks and the arm he had about her waist. Of course, given the busy minds and puritan values around here, a formal announcement might be best.

Jamir actually scowled at Blue when they told him their news, but his face softened when he looked at his employer. "A thousand blessings on you," he said, and kissed Gem on both cheeks.

Xera entered the kitchen and looked at them all with interest. "What did I miss?" she asked.

"We're officially courting," Blue said.

Xera's brows rose. "Well, fast work! What was that, seconds? Let's hope you aren't as speedy in all your doings!"

Gem blushed. "Xera! That's tavern talk!"

"Yeah, you hear a few things in the taproom," Xera agreed cheekily. "But congratulations to you both. Won't hurt my feelings if you speed things along, either. I want to get to the academy before I die of old age." She stilled Gem's imminent protest with a bone-crushing hug, which hastily lightened at her sister's pained squeak. "Sorry! I forgot about your shoulder."

Gem grunted and rubbed it, but she forgot her annoyance when Blue's hand found her lower back. "It's all right," she said.

Xera clapped her hands. "Great, so let's celebrate!

I say we go out to eat. Love your cooking, Jamir, but I'm in the mood for chocolate."

"Sorry, Xera, but I want your sister to myself for the day," Blue spoke up. "I'd planned to go find Brandy and tell her, then take Gem out for a while. She needs a break from this place."

Xera didn't argue. Brandy proved elusive, however. After an exhaustive hunt, Gem and Blue found her in the back lot, talking to a tall Kiuyian man. The pair glanced up as Blue and Gem approached.

Brandy smiled. Gem was startled by the lightness in her sister's expression as she said, "Gem, you remember our old neighbor M'acht?"

"Match," the man corrected. He looked at Brandy with a rueful smile. "I've been with the miners too long. A man can't introduce himself as 'M'acht' and expect anything but ribbing." Pronounced Mah-ach-EE, his Kiuyian name had an unfortunate similarity to a popular girl's name. Not that he looked in the least girlish. His pale green hair was longish but not feminine, and he was dressed casually in a short-sleeved shirt and canvas pants. The boots on his feet were scarred from heavy use.

Brandy looked surprised. "Bet your father loves that. He was always such a stickler for tradition."

Match's green eyes darkened. "My father has no say in it now."

"Oh."

The word was a cross between wonder and . . . admiration? From Brandy? Gem regarded her neighbor with more interest. "Match. It's been a while," she said. "You shipped out what, two years ago?"

"Three and a half," Brandy supplied. "You remember, it was the night of that big electrical storm."

"Oh, right," Gem agreed, though she remembered no such thing. "So you decided freight hauling didn't agree with you?"

"Something like that. I hear my younger brother's been giving you grief. Setting fire, stealing . . ." The Kiuyian blushed.

"It's been an exciting season," Gem admitted. Unwilling to discuss it, she gestured to Blue. "This is Blue, my . . ." She stumbled, unused to introducing him in the new way.

"Boyfriend," Blue supplied, shaking Match's hand. "Nice to meet you." He met Brandy's surprised gaze and added, "We were coming to tell you we've begun courting."

"Oh." Brandy seemed at a loss for words. "Congratulations, really. You make a lovely couple." There was an awkward pause.

Match looked kindly at Brandy. "You used to make a fabulous spiky melon soda, as I recall. Been brewing up anything interesting lately?"

Brandy stiffened. Her face turned pale. "I-I'll see you later." She turned her wheelchair around and left.

Match gave Gem a surprised look, then raced after Brandy. "What'd I say? Brandy? Bran? Stop that!" He stepped in front of her chair with an annoyed expression right at the doorway. "We're not kids anymore. You'd think we could go five minutes without fight—Are you crying?" He looked more closely.

"No!" Brandy turned her face away and tried to go around him. "Leave me alone!"

"Maybe we should leave them to it," Blue suggested. He put his hand under Gem's elbow and tried to escort her away.

Torn, she shook her head. "Wait."

Match knelt by Brandy's side. "Hey, I'm sorry. Whatever I did, I didn't mean to hurt your feelings."

"Haven't you heard?" Brandy demanded, sniffling.

The Kiuyian shook his head. "I've only been home an hour. I had time to walk in the door and fight with my dad and that was it. Want to tell me about it?"

"*Now* we can go," Gem said, allowing Blue to lead her off. She glanced over her shoulder as they walked away. "I hadn't realized she still liked him."

"Liked?" Blue glanced at her, and there was amusement in his eyes.

"Cared about him. They used to fight all the time, but I always knew she favored him. She got very quiet after he left." Her eyebrows drew together. Match's home life had never been very good. She'd been rather relieved when he left because it reduced the fighting next door. Now she wished she'd paid more attention to how Brandy felt.

"I think it's time we got out of here," Blue said, glancing at her face. "I'm determined to make you smile today."

She smiled just to prove she could.

"Better," he responded. "We'll see if we can up the wattage a little."

He took her to lunch at a colorful Outlander restaurant, and introduced her to a hot stew with the power to set her mouth aflame. Afterward he took her to the tree-lined shores of Lunar Lake and bought her a fruit ice. They walked along the sandy shores, enjoying the sun and each other.

"I can't believe this place was once a barren asteroid. Makes me really appreciate all they've done with it." Gem looked around at the birds fluttering in the trees, the water ducks and distant dolphins at play. "I should ask the gardeners here how they do it. Flowers struggle in my garden, but here they've got entire bushes and trees blooming their hearts out."

Blue grinned. "Maybe you were meant to stick to inn-keeping, not farming."

She grimaced. "Why do you think we hire that out? Seriously, this is a great place. I don't know why I haven't come here more often."

"You work too hard," he said simply. "We'll have to make a habit of this."

She looked at his smile and wondered what else they could make a habit of. Just being with him felt like a reward.

"That looks like fun," he said, shading his eyes as he looked over the lake at a pair of personal watercraft. "Do they rent those around here?"

"I don't know. I've never been," she admitted, but he was already walking toward a pier not far down the beach.

As they got closer, she could see several of the watercraft tied against the dock. She was dubious when Blue talked to the owner about renting one, and said, "I don't know how to drive that thing."

"I'll teach you. It'll be fun," he assured her. He handed her a life vest and boating shoes. "Let's go."

He motioned for her to sit down on the seat and gestured to the controls. "This is your power switch and this is the throttle. The rest you'll figure out as we go along."

"Sounds easy enough . . . if I had two arms!"

Blue laughed. "Don't worry; I'll be your left arm. Power up."

Now that she was actually on one, she was getting into the idea. She grinned as they idled away from the dock, then gave a whoop and slowly increased speed until she was going flat out. It was easy on the calm water.

Blue matched his steering to her actions, and they gradually arced back the way they'd come. This was great! But as Gem tried a few tight circles, ignoring the discomfort in her shoulder, she accidentally gunned the throttle. Her butt hit the water before she even knew she'd been thrown off.

Ack! Flustered, she bobbed up and spit water out of her mouth. For a moment all she could see was wet hair and water, but when she swiped at her eyes, there was Blue's laughing face. He was floating in the lake next to her.

"I wish I had that on video," he said. "You okay?"

He helped her swim back to her machine, which had automatically stopped when she fell off, and steadied her as she crawled back on. He looked at her closely and said, "I think we'd better head in. You look kinda green—and I don't just mean your hair."

Her smile was lopsided. She'd have to remember to strip the dye out when she got back. At least the dye on her lips had faded.

She shook her head. "The shoulder is acting up a little, but I'm enjoying this. I hate to stop." She didn't want to admit the pain was making her slightly queasy. She was glad he'd suggested the whole excursion.

"Don't worry. We'll do it again," he reassured her, and turned them back toward the dock. "If you're nice, I'll even treat you to dinner. Maybe something greasy . . ."

She wrinkled her nose at him. The man was cruel.

As both of them were covered in sand and soaking wet, Blue had to give a transport cabbie a big tip before they could get a ride home. By the time they got back, Gem's hair was drying in stiff spikes.

Xera grinned as they walked in the door. "What happened to you?"

Gem exchanged amused glances with Blue. "He introduced me to water sports."

"Wow! You're making me jealous!" her sister grumped good-naturedly. Then, "Hope it won't throw a damper on things, but ol' sour face is waiting out in the taproom. He wants to speak with you, Blue."

"Who?"

"Azor," Xera clarified. "I hope it won't take you long to change into new clothes, either. He's making the customers nervous."

Chapter Nineteen

Azor glanced up from his ice water as Blue slid onto the chair next to him. "For a man who spent yesterday the way you did, you look happy," the Kiuyian policeman remarked.

"I made an effort to enjoy the day," Blue replied, taking a sip of a beer. "I hope you're not bearing bad news, because I'd planned to enjoy the night, too."

"No bad news." Azor looked at him thoughtfully. "There's a rumor going around that you plan to resign your post."

"It's more than a rumor. I've given enough years to the job. It's time for something different."

Azor seemed skeptical. "You plan to become a farmer?" He glanced around the bar. "Or an innkeeper?"

"Careful." Blue wasn't going to take any guff.

Shrugging, Azor inclined his head. "It'd be a nice family, if they could just stay out of trouble."

Blue laughed. "I like trouble. It keeps me young." He leaned back in his seat and added, "What's eating you, man? You look beat."

Azor leaned back himself. A little of his weariness

showed through. "It's been a long month. If ever I were tempted to resign, myself, it would be now."

Blue shook his head. "That's not you. Not from anything I've ever seen, at any rate. Maybe . . . How long has it been since you took a vacation? Even a man who loves his job can get burnt out."

Azor was silent a moment. "I can't remember."

"Put in for one, then. Find a likely lady and spend some play time with her."

The remark won Blue a slight smile. Then Azor admitted, "As if I know any I haven't arrested at one time or another. And I can't date another cop—those relationships always end badly."

"It's true you're not going to find a girl hanging out in dark alleys or at your desk. You need to socialize more. Even this bar has the occasional possibility."

Azor glanced around. His eyes fell on Brandy, however, who'd wheeled through the door and was speaking to Jaq, the barkeep. The old man seemed to have weathered the recent troubles with his usual calm. A thoughtful light appeared in his eyes.

Blue glanced over but didn't say anything. It was impossible to judge what his companion was thinking. A word of caution seemed in order, though. "She seems to have an interest in her Kiuyian neighbor, Match. Remember the kid who set fire to the place? His big brother is back in town."

Azor glanced at him.

Blue shrugged his good shoulder. "Doesn't hurt to know the lay of the land," he explained.

"She's in the middle of a sticky situation," Azor reminded him. "And I'm a professional."

Reminded of his relationship with his own woman, Blue's lip curled. "Aren't we all?"

Gem's entrance was well timed. Blue snaked an arm around her waist as she neared their table, and he sat her on his lap, careful not to disturb her bad arm. He kissed her hello. "You look hot, baby doll."

"Blue!" She blushed and wriggled off his lap onto the chair beside him. Her sling made it awkward. "Behave."

Blue waggled his eyebrows to make her laugh. "Not too long, though," he promised.

Gem glanced at his companion. "Captain Azor."

"Ma'am."

"And you wonder why you have no dates," Blue chided. "I'm trying to convince him that he needs some downtime."

Gem eyed the dour detective. "You have a point."

Azor returned her comment with a droll stare.

"Anyway, I thought we could go out to eat, maybe take in a show," Blue suggested to his new girl. "They have a display of prototype spacecraft set up at the spaceport, and—"

Gem laughed. "That's your idea of a show?"

"You don't like ships?" he asked.

She shook her head. "They're fine. You just surprised me." She looked thoughtful. "Come to think of it, I've never gone to that sort of exhibit."

"Just one of the many firsts to come," Blue promised lazily, his smile telling her exactly what areas he planned to explore first.

Azor shook his head. "I think I've had enough entertainment for the night. I'll see you around," he said.

"Don't go," Blue teased. "We haven't even begun to be entertaining."

"Lovers," Azor muttered. He stood, then wound his way through bodies toward the door.

"Has he always been that cheerful?" Gem asked.

Blue shrugged. "Since the police academy, at least. He was the first Kiuyian I ever met. I thought they were all like him until I'd seen a few more. Speaking of that, there's your neighbor."

Gem glanced over and saw Match at the bar, talking to Brandy. It didn't take long for the two to head off toward the kitchen hallway, but instead of going right, they both turned left toward the brewery . . . or the family apartments.

"I'm not sure about this," Gem remarked uneasily.

Blue considered. "You don't like him?"

Gem chewed her lip. "It's been a while since I've seen him. I don't know if he's the same. It'd be a rough family to marry into."

"You think it'll go that far?" Blue asked.

"I don't know. Depends, I guess. Brandy's clearly still hooked on him." She rose from her seat. "I think I'll see what they're up to."

Blue rose with her. "Are you sure they want a chaperone? I know *I'm* not fond of them." He sent her a playful, flirtatious glance.

"It's different with us."

"Uh-huh."

Blue placed a hand at the small of her back. She was wearing a black satin wrap shirt with long sleeves, and the thin material felt delicious pressed against her warm skin. He'd have to buy her a satin nightie sometime. Maybe they'd get one tonight. Visions of her modeling garments for him came to mind. It was a provocative and not immediately gratifying experience.

Brandy and Match were just about to slip down into the brewery when Gem caught up to them. "Hey, sis. Whatcha doing?" she asked casually. "Showing off the new additions?"

"Trying to," Brandy said with a trace of irritation. "I thought you were going out."

"Pretty soon," Gem agreed. "You've reminded me that I never gave Blue a proper tour, either."

Match opened the door for all of them.

If Brandy was hesitant to enter, no one blamed her. The last time she'd passed through those doors, she'd been carried out. Finally, she smiled grimly and wheeled herself in.

The overhead lights came on automatically as the foursome entered. Huge copper vats lined the walkway, gleaming as if recently polished. Stone tiles lined the floor underfoot, but shadows hid in the space between kettles.

The place had been cleaned up, but Blue noticed Brandy looked away as they passed the pipes where she'd been tied. His own gut tightened as he remembered how she'd looked. He'd seldom seen anyone so brutally hurt. The last time had likely been in that prisoner of war camp. He shook his head to dislodge the memory. Why had Gem thought this was a good idea?

Brandy took a deep breath as they neared a workbench. "This is the heart of it. I've spent many hours in here tinkering with brews."

"But no soda? Tell me you haven't given up on my favorites," Match teased. "I can't tell you how much I was looking forward to a fruit cream."

Brandy smiled slightly. "I haven't made one of those in years."

"Is it hard? You could teach me to make my own," Match persisted.

Brandy laughed. "Now? Don't you have anything better to do?"

"Can't think of a better way to spend my evening," he replied with a smile.

Brandy shrugged. "Why not?"

Blue sent Gem a questioning look. She must have interpreted it correctly, for she said, "Sounds like you two are going to have fun. Blue and I had better be going or we'll be late."

"'Bye," Match said absently. Brandy just nodded as she went in search of her recipe book.

Blue snorted as soon as they were out of earshot. "Going to be a wild and crazy night for those two," he predicted sarcastically. "I don't know, maybe they can get creative with her in a wheelchair, but I have my doubts."

She glowered at him. "Hey, it's a big sister's job to be protective."

He slung an arm around Gem's waist and bumped their hips. "Aren't I glad you don't have a big sister."

Gem sighed in contentment and leaned back against Blue's chest, which filled him with pleasure of his own. They'd dined at an elegant restaurant, then rented a private pavilion overlooking the lake. Stars twinkled overhead and reflected back in the cool waters. They'd doused the torches and reclined on velvet pillows, the better to see the fireflies. He knew she'd seldom felt so peaceful.

Blue toyed with her hair. "What are your dreams? If you could do anything at all, what would it be?"

She stretched lazily as she thought. "Hm. Right after make love with you, you mean?"

He choked. "I thought we were trying to behave!" It was unusual for her to bring up something like that, which could only mean she was thinking of him in terms of her future husband. His heart warmed just thinking of it.

"And you're doing admirably, but don't think I haven't noticed that thing poking my back."

A man could only take so much provocation. He growled and started to drag her down.

She laughed and held up a hand. "No, no! I'll be good. Let's see, if I could do anything . . ."

He waited, torn between kissing her into silence and hearing her answer. If she stalled much longer he'd settle for silence.

"I think I'd like to spend more time with you. Just like this, just . . . playing."

"That's it? You've never had a yen to skydive or explore the galaxy?"

She snorted. "I have action and adventure every day of my life. Believe me, there's never a dull moment around The Spark. What I'd like is more time to myself, just resting. I'm not complaining, but I never got a chance to just be a kid, you know? After my father died, I tried to fill his shoes. The business needed a leader and my sisters needed someone to watch over them. I couldn't be Mom or Dad, but I could be dependable, a confidant . . . *there*. It's what my father would have wanted, and I was glad to do it. It just came at a cost."

He nuzzled her hair. "You lost your chance to run wild yourself."

"I don't know if I would have been wild, but I did grow up fast. I just want some fun now."

He tickled her ribs. "And you want it with me." Satisfaction filled him, bone deep. He'd never been someone's idea of rest before. He found he liked it, liked the way she defined their relationship. He'd had his share of adventure, too. He wouldn't mind a chance to hang around with her, just being himself.

A shadow dimmed his mood as he considered what she knew about him. Maybe it was time he gave her more details so that she knew exactly who he was. He wouldn't want her to claim he'd omitted facts later on.

He began slowly. "I grew up in a house a lot like Match's." She turned her head slightly, listening. He forced himself to go on. "It wasn't the best way to learn how to be a man, and I was always in trouble. I wasn't that much different from the young punk next door."

"You ever set fire to someone's home?" Gem asked. It sounded like she doubted it.

He snorted. "No, but I swiped stuff from stores, got in fights, that sort of thing. It was probably a good thing I ended up in the military—I think they saved me."

"So you *were* in prison?"

"Juvie. I got sent to a military academy once I hit sixteen. There wasn't a regular school in the province that would take me by then. I'd been kicked out of most of them."

"No prison. Juvie," she said to herself, as if memorizing the new truth. "And you went from that academy to special ops?"

"And from there to war and prison camp. After that, I joined the police."

"And finally ended up at The Spark," she finished. She was quiet for a little while. "In all that time, was there ever someone else? A romance?"

He shifted uncomfortably. Telling her the truth and telling her the whole truth were two different things; she really didn't need to know about his playboy past.

"There were a few ladies, but never anyone who lasted, you know? Work got in the way. To be honest, I don't think I was ready to get serious about anyone until I met you. There are a lot of shallow women out there. You were different."

That he'd been drawn to shallow women didn't say much about him, either. She'd changed him. Gem might be unhappy at being forced to mature quickly, but it was one of the things that had drawn him to her. She was exactly what she appeared to be: steady, practical, loving. She was strong enough to carry her sisters and the inn, and tender enough to share the load with someone like him. Her responsibilities hadn't made her cold or totally self-reliant. It made a man proud to be associated with a lady like her. Being a part of her team made him feel like something special.

Gem sighed, paused, and clearly wanted to make a confession. She finally said, "There are rough times ahead. Business has fallen off because of the trial and the recent difficulties. Jean Luc's beer is no longer here to sell, though maybe we can make something roughly similar—but legal. I'm sure Brandy's brews will be good."

She shook her head, thinking. "It's going to be hard to overcome the bad press, even though I know we'll be okay in the end. Brandy is going to have it rough for a couple of years, no matter how talented she is. Xera kept talking about leaving for the academy, and now she has to. Her reputation's ruined, as we both know." She paused. "Things like that, Blue . . . Well, I just want you to be sure of what you're getting into."

Blue pulled her close, then down to the ground and leaned over her so that she could see his face clearly. "Woman, this is the only time you're allowed to bring this up. The answer is yes, yes and yes. Enough said." He kissed her firmly to show that he meant business, then kissed her just because he liked doing so.

She melted like honey on his tongue, burned a trail straight down to his groin. He shifted his thigh over hers and deepened the kiss. The woman could spark a fire in him that obliterated all thought of caution. His lips wandered a path down her face, lower to her ear. She snuggled into his caress—

The overhead lights came on suddenly, ruining the moment. They blinked, momentarily blinded.

Gem groaned. "The automated chaperone kicked in."

Blue exhaled in disbelief. "Automated cha— What kind of a barbaric planet *is* this?"

She heaved a sigh and sat up. "I guess we should head home."

Blue rose and helped her to her feet, grumbling. His pants were achingly tight. No amount of adjusting helped to make them comfortable. "You're giving me blue balls, woman," he complained, but it was good-naturedly.

She gaped at him, then laughed in embarrassment.

He gave her a rueful smile. "I never said I was a gentleman," he muttered. Then he wrapped his arm around her and led her from the pavilion. Automated chaperones? He said a few choice curses in his head. What were the odds they could at least find a quiet corner at home?

Not good, as it turned out. They were walking up the drive when Blue's communicator buzzed. Of course, it was a call he was glad to take. "Zsak! How are you, buddy? I was going to come see you in a little bit. You were sleeping hard when we came by this afternoon."

Zsak's face on the view screen was tired and pale, but he smiled. "I knew you were there, but these meds have me in and out. Thanks for the flowers . . . I think. Is that the sort of thing you're supposed to bring a guy?"

Blue flashed the screen at Gem. "It was her idea. Use them to bribe the nurses to get something good to eat."

"Haven't seen anything here that wouldn't eat me first," Zsak slurred ruefully. "I could use something decent, though. They won't let me order out."

"It's on the way. You want me to raid the kitchen here, or was there something special you wanted from somewhere else?"

Zsak laughed. "If it irritates that little cook of hers, I'm in. Whatever he least wants to give up. You know I like The Spark's food."

"We'll be up with it shortly," Gem promised. "See you soon." She glanced at Blue and gestured that she was going to head to the kitchens.

Blue nodded, waited until she was out of earshot and told Zsak, "You can congratulate me on my new girlfriend, by the way."

His partner grinned. "About time! Good work, buddy."

"Thanks. I'm a lucky man."

Zsak hesitated. "How are her sisters doing? Has the press backed off? How's everything?"

Blue's smile faded. "Everything's mostly okay. Her sisters came out of it a little banged up, but they're fine. I was more worried about y—"

"I bet they are okay," Zsak interrupted. "They're a tough bunch. They'll get through anything." He winced as he shifted, trying to get comfortable. "Blasted shoulder feels as if somebody ripped it off."

Blue grimaced at the black joke. "The doctors said it should be as good as new after it heals."

Zsak grunted. "I hate physical therapy."

"We'll find you a pretty coach. Either way, I'll be there for you."

"Thanks, but you don't need to do that."

"I owe you," Blue said. "And I'm sure the ladies feel the same. You're a hero. Live with it."

"I will if you will. Now, listen, I'm going to nap until you get here. See you soon." Zsak hung up.

Blue looked at his communicator for a moment and then smiled. Zsak was going to be all right.

Chapter Twenty

They met Azor leaving Zsak's floor in the hospital as they were coming up in the elevator. He looked uncomfortable as he spotted them, then resigned.

"Business or social call?" Blue asked, alert for trouble.

"Paying my respects," Azor replied coolly. "I see you're doing the same. I won't keep you." He nodded and walked away.

Gem studied the detective's retreating figure. "He keeps this up and I'm going to think he has a heart."

"Not quite, but he does have a softer side." Blue winked and took her good hand, and they proceeded to Zsak's room.

Zsak was awake and appeared thoughtful. He smiled when he saw them. "Hey! Nice to see you." He grinned as Gem set a basket on the table next to him. "Is that for me? You shouldn't have."

She laughed at his fake surprise. "We brought pocket pies and a new batch of Jamir's fresh-squeezed berry punch. I figured beer is probably a no-no right now."

"Don't tease me—I could use a cool one right now.

Those pies look great, though. You wouldn't believe the pap they serve here."

"Yeah, none of us was too thrilled, either. I bet I could make a fortune on bootleg dinner deliveries." Gem laughed.

"Count me in." Zsak moaned around a bit of steaming pie and added, "Oh, this is better than sex."

"You're out of your head!" Blue told him in mock alarm. "But it's probably just the drugs talking. You'll come to your senses when they wear off."

Zsak laughed, then winced. But if he was in pain, he didn't let it interfere with his appetite. He polished off one pie and reached for another.

"We saw Azor as we were coming in," Gem remarked.

Zsak smiled. "He's not such a bad guy."

Blue shrugged. "Too bad Brandy's in love with her neighbor. I'd try to set them up."

Gem looked at him with mild alarm. "Don't be starting trouble, boy."

He exchanged grins with Zsak but promised, "All right. I'll behave."

"That would be nice. The last thing I need is the uproar pairing the two of them would cause. Can you imagine? Besides, they'd never last."

She looked so disturbed by the idea that Blue decided to distract her. He put a casual hand on her hip. "The real question is, how long will it take you to say yes to marrying me?"

She stared at him. "Is that a formal question?"

"You knew my intent," he reminded her. Then, aware that Zsak was absently polishing off food as he watched, as if this were a dinner drama enacted for him alone, Blue leaned forward and rubbed noses with her. "Think it over. Get back to me."

She smiled, clearly amused. "You make it sound like a business proposal."

"I'd like to make you a different type of proposal," he replied.

Her smile grew larger, but she saw through him. "You're trying to distract me."

"Is it working?"

She gave him a gentle kiss. "I'll let you know."

There was more than one way to interpret that, and Blue's heart felt lighter just thinking about it. He turned to Zsak and asked, "So, anything good on TV?"

It was really late when they got back home. Both Gem and Blue were tired, so it wasn't as difficult for her to kiss Blue good night as it might have been. The process only took fifteen minutes or so.

Blue rested his forehead against hers as they snuggled against the entryway wall. The door was open, and no one could see into her apartment from this angle. Blue didn't say anything, but she could guess his thoughts. He wouldn't say no if he were invited in.

She didn't want to say no anymore. She wanted the right to keep him here. "Blue?" she said.

"Hm?"

"I'll marry you."

For a sleepy man, he suddenly looked alert. "You will? When?"

She laughed. "I guess it had better be soon. If I had a daughter hanging out with a man like you, I'd lock her up."

He grinned. "Make it tomorrow, then. Or . . . do you want a big wedding?" He looked suddenly grim, as if contemplating something agonizing. Few men cared for big to-dos, she knew. At least, few on Polaris.

She smiled and toyed with his shirt. "Let me sleep on it. I can't make a decision like this when I'm tired."

He looked at her fondly. "Sometimes I love your practical side, and sometimes . . ." He shook his head and gave her a final kiss. "You know I won't sleep tonight."

"I hope I will," she said, laughing at the hot once-over he gave her with his eyes.

He edged out the door with extreme reluctance, then caught it when she would have shut it. He peeked around the edge. "You won't change your mind?" he asked.

"No, Blue," she told him, touched. "I love you."

He froze, then pushed the door back open. His gaze was piercing. "You do?"

She couldn't help the joy that welled within her. She beamed at him. "Would I marry you if I didn't?"

Her gasp was muffled as he pulled her into his arms and slew her with a kiss. He inhaled her as if she were oxygen and he couldn't breathe. He was drowning and she was a lifeline, but she was going down, too. If he asked to stay she wouldn't say no.

Brandy wandered out of her room with a yawn. She paused in wheeling her chair to say, "Ew! I see I'm interrupting something."

Blue came up for air. His hair was ruffled from Gem's fingers and his eyes were dilated, but he told her, "Gem's agreed to marry me."

Brandy rubbed her eyes, surprised. "Already?"

Summoned by the conversations, Xera came to her bedroom doorway, blinking in the light. Her hair stood up at crazy angles. "What's up? You two are getting married? Already?"

"I see they're not surprised by the if, just the when." Gem giggled. "I should make them wear yellow just for that."

Brandy and Xera looked at each other. "Elope," they said in tandem.

"I'll have the justice of the peace here first thing in the morning," Xera said dourly. "I will not wear yellow—or pink, for that matter. The more I think about it, the more in favor I am of not giving you time to plan a party. You'll just work yourself down and run us around, and . . . no. Just *no.*"

"Agreed," Brandy said, folding her arms. She looked at Xera. "How about we just tell Jamir what's up and have him plan a nice lunch just for family? I guess Blue could invite a few friends, too," she added, casting a doubtful look his way.

"Seeing as how he's the groom," Xera agreed dryly. "Let's get to work." They headed to the couch and got out a tablet to keep track of their plans.

"Looks like they don't even need us," Blue said with a grin. "I guess your sisters are good for something after all."

"I heard that!" Xera called, but she didn't look up.

He sobered and looked at his beloved, soon to be his wife. "You don't mind, do you? Would you like something else? Would you like to handle the plans?"

She gave him a wry smile. "They may have a point.

If I got involved I'd probably spool out of control, turn the thing into an *event*. It's better to keep the focus on us."

"I'd like Zsak and Azor there," Blue admitted. "Maybe a few other people."

"Anything you want. Can you arrange a teleconference for Zsak? I doubt the doctors will let him out for this."

"I'll make something happen," Blue promised. He kissed Gem softly. "I'd better go."

Gem watched him leave, but it was easier this time. After all, soon he'd have the right to stay. She couldn't wait for the chance to call him her husband, for him to truly be her lover.

She grinned, remembering how she'd once thought he was just a shiftless drifter. If someone had told her then that Blue would become her best friend, she would have thought they were drunk. Now, she was impatient to bind him to her in the most intimate, most enduring way of all.

She glanced at her sisters as she heard Brandy mutter, "Honeymoon suite? I am *not* sleeping next to newlyweds."

"Already made the reservations," Xera replied. There were advantages to owning your own inn.

"Flowers, cake, wine?"

"You, Jamir, Jamir. I'll take the invites," Xera said, efficiently entering data into a spreadsheet. She turned to Gem. "Might as well get some sleep. We'll be up a while."

Grinning at their dismissal, Gem waved good night. She thought they were enjoying themselves. Maybe it was good for them to be in charge for once.

She'd have to think about that, but tomorrow. For now, sleep sounded like heaven.

"Wake up!" someone ordered. The bed vibrated.

Gem's eyes snapped open. Xera was bouncing on the edge of the mattress, grinning like a fool.

Gem groaned and rolled back over. "What time is it?"

"Time to get married," Xera announced, gleefully stripping off the covers. "Blue's been here twice already. He's convinced you'll change your mind if he doesn't get a ring on you, quick."

Gem muffled her laugh in her pillow and tried to curl up. "Five more minutes."

Cold water hit her in the face, making her gasp. She leapt out of bed and tried to catch her sister, but Xera ran out of the room and leapt behind the couch. She grinned. "You'll never take me alive!"

Gem chuckled and dodged right and left. "I'll enjoy trying."

A whistle split the air. Gem whirled, suddenly conscious of her short nightshirt. Blue stood there, a grin on his face. His eyes took in her legs and one particular point of interest in between.

"Don't stop on my account," he told her. "I'll even help." He took the right flank, boxing Xera behind the couch.

Gem grinned and stalked left. Pinned, Xera had no choice but to leap forward and dash for the door. She might have made it in time, but Blue sent a pillow sailing after her. It crashed into her legs, sending her sprawling. She rolled over and gave him a mock glare.

"Gotta watch your back," he remarked, amused.

She snorted and hauled herself upright. Heading for the door, she muttered, "You've got five minutes to say good morning. Don't get carried away."

"Five minutes? She has no imagination, or she'd never leave that long," Blue scoffed. He took Gem in his arms. "Good morning." He kissed her possessively, ran his hands over her back. They sank lower on her body, squeezed her rump, surprising a gasp out of her. One hand rose and cupped her face, then slid down between her breasts, over her belly. She felt him grin against her mouth as he hooked her leg higher, settled it around his hip. She formed a question against his lips, then abruptly gasped. His fingers slid under her panties and deep, deeply home.

He sighed against her mouth as his fingers worked. "Five minutes, love."

She gasped in shock and pleasure. If he meant to reassure her that he could only do so much, he needn't have bothered. She'd forgotten all about her sister.

Tension rose, sweet and hot. Those fingers! His mouth against hers, breathing in her cries. A climax hit so hard and fast she thought she'd fall. Her vision went black. A star shower burst behind her eyes, sparked as far as her fingers and toes. Oh, the man could kiss! Among other things.

He came up for air. One look at her face and he smiled like a hungry predator. "Lady, you should be bottled. One taste of you and a man is drunk."

She shuddered with aftershocks from the pleasure he'd brought her. It was cruel of him to draw his hand away so slowly, the touch causing even more sparks. She moaned and nuzzled closer in protest.

"Time's up!" Xera said, coming in through the

door. "Behave yourself and go get dressed, sis. You'll have him to yourself soon enough."

Blue grumbled good-naturedly as he escorted Gem to the door of her room. It disguised the fact that she would have stumbled without his support. He kissed her quickly and handed her into the room, then shut the door behind her.

There were a lot of cops at the ceremony, including Chief Blackwing, who greeted her warmly. She wasn't too surprised to see that Zsak was Blue's chosen best man for the hurried ceremony, wounds or not, or that he was dressed in his best. She was surprised to see his image broadcast from a portable computer held by none other than Jamir. The Latq cook grinned broadly, showing off sharp white teeth. All four feet of him stood straight at attention, proud to be a part of the ceremony. His milky skin was pink with pleasure.

"Zsak is his new hero," Xera whispered in an aside. "He can't in good conscience like Blue, so Blue's partner is reaping all the benefits for them keeping us safe."

Gem exhaled in amusement. She really did have a great cook.

The surprises continued. Azor was to marry them, using the authority granted to him by his rank in the police department. He looked dour but handsome in his dress uniform, and an electronic tablet was held loosely in one hand.

"If he weren't a cop, he'd be almost date-worthy," Xera said in approval. "He's got a really nice butt."

Gem gave her a scandalized look.

"What? For that matter, your man's got what counts,

too." Xera grinned wickedly. She was enjoying her task of standing up with her sister, though her outfit of a navy silk wrap shirt and black pants were definitely not typical bridesmaid attire.

Brandy didn't seem to mind her role as observer, especially not with Match at her side. They made a cute couple, Gem thought, though she had to wonder if it would last. While his attention was flattering for Brandy, her sister had to know he wasn't the kind to stick around. He might be a gentleman with her, but Gem had asked others. He had a reputation as a lady's man and a taste for dangerous sports. She'd ask him later if the rumor was true about him shipping out as a pilot for the big freighters. If so, he could be gone for months at a time. Gem rather thought Brandy needed someone who'd stick closer to home.

All that was a matter for another day, however. Blue smiled at her, and Gem forgot all her plans. Her family could wait. Today was for her man.

The taproom was bursting with flowers, some from their own garden, and the lights had been set on twinkle. Jaq escorted Gem up the makeshift isle as her employees, family and friends looked on. He smiled proudly and winked as he handed her off to Blue, then returned to his seat.

They stood before Azor and looked at him expectantly. With due gravity, he glanced at his tablet. "Dear ones, we see before us now a loving couple . . ."

Gem looked at Blue and lost track of the words. In her heart she already belonged to him.

At the culmination of the ceremony, Blue was instructed to kiss his wife. He obliged with a hungry embrace that brought wolf whistles from everyone watching. Gem was cross-eyed when it was done, but she was grinning. Her husband was making her look forward to what came after the vows.

Jamir shooed the guests into the banquet room where he'd set up an impressive buffet. He hauled the computer with Zsak's image carelessly under his arm and set him at a place on the table. He'd already sent a huge delivery of food to Zsak's hospital room so the man could share in the feast. To hear Zsak tell it, that was the most important part of the celebration, anyway.

Gem shared in the toasts, but she stuck with a single glass of wine and ate lightly. There'd be plenty of time later to sneak down and raid the leftovers, or better yet, order room service. She laughed, thinking that was a service she'd never used, despite owning this inn forever.

Blue glanced her way, a smile in his eyes. "What's the joke?"

"Just thinking of the changes married life has brought. I've never ordered room service."

His eyes sparked. "I like where your mind's going. Today definitely seems like a good time to start."

She looked at him with mock innocence. "But the kitchen is so close."

He leaned in closer to whisper, "Trust me, baby, you're going to be far too exhausted to walk three steps."

She flushed, but couldn't help mocking him. "You have a high opinion of yourself."

"You can judge for yourself later. I think I'll be inspired to reach new heights."

Zsak snorted, and even Azor gave an abbreviated laugh. There were general snickers around the table.

Gem eyed her husband uncertainly. She was fairly sure she understood what he was talking about. Unfortunately, she was also rather new at this type of repartee and couldn't think of a timely retort. She settled for a quelling stare.

He guessed her issue and said lazily, "Don't worry, sweetheart, you'll get better with practice. Luckily, I'm a firm believer in practice." That began a fresh wave of giggles from the peanut gallery.

Gem had had enough of being teased. She knew her friends and family well enough to know they could go on for hours and never tire. There was only one way to spike their guns. She placed her napkin on the table and stood up. "Maybe it's time to put your money where your mouth is."

Sudden silence fell across the table. How satisfying. She'd shocked them speechless.

Blue's eyes flared. He rose with controlled grace from his chair and looked down at her. "What a fine idea," he purred.

She had an instant of trepidation. Maybe it wasn't a good idea to get him too excited. It was too late to back down, though. He extended his hand and she placed hers on top. He glanced at their guests and said in farewell, "Enjoy yourselves."

"Not as much as you will," someone murmured as they left. Gem thought it sounded rather like Zsak.

Chapter Twenty-one

The honeymoon suite, as Gem knew but had never experienced, boasted a huge bed and a roomy tiled tub with space for two. The coverlet on the bed was white eyelet, and underneath were sheets of red satin. Fresh flowers in shades of cherry and pink perfumed the air. A crystal chandelier sparkled on the ceiling, and crystal sconces held lights on the walls. Plants dotted the room for atmosphere and there was a small fridge full of refreshments. A table for two sat near a large window with sheer drapes for allowing light, and heavy silk for privacy. A bowl full of fresh berries sat on an ironed tablecloth, ready to be savored.

"I'm impressed," Blue remarked, looking around. "I want to steal your decorator."

"You already have." Gem smiled and slipped her shoes off. It was a warm day and she enjoyed the feel of the cool tile under her bare feet. Her ivory and burgundy dress felt silky against her calves, heightening the sensuality of the moment. It was the first time they'd been alone with guaranteed privacy and the blessing of all concerned. It felt odd.

"Someone left a present on the bed," Blue commented. "Wonder what it could be?"

Gem took the hint and went over to examine the package. It was wrapped in gold foil, and she raised an eyebrow at the card on top. "It's a joint gift from Zsak, Jaq, the staff and my sisters." She hesitated, eyeing the two-foot by three-foot package. "This could be interesting."

Blue sat on the bed, clearly amused. "Let's find out."

"You know what this is," she accused.

"I might have heard a rumor. Go on," he urged. "I'm dying of curiosity."

She opened the box and peered inside. She couldn't help a laugh as she held up a pair of fuzzy purple handcuffs. "The tag says they're to keep you in line."

Blue smirked. "Inevitable cop humor. Must be from Zsak. He was never very original."

She raised a brow, both at his comment and at the next item. "Chocolate body paint and honey?"

He grinned. "How sweet."

She rolled her eyes. "Someone has too much time on their hands." She stared quizzically at the next item, a stack of embroidered handkerchiefs. "At least someone put in something practical."

Blue smothered a grin and placed the kerchiefs on the nightstand. He doubted she had a clue yet, but she would later. He could almost picture her blush.

Suddenly, he was tired of looking at naughty gifts. He had his wife, a bed and a quiet room. Though he'd admired her dress the moment he saw it, suddenly he was dying to slip it off.

She glanced up and stilled. A tint of color kissed her cheeks. There was shyness there, but no fear. She was ready, too.

He placed the box on the floor. At her questioning look, he murmured, "I don't really think we need these, do we? I'm not in the mood for toys."

Her lashes dipped as she glanced down self-consciously, but she came into his arms easily enough. In spite of his earlier teasing, his kiss was gentle, reassuring. He showed her a tenderness he'd rarely shown another woman. Making love had never mattered so much, and he wanted to do this right.

She seemed to approve of his technique. With every soft caress, she snuggled closer, wordlessly demanding a little more. He kept his touch light, relaxed yet passionate.

Soon she was the aggressor, pushing him over on the bed to kiss him deeply. It was awkward with her arm in a sling, but she was determined. As long as they were careful, the pain meds would prevent her injury from interfering with their pleasure.

She didn't seem to notice his busy hands sliding the silk ever higher up her legs. He lightly stroked the insides of her thighs. She stilled, then dropped her head to his shoulder with a little moan. Utterly limp, it was obvious she'd become too dazed with passion to do anything other than enjoy.

He smiled against her mouth as he rolled her onto her back. She blinked, momentarily startled, then relaxed under his kiss. Her eyes were glazed, slumberous with pleasure as his mouth toyed with her ears and then drifted down her neck. She was a little shy about her breasts and tried to cover what he bared, but her concerns melted away as he sucked the screening fingers into his mouth one by one, laving her exposed breasts as he went. When she was utterly boneless, he guided her hand to his shoulder and had his way, teaching her the many pleasures of a man's mouth on her nipples, the fiery chill of a silken tongue.

She conceded his expertise with a soft moan, turning her head restlessly. It must have been a further torment with her bound arm, which, though it remained unable to pain her, forced her to remain as still as possible. A soft nip of his teeth caused her to arch upward, thrusting her chest toward Blue's mouth. He rewarded her with a quick kiss to one nipple, then buried his face between her breasts and licked his way down her belly. She liked that well enough, twisting beneath his gentle onslaught. She stiffened, though, as he approached his goal. Her hand tried to cover that, too.

He paused, then settled between her thighs. His hands idly stroked her hips as he gazed up at her. She looked tensely back.

"Put a couple of pillows behind your head," he instructed.

"Why?" she asked.

He just gazed at her until she complied, allowing him to help her. "Good, now I'll walk you through this."

Her eyes widened at his words and she tried to squirm away. He easily held her still until her thrashing stopped, then met her eyes. "We're going through this together. I want you to see what I do, to know I'm only going to give you pleasure."

"It . . . it seems so . . . wrong," she whispered.

He smiled against her soft inner thigh, knowing she could feel his mouth curve. "It brings me pleasure. It will bring you great pleasure." He met her eyes and said softly, "I like the taste, honey."

She shivered at his endearment. Her head fell back, and her eyes closed.

He smiled and reached up to tweak her nipple. Her eyes popped back open. "Watch, darlin'," he commanded. "I want you to acknowledge what I'm doing. I want you to give up your fear."

He gently parted her, then leaned forward and gave her most sensitive petal a little lap. She flinched, but not in pain. Her breath caught.

He kissed her, then spread her farther with his fingers and placed a soft, deliberate kiss there, too. She exhaled with a shaky little hiss. He inserted his tongue slowly inside and took a deliberate taste of pure woman. She collapsed on the bed, her eyes closed with the intensity of this new pleasure, but he didn't mind that she wasn't watching now that he'd gotten what he wanted. Her legs had fallen open to him; her fear had faded. This was what he had intended.

Yes, this first time he wanted her boneless under him. He didn't want her thrashing and tense, not even in passion. Not yet. For now, he wanted her soft and open, drenchingly wet to ease his way. He didn't want to hurt her.

Patiently, he coaxed her with his mouth, soothing when she got too intense, encouraging her soft pants and helpless little hip thrusts. When she'd tossed the pillows aside and was thrusting insistently against his mouth, he moved up and slipped inside her. She was breached before she realized his intent.

Gem gasped as she felt him slide inside. Her eyes wide, she stiffened at the feel of the huge thing inside her. Her legs wouldn't close; Blue was wedged too deep. It hurt— but not as much as she'd feared or heard. There was something else there with the burning: a deep need to move.

She and Blue got rid of the pillows.

He rocked her with his body and she sucked in air. His tongue teasing along her neck made her quiver. By the time his mouth dropped to her breasts, she was squirming under him, wordlessly begging him to move.

He took her nipple in his mouth and gave a tiny thrust. She tightened her legs on him and held on tight. He growled his pleasure and began a slow, easy rhythm that made her hotter than exploding rocket fuel. Her nails scored his back, though she tried not to hurt him. The pleasure built and built . . .

A scream tore from her throat as climax hit hard and fast. She was unprepared for the intensity, or for his matching shout. It hurt when he lost control and pounded into her, but she was unable and unwilling to stop. Having him there, in her, with her . . . There was nothing finer in the world.

Finally he came to a shuddering stop. He supported his weight but wouldn't move off her. "Do you mind, baby? I don't want to give this up."

Mind? Was he crazy? "Stay," she said, and it took an effort.

He smiled against her neck. "Not too bad, was I?"

She grunted.

His smile grew, and that wasn't all. He hummed in satisfaction as he moved in her.

Her eyes opened in surprise. "Now?"

"Apparently." He nibbled on her breasts and took the nipples in his mouth the way she liked. Any protests she might have had raised died unspoken, though she did wince.

He paused.

"No." She shivered under him and took a firm grip of his butt. He didn't seem capable of argument.

Some hours later, Gem opened her eyes and hummed sleepily. Who'd known naked skin felt so good against satin? Better yet was the warmth of the man against her back. He'd shown her the pleasure of many new sensations that afternoon. Thanks to him, she'd discovered the feel of leashed power as a man moved over her, the patience a man could share. Seeing that side of him had been a gift in itself. Who'd believe her if she told him how tender Blue could be? Lovemaking could be such a revelation.

Her husband's arm draped over her stomach, pulled her back into a gentle hug. "Good morning . . . or whatever time it is. Sleep well?"

She made a sound of agreement and rolled onto her back, only to wince. It wasn't just the tenderness inside her sex; some of the muscles they'd worked had never been used before.

He smiled and gently combed his fingers through her hair. "Sorry about that. A hot bath will help. Why don't I get it started?"

He rolled out of bed and sauntered toward the bath, unconcerned with his nakedness. She discreetly peeked even as she drew the covers over her own chest. Nakedness was still foreign to her.

Hunger was an old friend, though, and she finally slipped out of bed, using his discarded shirt as a covering. She was standing at the table, one hand holding his shirt closed and the other popping berries into her mouth. He leaned a hand against the low dresser and grinned. "Now that's a view."

She flushed and glanced away from all that bare skin. "I was hungry."

He sauntered closer and wrapped her in a hug. "Let's take these with us, then. You can feed me while I show you how much fun soap can be. Afterward, we can order room service." He picked up the bowl and coaxed her into the bathroom and out of his shirt.

Room service didn't come until much, much later.

They enjoyed a leisurely meal while watching the sun set through the open window. He'd thrown on some pants, but wouldn't let her wear anything other than his shirt. A warm breeze teased the curtains, bringing the scent of flowers. It was a perfect evening.

"I think I'm going to have to plant lots of flowers on the farm," Blue said thoughtfully. "And we'll definitely need a room with big windows."

She glanced at him with mild surprise. "You want to live there?"

"At least part of the time. You might like to get away from your sisters, and I might like to steal you away from the business sometimes."

"Hm. I hadn't thought about it." Didn't want to, if the truth were known. There was enough going on for the moment.

"Think about it later," he advised. "We can go over plans together when we want. I'd like time to daydream with you first."

She smiled. "That's different. I'm used to having time limits imposed on me. Everyone wants things decided yesterday."

He grinned and hooked his foot around her ankle playfully. "You want a time limit? Take a couple of years, for all I care. It's not as if we'll be homeless in the meantime."

She closed her eyes in blissful pleasure. His foot was stroking her calf. "I'm tempted to move in here permanently."

"Might be a good idea. Your sisters won't appreciate our keeping them up at night. You're a noisy novice," he said with a wink.

"Novice? Are you looking for a black eye?" she demanded. "It didn't seem that complicated to me."

He smirked, just to tease her. "You can't claim experience until you've done it with handcuffs—twice."

"Twice?" she choked. Sarcasm was difficult to pull off when wearing a blush.

For an answer, he leaned forward, a definite glint in his eye. "First, I would close the curtains . . . or maybe not. This is my daydream, after all. After that, I'd take you to the bed . . ."

His words conjured up a fantasy, and it was as erotic as performing the act. Gem squirmed as her mind took her into his dream. His tale had them headed for the bed.

The first time involved a strip search. When he was satisfied she wasn't hiding anything, he cuffed her hands behind her back and bent her over the bed.

The second time had her on her back with her hands cuffed to the headboard. He really took his time then.

The third time—yes, there was a third time; he was *very* inventive—had her on top with her hands cuffed behind her. Since he'd toyed with her for a good half hour beforehand, there was a long pause before she was allowed full penetration, and she was desperate for it. She made little whimpering sounds and tried not to thrash as he slowly lowered her onto him. Wet and slick, she was able to ignore any tightness of her body. He'd made her so crazy by then, she would have bit him if he'd suggested they stop.

Blue cupped her hips in his hands and guided her onto him. With her hands behind her back, her breasts thrust forward, she was helpless to prevent his teasing tweaks. With a wild cry she threw herself down and kissed him desperately until he grabbed her hips and finished them with a few wild thrusts.

Gem drew a trembling breath at the culmination of his story, frustrated that they hadn't yet acted out any of his words. She was aching in the place he'd so thoroughly described. When his fingers came exploring in truth, there was plenty of dampness there. Blue smiled and closed the curtains, then had her climb onto his lap.

She was ready to concede she wouldn't be able to walk to the kitchens for a long while yet to come.

Even newlyweds couldn't make love forever, so they ventured outside the next day. Not that Gem did any work. Even if the inn had been beset by several serious financial concerns, she would have been useless to help. Her new husband occupied her every thought, her every moment. Her marriage so far felt like being trapped in one eternal, wondrous daydream. Every time their eyes met, sparks would fly.

Life was very, very good.

Chapter Twenty-two

Sometime on the third day, Gem got restless. Unused to so much inactivity—or at least activity of an entirely pleasant sort—she started to involve herself again in business. She chose little things, of course, activities she could drop on a whim—or at the crook of Blue's finger. One had to have priorities, after all.

Xera had waited a bit to announce her pending departure. "The ship leaves next week," she informed her sisters over breakfast. "It seems like I've waited forever."

Gem felt a bit of sadness, but it was tempered by Blue's presence. With him there, change didn't feel so bad. "I'm happy for you. Is there anything special you'd like to do over the next few days? It might be a while until you get back home."

Xera didn't answer right away. They all knew it would be difficult to do anything in public. Though the media were less persistent than before, scandal-mongering reporters still dogged their steps. Not only did she have to deal with those Polaris inhabitants who shunned her, but also some merchants felt free to ban her from their premises. Serving women with reputations was bad business, they claimed.

After a moment of thought, Xera suggested, "Why don't we find Brandy and ask her for suggestions? We could have a family night, maybe even a party with just us and a few staff." Staff were a safe bet, for any who'd had problems with the scandal had already quit.

"We could invite Match, Zsak and Azor," Gem suggested.

"You think Azor would come?" Xera seemed skeptical.

Gem shrugged and glanced sheepishly at Blue. "He's growing on me. Maybe I pity him. Believe it or not, he seems kind of lonely."

Blue choked on his drink. When he could speak, he warned her, "Don't ever tell him that! I don't think his ego could take it."

Xera slid back her chair. "We'll worry about him later. Are you coming to find Brandy, Blue?"

He shook his head. "I want to check on the experimental plants I started in the garden. I'm trying the new 'black gold' technique. You know, the one where they use granulated charcoal to boost plant growth? It's supposed to be far superior to compost or organic fertilizer. It could be a huge help on the farm. It wouldn't hurt to boost your yields here, either."

Xera's eyes were already glazing over. "Great," she interrupted. "Good luck with that. Gem?"

Gem grinned and kissed Blue's scratchy cheek. He hadn't shaved that day. "You know *I* like to hear about it, hon. Why don't you find us when you're done? You can fill me in."

He whispered something in her ear that caused her to blush. She pushed at his shoulder playfully and joined her sister.

"Who knew you'd end up marrying a farmer?" Xera teased. "I swear I'll barf if I have to hear anything more about crop yields and soil fertility."

Gem smirked. "Just as well—he's *my* farm boy, and boy, can he sling hay."

Xera made an amused yet exasperated face. "Roll in the hay, more like. We've barely seen you two in days."

Gem lifted a shoulder, a satisfied expression on her face. "Marriage agrees with me."

"Huh." Xera admitted, "You do seem happy."

Gem's face glowed. "I'm so glad I married him, sis! I'm sure we'll have our share of arguments, but we're both willing to do what it takes to keep this marriage strong. He's a good man."

"Good to know. Now, where's our sister?"

Gem and Xera looked in their apartment first; then they headed to the obvious next place, the brewery.

"Think we'll find Match there, too?" Xera asked. "I swear, I'd suspect them of having an affair if she weren't still so banged up. You'll have to have a word with her about a chaperone—especially now." Her tone was matter of fact, but her face betrayed her solemnity. This was no small matter. That she was asking Gem to do the talking showed that she'd feel hypocritical bringing it up. Her indiscretion had hurt both her sisters, and it still stung.

"Sure. Maybe." Gem wasn't about to fuel any of her sister's self-recrimination. Fortunately, they'd reached the door to the brewery, which made a good distraction. She held it open. "After you."

Xera strode through, calling Brandy's name. "We need your input for what we're going to do tonight!"

She spoke loudly to the air, assuming her sister was inside. After all, there were only so many places a girl on house arrest could go. Besides, there was a light on at Brandy's desk, at the end of the vats.

As they got closer, they could see the back of Brandy's chair. Their sister was sitting at her desk, facing away from them. She didn't respond to their calls.

"Are you sleeping?" Xera muttered when she got close enough. She spun Brandy's chair around, then gasped. Brandy's head lolled to the side. Her eyes were blank and staring. Gem felt her gorge rise.

Xera cursed and felt for a pulse. "She's alive!"

"Yes, but not for long," a new voice said.

The lights went out.

Blue's plants were doing even better than he'd hoped. Pleased, he entered the kitchen, eager to tell Gem all about it. He had high hopes for the girl. She might have grown up a tavern owner, and disavowed all knowledge of gardening, but she was smart and extremely interested in everything he did.

She enjoyed hearing about his experiments and plans—probably because they were business-related, and she had a particularly apt mind for business—and encouraged him to try out many new ideas, as long as he didn't discard what worked in the process. Cautious, she was. She'd never have made the risky investments that had led to his success, but her slow and steady approach had reaped its own rewards and he didn't fault her. He was more cautious these days as well. A man was less inclined to make omelets with his nest egg.

She wasn't in the taproom, but Azor and Zsak had come in. He greeted both men with surprise. "Hey!

You didn't tell me you were getting out of the hospital." Since a hug was out of the question, even if he hadn't been afraid Zsak's arm would fall off, he settled for a hearty (opposite arm) forearm clasp.

Zsak grinned. He looked a bit pale but otherwise sturdy. "I couldn't take it anymore. I threatened mayhem if they didn't let me out. Luckily, Azor stopped in and gave me a ride back here."

Azor looked unhappy. "I wouldn't have visited if I'd known he would go AWOL at the first sight of someone he knew. He jumped out of bed and demanded his clothes."

"I would have walked out in that stupid gown if they hadn't fetched them," Blue's partner said without remorse. "Azor was a handy ride. Wasn't going to pass that up." He plopped a bag on the bar and spoke to Jaq. "Hey, stick these somewhere safe, could you? They loaded me up with enough meds to choke a donkey."

He glanced around and said to Blue, "Where's your lady? I want to tease her about marrying you when she could have had me."

Blue snorted but wondered the same thing. "I was just looking for her. She and her sister went hunting for Brandy. Have you seen any of them, Jaq?"

Jaq shook his head as he wiped the bar. "Haven't seen Brandy since first thing this morning. Said she was going to be in the brewery. They probably found her there."

Blue got a sudden uneasy feeling in his gut. It was probably nothing, just déjà vu. After all, he'd been to the brewery a couple of times since they'd found Brandy and Jean Luc, and nothing bad had happened.

Azor and Zsak stilled at his expression. Cops themselves, they were attuned more to his unease than to any other stimulus. Paranoia ran in the profession.

"You want me to come with you?" Zsak offered.

"You're in no condition to handle trouble," Azor said with a dismissive glance. "I'll go."

Blue tried to wave them off. "It's fine, guys. There's probably nothing wrong. Why would there be?"

"Well, why don't we use the security system to check for them? Rather than running around looking, we can screen the whole premises. I've got time, and Gimpy here isn't doing anything special," Azor suggested reasonably. Though he didn't say it, he may have thought, as Blue did, that manning the security system would keep the still-recovering Zsak out of harm's way. He had no business getting physical if there was something wrong.

"Hey!" Zsak protested the nickname Gimpy, but was ignored.

"If you're determined," was all Blue said, but privately he was glad for the backup. His paranoia had paid dividends more than once, and these guys had likely benefited from similar gut instincts.

Minutes later they were searching each of the security screens Blue had set up, while the office manager looked on in mild annoyance. They'd have to move this stuff one of these days. Although the need was no longer acute, Blue was a firm believer in good security. However, that didn't mean it necessarily belonged in the manager's office.

"There," Zsak said quietly. "They *are* in the brewery. Or at least Brandy and Xera are." And it was worse than Blue's instinct had imagined.

He took a steadying breath. He could just see

Brandy lolling in her chair near her desk, either seriously hurt or dead. She stared at the ceiling with a vacant expression. Xera was on the floor next to her, her arms bound behind her back. She'd been secured to one of the heavy legs of a nearby bench. She had a killing expression on her face, and she stared intently at something or someone.

Zsak panned the camera around. He stood straighter as it passed over Gem. She was upright against a pipe, her arms behind her. Her eyes tracked someone just out of sight, surely the same person at whom Xera had been leveling such loathing.

Zsak adjusted the view. "No way!"

"Kiyl?" Blue clenched his fist in shock. He wanted to wrap it around the man's throat.

"But . . . he's dead," Azor said. "We saw him die."

"We saw a flash. Your men and his body disappeared. But that's him, Azor," Blue murmured.

Azor nodded. "He duped us, somehow. That flash must have been a distraction, and maybe he changed form and flew away. Amazing—even jacked up on drugs, he shouldn't have been conscious after being shot with a stunner like that. I wonder what he used to counter the effect?" He got out his communicator to call for backup.

Zsak shook his head. "Some kind of military hardware, maybe? What I want to know is, is there anyone else in there now?"

There *was* someone else present. In the shadows behind Kiyl they spotted another Kiuyian, but it was Match, and he was secured like Gem. His head lolled forward. He twitched from time to time, as if fighting for consciousness.

"Out!" Azor ordered The Spark's office manager;

Tam Rasheed would just be another body in the way when his men arrived. He looked at Zsak. "Put your earset on. You're coordinator. I want you feeding my team data as they converge. Keep Blue and me updated. We're going in."

Blue was already opening a locker and extracting equipment he'd stashed there a month earlier. Guns and dragonskin riot gear armor were soon piled on the couch. Azor looked impressed.

Zsak shushed them and dialed up the volume on the security camera before he fumbled with an earset, putting it on one-handed. They could all hear talking.

"—was going to leave them like this and call in a tip, but this is too good to pass up. Why settle for ruining your sister when I can kill you all?" Kiyl's eyes gleamed in excitement as he paced. His skin was scaled with dragonskin, like it had been when he'd fought Zsak. He'd transformed his hands into having freakishly long fingers with razor-sharp claws, and he waved one of those in Gem's face. "Do you know how painful it was to regrow this hand, you little bitch? Your boyfriend will pay for that."

"Leave her alone," Match mumbled. It was barely audible. He couldn't lift his head.

Kyil laughed and turned toward his fellow Kiuyian. "What's that, *shatungu*? I don't take orders from a useless piece of meat like you. You can't even change, can you? Even your little brother is more of a man than you. No wonder your father hates you." It was apparent the two knew each other, or Kiyl had taken the time to scout the neighbors. Something personal like this, though . . . It seemed Kiyl knew someone in the household.

"What'd he call him?" Zsak asked.

Azor looked grim. "It means 'Man who can't change.'"

"Plan?" Blue prompted as he finished strapping on his armor. He had a gun but was smart enough not to run out, guns blazing. He knew his wasn't the coolest head just then. Azor was many things, including calm under pressure, so he was the right man from whom to seek advice. Besides, he was a Kiuyian.

Unwisely, Match returned an insult. Maybe the drugs had diminished his judgment. Either way, Kiyl grabbed his hair and yanked his head back to expose Match's throat.

"Haven't you learned not to taunt a hunter? Your kind isn't fit to live. Pitiful throwbacks. I should kill you, but . . ." Kiyl suddenly smiled, and it was a chilling sight. "Maybe I'll make sure you can't breed instead." He stepped back and raked his claws down in a sudden flash.

Match screamed. The attack had created a shallow trench of blood over his belly and down the front of his pants. Kiyl stood back, watching him thrash.

"We can't wait for backup. I'll provide the distraction," Azor said in a sudden decision. "Blue, go to the front of the brewery and wait for Zsak's signal. I'll slip in the back."

"That could be dangerous if he sees you. He might kill someone," Blue warned.

Azor's smile seemed strangely amused. "I believe he'll be too busy. He'll never be able to resist."

Gem stared, desperately wishing she could stop the blood. Even with Kiyl's drugs in him, the pain must have been bad. Match kept moaning like a wounded animal.

Kiyl moved near her, unholy satisfaction in every line of his face. "You see what I do to your friends? Imagine what I'll do to your boyfriend," he promised.

"What did I do to you?" she replied.

He grabbed her chin, his long fingers making a cage around her head. "You stopped sending out Pax. I was getting filthy rich off the stuff. Plus, it was my favorite drug. Nothing like it. You snatched it away and then sicced the cops on us. You're a bad luck charm, lady, and you're going to pay."

Gem tried to keep her voice even. "Didn't you follow the trial? We were found innocent. My sisters and I didn't really have anything to do with the Pax—that was all Jean Luc."

He gave her a shove that banged her head against the pipe. His disgust was apparent, as was a small seed of admiration. "Yes, I saw that was reported. You paid them off. My father did it all the time." His eyes turned savage at the reminder. "Your cop boyfriend sicced them on *him.*"

Clearly, there was no reasoning with him. One moment there was lucidity, the next, pure demon. The Kiuyian had cooked his brain on one too many chemical cocktails, it seemed, and now he was dangerously unpredictable. Not that he'd been safe beforehand.

Someone entered through the back. The sound of the opening door was so unexpected that everyone looked—everyone but Kiyl. He immediately jumped for Gem and placed his claws in a delicate position. "Step wrong and she'll be smiling through her throat," he snarled at the shadows.

"Hey, man, it's just me," a youthful voice said.

Match's brother Bijo appeared, stepping into the light. He glanced nervously around. "Hey, I thought you were just after the cop. What are all these guys doing here?"

"None of your business. Why did you follow me?" Kiyl demanded. Losing interest in Gem, he stalked toward the boy.

Bijo started to speak, then caught sight of his brother. "What did you do to him?" he shrieked.

Kiyl intercepted the boy before he could reach Match. "Don't interfere."

"You told me you'd leave us alone if I helped you!"

Kiyl showed his teeth. "I lied. If you're not careful, you're next. Lucky for you, I still have a use for you."

Bijo shook his head and cursed.

Kiyl backhanded the boy, sending him skidding across the room. "You need a lesson in manners, kid." He took a step forward. But then another sound, one from somewhere in the pipes, caught his attention. He looked toward the vats. A pair of beady eyes blinked at him from the shadows.

Gem blinked, for she saw the same thing as her enemy. It was a green rabbit with outlandishly long legs and ears like salad scoops. She had no idea how it had gotten inside her inn.

Kiyl stared for a moment, then laughed. "What's this? Has your daddy come to see what's become of his boys? Is that the best you can do?" he called loudly to the rabbit. "You full-bloods are so proud of your purity, and this is your best? A rabbit! Compared to you, I'm a god! Watch what a *bastard* can do, old man." In moments he became a lean, armored carnivore of some type that Gem had never seen. His gray hide was covered with thick plates, and spines ridged his back. He leapt forward on four legs, black teeth snapping.

The rabbit released a horrible scream and bounced away. Kiyl gave chase, laughing maniacally.

Bijo used the distraction to leap toward his brother, pulling a knife and slitting the rope around Match's hands, then caught him as he fell. Ignoring the noise of the terrified animal, he slung one of Match's hands over his shoulder and dragged his brother toward the door.

Just before he reached it, the door burst open. "Get down!" Blue hissed, running inside, his gun leveled at the boy's chest. Bijo instantly obeyed, though he tried to go easy with his brother. Match groaned as they both fell. There was another horrible screech; then all went quiet.

Blue sprinted to Gem and cut her loose. He pressed his knife into her hand and pushed her gently toward her sisters. "I'll cover you," he said softly. "Try to get them out."

Kiyl, still in the carnivore form, slowly stalked out of the shadows. He shifted just enough to stand on his hind legs and speak. "Here you are, cop," he crowed. "I thought I was going to eat your girl before you even got here."

"Kiyl," Blue replied. "I'd have thought you would give up by now. You know there's no way out."

Kiyl's lips parted in a horrible black grin. "I'm invincible, fool. I got away once and I'll do it again. I even grew back my hand." He waggled his freakish claws in illustration. "I'm a god . . . a god of *death*."

But the death god didn't see what Blue was hiding. Bijo was behind him, and he was changing. The boy had talent. It only took him seconds to become a two-legged lizard with massive jaws and a powerful, clubbed tail. Only his arms remained humanoid, but they were clawed and thick with muscle.

He launched himself at Kiyl without warning. One snap of his jaws engulfed Kiyl's entire head, and the shape-shifted boy clamped harder as the villain thrashed. He even shook his head back and forth, flinging Kiyl's body around like a dog would a chew toy. Finally the Kiuyian's body landed some feet away with a sick, meaty sound. Bijo stared at him for a moment and then spat out Kiyl's head. It landed facedown with a wet thud. Blue could hear someone being sick. He felt a little off himself.

Bijo resumed the shape of a scrawny teen with a bloodstained mouth. He stared at Blue, then hurried over to his brother.

Again, the door burst open. Cops swarmed in. Bijo was forced to the floor before Blue called them off. Medics followed close behind.

Blue turned to his wife and family to see the damage. Xera was free and scowling as medics swarmed over Brandy. Gem's youngest sister seemed mostly fine now, although she didn't enjoy the medics' attention. She kept insisting she was okay.

Gem hurried close for a hug. The embrace was brief if heartfelt. "I've got to find Azor," Blue told her, and raced toward the vats where the rabbit had disappeared.

His friend and colleague lay naked on the floor in the shadows. His long green hair spilled loose and blood streamed out of bone-deep claw marks on his thigh, shoulder and back. Blue yelled for the medics.

Azor smiled grimly. "Is he dead?"

"The neighbor kid got him. Bijo," Blue explained.

Azor grunted. "I saw him when I was still outside, heading for the door. Kid got involved before I could warn him."

"Relax—he came in useful." Blue paused, then asked, puzzled, "Why a rabbit?"

Azor grinned. "I told you he'd never be able to resist. If I'd come in looking like a bigger monster than he was . . ." He trailed off as the medics swarmed him, flinched at their bright lights and ministering hands.

Blue got the drift. If Azor had challenged him with brute force, the killer might have tried to hide behind his hostages. Only by offering him an even more attractive prey had Azor been able to ensure that they could get Kiyl away from his captives. Smart.

When the storm of cops and medical personnel finally cleared, the Harrisdaughter family gathered in their apartments. Zsak had followed Azor to the hospital for the first watch. The medics had decided to let Brandy's system clear itself of Kiyl's drugs without intervention, because that was the safest route. As soon as she was able, however, her sisters vowed to take her to the hospital. She was impatient to see Match.

"It could have been much worse," Blue explained. "From what I understand, Match should be able to regenerate much of his missing . . . parts . . . with a little help. They still have to patch him up and stop the bleeding, though. And infection is always a problem without medicine." Blue held Gem on his lap as she sipped hot tea. They'd been sitting that way for quite a while. He wasn't in the mood to let go.

She stirred. "We should go to the hospital."

His arms tightened. "Not yet. Zsak will let us know as soon as our friends are ready for company. It's just as easy to wait here. Besides, Jamir is still trying to soothe your shock with food. You wouldn't want to duck out on his mothering, would you? He hasn't even finished the cookies yet!"

She made a face at him, but his joke lightened the moment. She shivered, and he knew she was remembering how Kiyl had died.

"Couldn't have happened to a nicer guy," he suggested. "The bastard was destined for a bad end. I'm just sorry you had to see it."

"What will happen to Bijo?" Xera asked, changing the subject.

"I imagine he'll get off lightly. He's just a kid, and it sounds like his family was threatened. The thing with Kiyl was self-defense. We all saw."

Xera grimaced and looked aside.

Tough, fearless Xera. She had been the one to get sick earlier, when she'd seen their enemy's head ripped off. She was apparently strong but not hardened. For her sake, Blue hoped she'd never see worse.

"I'm going to check on Brandy," she said, rising. Brandy was surely fast asleep and oblivious, but Xera was compulsive about keeping an eye on her.

Gem set her tea aside and snuggled down into her husband's arms. "I'm getting a kink in my back," she remarked. "Maybe it would be easier to take a nap. You could leave the communicator beside the bed." She gave Blue a hopeful look. She wanted to comfort him.

He smiled into her hair. "Is that code, or do you really want to nap?"

She sat up and scowled.

He laughed. "I was just joking!"

She rolled her eyes and led him to her room.

Epilogue

It was two weeks after the episode with Kiyl that Azor again stopped into The Spark for a visit with Blue and Gem. Not that he entered the private rooms for the family. His preferred method of visiting was to come to the taproom and order an ice water, then wait for either of his friends to seek him out. While still reserved, he didn't let his part in the prior investigation surrounding The Spark keep him from socializing with them when he chose.

His mouth curved faintly upward as Gem slid into the chair next to him. "Gem," he said. "Please tell your cook to stop sending baskets of food to my apartment. My roommate has begun to ask embarrassing questions."

Gem exhaled in amusement. "You should ask him personally. I don't want to be seen as the bad guy. Ever since Zsak took that assignment off-world, Jamir has been at loose ends. He doesn't know who to cook for, besides our guests. I warn you, he can be stubborn."

Azor eyed her. "Hm. Maybe I can redirect him. The SWAT team might appreciate a few baskets of goodies."

Gem laughed. "Good luck!"

He allowed a half smile, then sobered. "I assume you've heard the news about Cirrus? The jury returned a guilty verdict. He's going to be serving some time doing hard labor in the mines. His assets have also been seized by the Polaris government. They're to be sold at auction soon."

Gem shook her head. "All his art, his house . . . I almost feel sorry for him."

Blue sent her a skeptical look.

"Yeah, maybe not," she agreed. "He had it coming."

She sighed and remarked to the others, "Did you hear that Blue and I are moving out to the farm for a while? He's calling it a honeymoon, but I think he just wants to see what's going on out there with his own eyes. That, and I think he'd like to get away from here for a bit."

Azor nodded. "Your sister Brandy will be in charge, then? I guess you should be glad she's under house arrest, because it gives you someone to keep an eye on the place so that you and Blue can get away. To . . . work on your gardening skills." He gave her a knowing grin.

Gem gave him a look, surprised at the detective's teasing. "Yes. Plus, I think it'll be good for her to get some experience being in charge alone. Nineteen's not so bad a time to start, especially not when you teethed on a business. Besides, she could use the confidence after all that happened. And since Jaq and Tam Rasheed are here, and I'm just a stone's throw away . . . Well, you didn't think I'd take my hands entirely off the wheel, did you?"

"No. I suppose you want something for Xera to come back to eventually."

Gem lifted a shoulder and shrugged. The gesture was somewhat sad. "Xera, come back? She may never. Who knows where she'll go or whom she'll meet in the GE? I just hope . . . Well, I just hope she ends up happy."

"She's not the sort to give up until she is," Azor replied.

Blue slid onto the barstool next to his wife. "Hey, Azor! You going to visit us on the farm?" he asked. He looked excited to go.

Azor gave his ex-colleague a sardonic look. "Am I invited?"

"Sure. Just come ready to work," Blue warned. "There'll always be something to do out there."

"I can see I'm going to want to rush right out." Azor glanced around and then admitted, "I heard your sister finally got out of her chair."

Gem smiled, giving a laugh of pure pleasure. "Yes! And thank God! I was ready to strangle her. She's such a crank when she's laid up. Speaking of which, how are you?" She looked embarrassed that she hadn't asked earlier, but Azor knew it wasn't from lack of concern. There was so much going on in her life, between her family, the inn and their new property, he was amazed she kept track of anything.

"I'll be back to work tomorrow," he admitted. "It would have been sooner, but my commander forced me to take the time off." He fought to hide his annoyance.

Blue rested an arm on the back of his wife's chair. He couldn't hide a small grin as he said, "Now, that's just cruel for a workaholic like yourself."

Azor grunted and stood to go. He was a little stiff. Blue stood with him, and he surprised Azor by clasping his forearm and giving a firm shake. "Stop in from time to time," he requested. His voice was full of unspoken emotion. "Seriously. You never know what we might have going on."

Gem huffed in dismay. "I don't doubt that. But no more adventures, please."

Blue put his arm around her. "Blame your dad. He never should have named this place The Spark. It was just asking for trouble."

"I'll tell him when I see him next," Gem replied, her voice a little tart. But then she stepped close and surprised Azor with a hug. "Thanks for everything."

A flush of bronze swept his cheekbones. "Um. Yes. I've got to go." He fled at a fast walk.

Blue glanced at his wife and laughed. "You're going to ruin the old boy," he observed. "I don't think he's been hugged since he was in nappies."

"He has potential," Gem replied stoutly, and there was a teasing glint in her eye.

Blue pulled his beloved close and whispered in her ear, "Not as much as I do." He wanted her always to remember that.

"Maybe you should prove it," she whispered back, and she bit him.

Blue growled and led her toward the door. The inn wasn't the only thing around here that was trouble. The Spark had indeed led to a fire. It had started with a clandestine drug-smuggling operation and grown into assassination attempts and kidnapping, but it had also led to him finding the love of his life. There was no question that their passion was a blaze that a lifetime of lovemaking would never put out. There was nowhere else in the galaxy that he'd rather be.

Autumn Dawn
NO WORDS ALONE

As The Only Woman In A Team Of Marooned Explorers, Whom Do You Trust— Your Friends...Or Your Enemy?

Crash-landing on a hostile planet with a variety of flora and fauna intent upon making her their lunch was Xera's most immediate concern, but not her only one. The Scorpio, sworn enemies of her people, were similarly stranded nearby, and Xera didn't trust the captain of her team of Galactic Explorers. He was belligerent and small-minded, and he'd already caused one unnecessary death—Genson's. Xera was the translator, and she should have been the first sent to deal with the Scorpio. Even if she was a lone woman and they were some of the galaxy's most merciless soldiers.

For, on this inhospitable world, the warlike Scorpio were their only chance. And in the eyes of the aliens' handsome leader, Xera saw a nobility and potency she'd never before encountered—a reaction she knew her male human companions would despise. A future with Commander Ryven was...something to consider. But first she had to survive.

ISBN 13: 978-0-505-52801-8

ICE

SOMEONE IS WAITING

Most people find beauty in Alaska's austere mountains. To Kaylie Fletcher, there is only death—her whole family gone after a disastrous climbing expedition. Then again, maybe not. A raspy call in the middle of the night leads Kaylie to believe her mother might still be alive. For now...

SOMEONE IS WATCHING

A strange message in a bar. A bloody knife. A fiery explosion. There's a killer inching closer, but Kaylie has nowhere to run. Except straight into the arms of Cort McClaine. The rugged bush pilot is too much of an adrenaline junkie to be considered safe, but Kaylie can't resist the heat of his touch amid the bitter cold.

SOMEONE WILL DIE

Caught in a high-stakes race against a murderous madman, Kaylie and Cort know that with one wrong step they'll be...iced.

STEPHANIE ROWE

ISBN 13: 978-0-505-52775-2

Tracy Madison

A Stroke of Magic

You know how freaky it is, to expect one taste and get another? Imagine picking up a can of tepid ginger ale and taking a swig of delicious, icy cold peppermint tea. Alice Raymond did just that. And though the tea is exactly what she wants, she bought herself a soda.

ONE STROKE OF MAGIC,
AND EVERYTHING HAS CHANGED

No, Alice's life isn't exactly paint-by-numbers. After breaking things off with her lying, stealing, bum of an ex, she discovered she's pregnant. Motherhood was definitely on her "someday" wish list, but a baby means less time for her art and no time for recent hallucinations that include this switcharoo with the tea. She has to impress her new boss, the ridiculously long-lashed, smoky-eyed Ethan Gallagher, and she has to deal with her family, who have started rambling about gypsy curses. Only a soul-deep bond with the right man can save her and her child? As if being single wasn't pressure enough!

Available July 2009!   ISBN 13: 978-0-505-52811-7

Tammy Kane

BREATH OF FIRE

"A fantastic new world of dragons!"
—Jade Lee, *USA Today* Bestselling Author of *Dragonbound*

When the dragon came to claim him, Karl knew his great plan had gone horribly wrong. If he had known the creature was real, he wouldn't have scoffed at the villagers…and he *certainly* wouldn't have been so quick to let them chain him to a rock. Mattaen Initiates trained as warriors, but no man could defeat a dragon.

"My name is Elera daughter of Shane. And you, Initiate, are my virgin prize."

She had vanquished the beast and named her price: one night with the virgin sacrifice she'd saved. He'd taken a vow of chastity, but Karl still had a man's needs—and Elera's sultry curves made him ache to taste his first woman. With a scorching kiss she shattered his defenses…and led him into a world of deception and seduction, where he'd be forced to choose between the brotherhood that had raised him and the woman whose courage set his heart on fire.

ISBN 13: 978-0-505-52816-2

TEKGRRL

A DARK SEED…

When she was 12, Mindy asked to go to the School like other gifted girls. Her parents sent her to another planet.

…HAS GROWN TO FRUITION

Today, Mindy's back on Earth. She's a mechanical genius with the Elite Hands of Justice, America's premier super-hero squad. She's been having headaches, though, and not just because her longtime crush is flirting with a teammate. It's not because she's pushing thirty. It's also not because of the contrary actions of the new Secretary for Superhero Affairs, ex-ally Simon Leasure. No, what's burning her brain is a past she can't remember, a past that has been erased. It's a memory surging closer—in flying saucers. Her worst nightmare is returning, big-time, and only she and her friends can stop it.

A. J. MENDEN

ISBN 13: 978-0-505-52787-5

COLLEEN THOMPSON

"[Thompson] more than holds her own in territory blazed by Tami Hoag and Tess Gerritsen."

—Publishers Weekly

In Deep Water

Ruby Monroe knows she's way out of her depth the minute she lays eyes on Sam McCoy. She's been warned to steer clear of this neighbor, the sexy bad boy with a criminal past. But with her four-year-old daughter missing, her home incinerated and her own life threatened by a tattooed gunman, where else can she turn? Drowning in the flood of emotion unleashed by their mind-blowing encounters, Ruby is horrified to learn an unidentified body has been dredged up, the local sheriff is somehow involved, and Sam hasn't told her all he knows. Has she put her trust in the wrong man and jeopardized her very survival by uncovering the secrets...

BENEATH BONE LAKE

ISBN 13: 978-0-8439-6243-7

✂ ☐ **YES!**

Sign me up for the Love Spell Book Club and send my
FREE BOOKS! If I choose to stay in the club, I will pay
only $8.50* each month, a savings of $6.48!

NAME: _____

ADDRESS: _____

TELEPHONE: _____

EMAIL: _____

☐ I want to pay by credit card.

☐ **VISA**   ☐ **MasterCard.**   ☐ **DISCOVER**

ACCOUNT #: _____

EXPIRATION DATE: _____

SIGNATURE: _____

Mail this page along with $2.00 shipping and handling to:
Love Spell Book Club
PO Box 6640
Wayne, PA 19087
Or fax (must include credit card information) to:
610-995-9274
You can also sign up online at **www.dorchesterpub.com**.
*Plus $2.00 for shipping. Offer open to residents of the U.S. and Canada only.
Canadian residents please call 1-800-481-9191 for pricing information.
If under 18, a parent or guardian must sign. Terms, prices and conditions subject to
change. Subscription subject to acceptance. Dorchester Publishing reserves the right
to reject any order or cancel any subscription.